FOR THE HONOR
OF
THE EMPIRE

Book 2 of
The Honor Trilogy

by

Andrew J Harvey

A Novel of the
Cross-Temporal Empire

Acknowledgments

My thanks to the following people without whom this book would never have been completed:

- Members of the Bassendean Writer's Group including, but not necessarily limited to: Inez, Julie, Ken, Mena, Punito, Sandi, and Theo.

- Doctor Sarah Burns who assisted me with backgrounding some of the more interesting people included in the series.

- Kathleen Gilles Seidel, who through her writing taught me to understand how to help broken characters recover from trauma.

- Wikipedia, which provided me with an initial start on many of the vignettes.

- My editor Sally Odgers, and my wonderful beta readers (Alan and Bianca).

And lastly, my wife, who put up with me burbling on about the latest issues with my two protagonists while they fell in love, fought villains, and generally ignored the plot I had so carefully created for them, and who also provided a final check on my manuscript. It should go without saying that any remaining errors remain solely the fault of the author.

Table of Contents

1

IS MISS PERIC GOING TO BE ALL RIGHT?

(Sunday: Mainline New York)

"Good morning, Miss Peric," the chauffeur said, as he opened the front door for her.

Louise turned away from her study of Central Park's elm forest drowsing in the warmth of the early morning sun, just beyond the long, graveled driveway that led down from the house to the Avenue that ran along the side of the park. "Rolf, what are you doing opening doors? Shouldn't you be polishing the Rolls or something?"

"This is one of those 'somethings'," he explained with a smile and closed the door against the screech of a tram turning into Fifth Avenue from its route down Seventy-seventh.

"Are they in the dining room?" she asked, starting for the open French-doors on the far side of the main hall, and ignoring the massive granite staircase that rose three stories from the floor.

"They are."

"Don't bother announcing me," she said over her shoulder.

"Morning, Markus," she said, as she breezed into the room. She inspected the spread laid out on the sideboard for breakfast, wondering if she'd have time for a danish. "What are you doing here? I thought you were still in Naisre."

Markus looked up from the coloring book Jessie, his eight-year-old daughter, was working on from his lap. Given that the table was large enough to seat twenty-four, and they were the only two in the room, the room appeared, to say the least, underutilized. She wondered why they weren't using the smaller dining room. The answer, she suspected, was Mrs. Mack. The diminutive housekeeper had a powerful sense of propriety.

Markus blinked at Louise's appearance. Despite the earliness of her arrival, she was wearing a long black beaded net evening dress. "I got back last night," he said. "It's a bit early for you, though, isn't it?" He glanced at the clock on the mantelpiece that still showed eight. "Or is it late?"

"The dress? I have the day off, so I thought I'd take Margaret shopping. And as it's such a beautiful day, I thought it deserved a beautiful dress." She glanced at the windows, where the silk brocade curtains had been pulled back and the windows opened to let in the early morning breeze. The dining room's polished oak floor glowed gold in the sunlight.

Jessie gave Louise an enormous smile. "Have you seen the kittens yet, Miss Peric?"

"Not yet, sweetheart. I hope you'll show them to me before I leave."

Jessie nodded and returned to her coloring.

"So, is Mags up?" Louise asked.

"I haven't seen her yet." He frowned. "I would have expected her to be up by now, though."

"No problems. I'll wake her."

At the top of the stairs, she rapped smartly on the door to her sister's third floor bedroom. "Margaret, come out, come out, wherever you are."

Her call was met with dead silence. After thirty seconds, she knocked again. "Mags?"

When there was still no response, she tried the door, only to find it locked. Her hands suddenly felt cold. "Margaret!" she called, rattling the door. "It's Louise, let me in."

"Louise?" It was Markus at the foot of the staircase. "Is everything all right?" Jessie clutched his hand as she stared up at Louise with wide, concerned eyes.

"No," Louise said. "The door's locked." She was aware of how stupid that sounded, but to put into words what she was afraid of . . .

Markus hurried up the stairs. "Margaret. Miss Peric?" he called, trying the door.

Louise bent to look through the lock, but the key was in it, blocking her view. Damn! Backing away, she looked over her shoulder to the ground floor where one of the ImpSec officers who'd been stationed at the house since the mail bomb attempt on her sister's life was looking up at them.

"You!"

The officer started.

"I need you up here," she told him. "Now!"

Behind her, Markus was rattling the door handle, presumably trying to force it open by sheer willpower.

The ImpSec officer took the stairs two at a time, talking into his radio as he did so.

"My sister's not responding," Louise said, as he arrived, slightly out of breath. "You need to break the door down."

"Are you sure?" Markus asked uncertainly.

"Yes — something's wrong."

Markus gave a nod and stood back from the door.

The officer lifted his foot and kicked at the solid, wood-joined door, causing the plate to splinter away from the jamb. Another kick and the wood around the plate and its reinforcement shattered, and the door slammed open.

Louise was through the door before it even had time to bounce back. Inside, she gagged at the stink of stale vomit. "Margaret!" she whispered at the sight of her sister lying in the large four-poster bed. Her sister's face was white, and vomit stained the bed-sheets.

She didn't remember moving, but somehow, she was across the room and checking her sister.

"She's still breathing," she said, relieved to feel the soft flutter of her sister's breath on the side of her cheek.

Markus had picked up the empty medicine bottle from the bedside table. "Sleeping pills," he said. He sniffed at the glass on the bedside table. "And vodka." He shook his head. "Oh, Margaret," he said, tenderly brushing a lock of her limp black hair away from her face.

"We need the doctor," Louise told the ImpSec officer, who had just returned from checking the en suite.

The officer nodded and headed downstairs at the run, calling loudly. But Louise was too busy trying to roll her sister onto her side to make out what it was he was saying.

"Jessie, out," Markus snapped to his daughter, and Louise looked up to see Jessie watching them from the doorway.

"Is Miss Peric going to be all right?" Jessie asked.

"I hope so," Louise said. "But you need to wait outside."

Jessie nodded reluctantly.

Louise and Markus shared a worried look.

"Miss Peric?" It was James, the butler, hovering in the doorway as he tried to take in what he was seeing.

"Tell one of the maids to get some fresh linen, and we need some light in here," Louise said, gesturing at the heavily curtained windows.

The butler nodded.

As soon as he'd gone, Markus looked at her.

"What?" Louise demanded.

"You don't seem very surprised by all this," Markus said.

Louise shrugged, unwilling to say anything.

Markus looked at her steadily, then nodded. "I'll get a cloth," he said, turning for the en suite.

He was still tenderly wiping Margaret's face when there was the sound of voices from downstairs. "That would be Doctor Castles," Markus said, a moment before the doctor with his bushy ginger sideburns bustled in.

Doctor Castles nodded curtly at them before pulling out his stethoscope to check on Margaret's breathing and heart. Apparently satisfied with what he heard he picked the medicine bottle up to check on its label. "Barbiturates," he said, making it sound like some sort of swear word. "Yes, that would do it." He peered at the vomit still staining the sheets. One finger prodded the remains of what looked like half-digested tablets. "Lucky she vomited, and lucky she didn't suck it back in."

"And who are you?" he asked, turning on Louise.

"Her sister."

"And has Miss Peric attempted suicide before?" he asked.

Louise hesitated for a moment, then shrugged. "I don't know," she admitted. "I know something happened at the end of the war that involved her in some sort of breakdown. But I was on the Mainline at the time, and Mama and Papa never talked about it."

"The war." He frowned, then shrugged. "Right, well, there's nothing more I can do for her at the moment. You'll need to have someone with her at all times. I'll arrange for a nurse to be sent round. She'll need to stay on the premises — I presume that won't be a problem, Mrs. Mack?" he asked the diminutive housekeeper, who had followed the butler back into the room.

"Of course not," Mrs. Mack said.

"Shouldn't you pump her stomach, or something?" Louise asked.

"There wouldn't be anything left in there to pump," he said. "This occurred when . . ." he poked at the stains again " . . . sometime last night. If you want to make yourself useful, get her into a clean bed and air this room. It stinks."

Louise watched him re-pack his bag sourly. As he closed the latch on his bag, he looked up.

"Assuming there's been no permanent damage, you may want to get your sister into see Doctor Helen Rubenstein. She's a psychiatrist who's done a lot of work with returned soldiers. I can give you a referral if you want one."

"Thank you, that would be helpful," Louise said. She frowned, working through what he'd just said. "Permanent damage?"

"I don't think there will be, but we can't dismiss the possibility until she wakes up."

"And when might that be?" Markus asked worriedly.

"Hard to say. It might be tonight or it might not be for a couple of days. The nurse will monitor her for me and will call me if there's any change." And then he bustled out again.

Louise scowled after him. "Oh crap," she said. "I'll need to tell Donald and get a message to my parents."

The piercing ring of the downstairs telephone interrupted her. "I'll see about moving her into one of the spare bedrooms while we get this one cleaned up," Mrs. Mack said.

Louise nodded, not really listening.

"Miss Peric?"

Louise looked to see one of the underhousemaids standing uncertainly by the door. "Yes?"

"It's your cousin, ma'am, the First Leader. He wants to speak to you."

"I'll keep an eye on her," Markus assured her.

"Thanks," Louise said, getting to her feet, wondering at the relationship between Markus and her sister. He *had* been staying at the house for six weeks now. Well, well, the ice princess had an admirer.

Downstairs, she took a deep breath before taking the telephone from James. She watched the butler leave the room, pulling the door closed behind him as he did so.

"Hello Donald."

"How is she?" her cousin and, for the last three years, First Leader of the Cross-Temporal Empire, demanded.

"Still asleep," she said, wondering why only bad news traveled so quickly. "The doctor said we won't know if there's any permanent damage until she wakes up, and that might not be for a couple of days."

"Do you know why? Was there a note?"

"I didn't see any note. And no, I don't know why."

"She didn't seem depressed?"

"No. I had tea with her a couple of days ago and she seemed fine."

There was silence for a moment. "You'll let me know as soon as something happens?" Donald asked. "I just can't get away at the moment. The Council of Leaders is debating rescinding the Edict on contact with advanced lines this week. And numbers are much too close for my comfort."

"That's fine. There's nothing you could do here even if you could," Louise said honestly. Having Donald here would probably make it easier to deal with her mother, but it would be unfair on him.

"Well, take care. And Louise — thank you."

Louise hung up the phone. Then, after staring at it for a moment, she picked it up again. "Notway embassy, Naisre," she told the operator. The sooner she let their parents know, the better.

2

WELCOME TO BEAUTIFUL PESH

(Wednesday: Sultan, Pesh)

The hotel bedroom smelled of rosewater and sandalwood. Jade considered the telephone on the side table nervously. "Are you sure this is going to work?" she asked in Arabic. "I mean, the number is almost four years old. Anything could have happened. He could have changed houses, or desks. Why would he still have the same number?"

Colonel Ferai considered her for a moment before shrugging his massive shoulders. "Apparently phone numbers are mobile here and stay with the individual. But we certainly won't find out if you don't try it."

His Arabic was atrocious, Jade thought as she nibbled her bottom lip. Jade knew the Colonel's first language was Phoenician, which Ferai claimed was quite close to Arabic, but Jade couldn't detect any similarity, and she'd understood Arabic was a pre-requisite for this mission. Ferai's home-line was the Mmbuto é, where the Phoenician civilization had escaped destruction during the third Punic war by establishing a colony in South Africa, but she had no idea why Imperial Intelligence had insisted on pairing her with him. She liked the man, but the one-eyed former colonel in the Mmbuto é Imperial Marines hardly merged into the background. His dark, almost blue-black skin was covered in intricate white tattoos and his height and sheer size made him stand out in any crowd. Though perhaps that was why

7

— he intimidated people. Jade had watched with interest how much effort people went to in pretending he wasn't there.

Taking a deep breath, she picked the phone up and dialed the number she'd memorized.

A cultured voice answered. "Yes?"

"Emre *Binbasi*?" she asked uncertainly.

"Emre *Kaymakam*," he corrected her.

"My apologies, Kaymakam," she said. His new title of Kaymakam would make him the equivalent of what . . . a Corps Leader? "We were not aware of your promotion."

"Who is this?" Emre asked. "And how did you get this number?"

"My name is Jade Carvello. Donald Clemhorn asked me to phone you."

There was a moment's stunned silence, then — "Where are you?" Emre asked.

"I'm at the Ayasofya Hotel — room 503."

"Are you alone?"

"I have one companion."

There was a pause, and Jade could hear Emre talking to someone in the background. "I'm in the car," he said finally, "just picking my sister up from her school. I can be there in thirty minutes. How do I recognize you?"

"We'll be in the foyer. You'll recognize my companion. A large gentleman with white tattoos." She grinned at Ferai, who looked at her impassively.

"Don't move. I'll be there in thirty."

"Well?" Ferai said, as she replaced the phone.

"He'll be here in thirty minutes." She stopped, suddenly wondering how he'd answered the phone from his car.

"So, we're got time for a coffee," Ferai said.

"Why not?" After exchanging four diamonds for the local currency at a jeweler a couple of hours ago, they could certainly afford it. She smiled at the memory of Ferai simply standing in the doorway, arms folded, as she negotiated a price. His presence had disconcerted the buyer so much that the whole haggling process had moved with commendable speed.

After purchasing their coffees, they took a window table in the hotel foyer which overlooked the street and the Danube just beyond it. They'd come through the portal a short distance outside Pesh that morning and had walked into the city. Jade had been too nervous to pay much attention to their surroundings, although she couldn't avoid noticing the damage from the last war. Now, with nothing to do but wait until the Kaymakam arrived, she had the time to properly consider the city.

It looked . . . sullen. The sky was leaden, and the Danube, gray-skinned and sodden, ran morosely between high embankments just beyond the street. On the other side of the river, Pesh's massive parliamentary building stretched itself along the water, while beyond it the Great Mosque was missing half its dome, an ugly reminder of the last war. At least the scaffolding erected around it promised some hope for the future. For some reason it made her wonder how Carlos was faring on Chikyù.

"There is no joy here," Ferai said quietly.

Jade nodded, tearing her mind away from her concern over Carlos, and back to her own worries. There were few cars on the road, and what people were out hurried past, heads down, their pinched faces drained of color. A squad of eight soldiers in tired looking fatigues trotted grimly past.

She had just taken her last swallow of coffee when a large silver vehicle pulled up in front of the hotel and a young man in a silk, dust-orange uniform stepped out. He was wearing pince-nez spectacles, a Cossack style cap, and a serious expression. Two motorcycles pulled in behind the vehicle, and at a nod from the young man, their two riders dismounted, unslung their assault rifles and came into the hotel. After a quick look around, one returned outside to report while the other took up position by the hotel's front door, his back against the wall.

Outside, the young man gazed at the hotel for a moment before bending down and helping a young girl out of the car. The girl was wearing trousers under a white ankle-length skirt and as she emerged, she adjusted her red fringed headscarf. She had short boots under her trousers. A dark felt sleeveless jacket decorated with golden embroidery covered her long white blouse and completed the ensemble.

Putting a protective arm over her shoulders, the young man ushered her toward the hotel.

"Looks like our contact has arrived," Jade said, rising to her feet, recognizing Emre from the description the First Leader had given them.

Ferai hoisted himself to his feet as Emre, now Kaymakam, entered the hotel lobby. As he noticed Ferai, Jade saw Emre's eyes widen momentarily. Then, seeing Jade, he came across, holding out his right hand. "Salaam," he said. "Jade Carvello, I presume?"

Jade nodded. "Emre Kaymakam?"

"The same. May I introduce my sister, Darda."

Jade took her hand. "I'm glad to meet you, Darda. Donald asked me to inquire as to your health."

Darda looked wide eyed at her, and Jade couldn't help a pang of jealousy at her gloriously large eyes set in a model's face.

"You may tell Donald she is well," Emre said on her behalf. "Her school was outside the main target area so avoided any significant damage. And how is Donald?"

"The First Leader is well. I understand he and Defella are expecting their first child."

The only sign of surprise Emre offered at the news that the penniless adventurer he had known less than four years ago was now First Leader of the C-T E, was a slight twitch to his left eye.

"Please pass my personal congratulations on to the two of them when you see them," Emre said, recovering quickly.

"And we should congratulate you on your promotion," Jade said. "May I ask what your new command entails?"

"My brother commands the entire Janissaries Corps," Darda said proudly. Emre looked embarrassed.

"A significant posting indeed," Ferai said. Jade nodded. The Janissaries served as the elite units of the Ottoman Empire and, given their primary base was in Pesh, also served as an equivalent to the Roman Empire's Praetorian Guard, with the power of hire and fire over the Sultan.

At Emre's puzzled glance at Ferai, Jade realized she had not introduced him yet.

"My apologies," Jade said quickly. "Can I introduce you to my companion, Colonel Ferai."

"Of the Mmbuto é line?" Emre asked.

Ferai nodded, surprised at being recognized. "Imperial Marines," he confirmed.

Emre salaamed shallowly. "I am pleased to meet you. Donald spoke highly of your ability." He looked around. "Do you have any bags?" he asked.

"Backpacks in our room," Ferai said.

"Would it be presumptuous of me to offer you rooms at our house? It's on the base and it would be more secure than here."

Jade looked at Ferai, who nodded. "I'll get them," he said.

"So, how badly was the city hit?" Jade asked as they waited. "It looked pretty bad as we were walking in."

"Ah, I was going to ask where your portal was," Emre said with a smile, before turning serious again. "Bad enough. We avoided getting hit by any biological or chemical weapons but got plastered by the kinetic weapons. The death toll wasn't quite up there with the Great War against the United Christian States, but it was close."

"That was what, thirty million people killed?"

"You know our history," Emre said, surprised.

Jade shrugged. "It was required reading during the war."

"We avoided those sorts of figures this time, but I suspect it was more by luck than good management."

"It still looks pretty bad," Jade said.

"If you think this looks bad, you should see the other guy. Cadiz was destroyed."

"So, what happened? We've always thought your war destroyed the line."

"About two hours after the destruction of our Moon Base, there was a coup in the United Tribes of the Great Plains which pulled them out of the war. There was some talk about a negotiated truce, but then those idiots on our esteemed High Command decided to ramp up the pressure and launched a raid on Cadiz. They detonated five thermobaric bombs over the city."

Jade frowned uncertainly. "Thermobaric?"

"It's a fuel-air bomb," Emre explained. "They were developed after the Great War as an alternative to nuclear weapons. As it turns out, it's a particularly effective weapon, so no more Cadiz. Spain immediately declared itself neutral, and the Angevin Empire followed suit."

Jade looked puzzled.

"England and France," he explained. "With the Angevins gone, the Etehad Sho'mali panicked and responded by pasting Prague and Berlin. Fortunately, we managed to hit them hard enough that their central command structure collapsed, and the war just sort of petered out. We certainly took a lot of damage, pretty significant damage," he admitted. "But at least we avoided the use of nuclear weapons this time." He broke off as Ferai reappeared, carrying the two backpacks. "Come on," he said, "let's go."

As they emerged from the hotel, the armed guard who rode shotgun in the front passenger seat opened the doors for them, then popped the hood on the back storage for the bags Ferai carried. Jade climbed into the car as the door closed behind them with a heavy thud. As she settled back into her seat, the car slowly pulled out from the curb. Jade was not entirely unsurprised at its lack of speed, given the amount of armor it was probably carrying.

As a thick panel of darkened glass rose to close the passenger compartment from the front of the vehicle, Emre adjusted his pince-nez. "So," he said, sitting back into the thick leather upholstery of the seat facing them. "Why are you here?"

Jade looked uncertainly at Ferai, who made a 'tell him' gesture with his shoulders.

Unfastening her jacket, she reached into her breast pocket and produced the small glass vial ImpSec had given her.

"What's this?" he asked, eyeing it uncertainly as she held it out to him.

"It's a particularly virulent potato virus," Jade said.

"And you give it to me, why?" Emre asked, making no effort to take it from her.

"Because we think it came from Sultan," Ferai said, his deep voice echoing around the back of the vehicle. "Ms. Carvello recovered it from some local terrorists, but intelligence indicates it came from Sultan. And given its particular . . . efficacy, we believe it may have been genetically modified. If so, the First Leader is hoping you can identify who might have produced it, and if there is an antidote. We simply don't have the technology."

"The tech *any more*," Jade corrected him. "The Hraffor from the Nayarit line who established the Empire could undertake quite sophisticated genetic manipulations. That was a hundred years ago, though."

Emre accepted the vial reluctantly, holding it up against the light to examine the dried dust it contained. "I can run some checks, but I may not be able to identify the source," he warned.

"That's all we can ask," Ferai said.

"There is another thing," Jade said.

"Oh?"

"The First Leader is interested in establishing diplomatic relations with Sultan."

Emre looked interested.

"The question, of course, is with who?" she continued.

"I see, I think."

"Our job is to establish where that embassy should be situated," Ferai said.

Emre's expression cleared. "Welcome to beautiful Pesh," he said, airily waving a hand at the ruined city outside the grayed windows. "Capital of the much reduced Ottoman Empire, the Northern Caliphate, and former member of the Etehad Junoobil."

3

Vignette:

A Brief Introduction to Sultan (1)

Sultan history diverged from the Mainline's in 735 CE when the Franks, who on the Mainline had successfully checked the Arabs at Tours only two years previously, were crushed at the battle of Bourges, giving the Arabs control over France.

In 841, Abu'l-Abbas Muhammad I ibn al-Aghlab, the fifth emir of the Aghlabid dynasty, and one of the greatest champions of the harb, captured Rome. Accepting the protection of the Holy Roman Emperor the Pope reestablished his papacy in Ingelheim and turned his attention to converting the north. The conversion of Harold Bluetooth, the King of Denmark in 965 to Christianity, ensured that Christian missionaries accompanied Leif Erikson to North America in 999, leading in turn to the establishment of the first European colonies in America.

In 1066 the British King (Stephen III) accepted Islam in exchange for aid against the Vikings. Stephen's conversion subsequently restricted Christianity to the very fringes of Europe and ensured that Christian missionaries focused their efforts on the new North American colonies.

Cyclopedia of the Cross-Temporal Empire

4

IT WOULD BE BEST IF YOU DON'T RETURN

(Sunday: Chikyù)

Sweat ran down the back of Carlos's neck, the coarsely woven linen shirt he was wearing sticking to the skin of his back under the heavy weight of his pack. Just how had he let himself get talked into this, Carlos thought, pausing for a moment to uncork his water flask. The leather had given the lukewarm water an unpleasant taste, and he had to force himself to swallow it. Recorking the flask he discovered that the heat had even softened the outer coating of the bees wax on the flask. Enough that came off on his fingers, and without anything else he could use, he had to wipe it off on his kilt.

He didn't even have the energy left to curse the weather, he thought, taking a moment to catch his breath in the shade of the nearest tree – or what remained of it. A fire had gone through since he was last here four weeks ago, clearing the undergrowth out and leaving the few trees still standing charred and blackened from the fire. The drought was obviously hitting hard, and the Mississippi was now impossible to navigate due to the lack of water in the river, forcing him to take the train, regardless of the threat that posed. At least the kilt was cooler than trousers. He smiled at that thought, wondering if that meant he was starting to get used to it.

But then he remembered what he was doing there, and shook his head – just what had he been thinking? He was a pâtissier, not some sort of James Fleming super spy. But when the head of Imperial Intelligence personally requests your assistance what else can you do? 'Nice and simple', she'd said. All he had to do was turn up at the Anarchist's base, go through their portal and activate the pinger ImpInt had given him. At which time the Empire should be able to get a fix on the line the Anarchists were using as the hub for their portal network. His eyes flicked to the watch on his left arm. "Yep, nice and simple," he muttered.

Taking a breath, he started up the road again. Not that it was much of a road, he thought sourly. It was barely more than a badly rutted track that meandered from tree to tree.

As he approached the top of the hill he checked his watch — quarter to six, good. ImpInt had stressed the need to only activate the pinger between six and half six. He squinted up at the setting sun and the small building nestled between the red maples that crowned the top of the hill. Unlike the white-washed picket fence and small flagstone path that had wound its way up the hill on the Mainline, the path on the Chikyù line defiantly remained a simple dirt track running beside a haphazardly erected split-rail fence in front of a small, gray stone building. A lone figure sat on the edge of the front porch, smoking a long-stemmed corncob pipe. The stink of mooter drifting down from the porch made Carlos wrinkle his nose.

Great – he thought sourly. He wasn't a big fan of the smell of cannabis at the best of times, and this one smelled like a weird combination of hoppy-beer and cabbage.

Still onwards and upwards. All he had to do was get through the portal and trigger the tachyon beacon so ImpInt could triangulate the line, and try not to get killed while he did so.

The figure on the porch raised his hand in greeting, and returning the wave, Carlos opened the gate and started up the track.

"Herman," Carlos said, surprised when he got to the top of the hill and recognized the tall anarchist with the carrot-colored hair he'd last seen in Mainline Pittsburgh.

"Carlos," Herman said, tapping his pipe out on the edge of the porch and standing up to take his hand. "We were starting to worry about you when you didn't turn up in Genessee. What happened?"

"Jade Carvello happened," Carlos said with a sigh, deciding now was as good a time as any to practice the story he'd agreed with ImpInt to explain his disappearance. "I'd met her a couple of times last month in New York and stumbled across her on the train. Turns out she works for the Rucker's Agency, and had managed to get hold of some of the potato virus. I liberated her of it, but it took me ages to lose her. I've got the box in my pack."

Herman raised his eyebrows. "I better get you through, then."

"I'm surprised to find you here though, Herman," Carlos said as the young anarchist opened the front door to the house and waved him in.

"Pittsburgh had become too hot for us," Herman said. "Sandy got transferred to New York, but they decided I was up for a promotion, so here I am."

Carlos looked round at the building's single room, sleeping bag unrolled in the far corner of the rough-hewn wooden floor, wood-burning stove in another. He considered the low table with two cushions in the center of the room, and held back his comments. Herman might consider it a promotion, but personally he would have preferred the comfort of running a safe house on the Mainline, to this.

Herman crossed to unlock the back door. "Come through," he said, bending over to insert the rod of clear plastic attached to a chain around his neck into the lock, and waving him through.

Inside the backroom, the heat from the portal struck Carlos like a blow. The windowless room was smaller than the one on the Mainline, but just as dominated by the shimmering soap bubble of light suspended between its frame against a sidewall.

"Shouldn't there be a guard here?" Carlos asked, looking around the bare room.

"There should be, but there's a bad flu doing the rounds, so we're short staffed at the moment. Here," Herman said, handing him a blindfold. "You know the drill."

Carlos nodded and slid the blindfold over his eyes. He hated how defenseless it made him feel. Herman took his arm, a gentle pressure on his elbow, the stink of the mooter he'd been smoking almost overwhelming in the confined space, and together they stepped through the portal. Despite the blindfold, his eyes flooded with light. Once again, time hiccuped, then the chaos of the portal spat him back out again and he stumbled at the slight difference in the floor level.

His watch was noticeably warmer, and he hoped there wasn't anything wrong with it. The techs hadn't said anything about any sort of heat discharge.

There was a moment of uneasy silence.

"What's wrong?" Carlos asked finally.

"Just waiting for the guard," Herman replied.

"I thought there was a permanent one here."

"We don't have *that* many resources," Herman said with a laugh. "There's permanent CCTV coverage though, and enough explosives in the floor to take out the portal and both rooms. All remotely managed from the control room."

That was way too much information when you were actually standing on the floor filled with all that explosive, Carlos thought.

Time seemed to pass extremely slowly without light, but finally Carlos heard approaching footsteps.

"Herman," a voice said. "Who have you got?"

"Hermandez?" Carlos said, surprised, recognizing the voice of his flatmate, and active member of the Anarchist's Armed Action Wing.

"Carlos? No, keep the blindfold on," Hermandez said quickly as Carlos started to lift the corner of his blindfold.

Carlos sighed but dropped his hands.

"What are you doing here, Carlos?" Hermandez asked. "You were supposed to meet me at Genessee."

"Jade Carvello happened," Carlos said, repeating his cover story. "You met her when she dropped by the flat once. It turns out she works for the Rucker's Agency. She recognized me on the train and tried to arrest me. I got away with her backpack, and when I went through it later I found a sample of the potato virus."

"You've got it with you?"

Carlos hefted his bag. "In here."

Hermandez sighed. "I wish you hadn't done that?"

"Why?" Carlos asked, wishing he could see Hermandez' face. It was maddening playing poker without being able to see any of the cards.

"We'd set her up. The authorities were to arrest her and find the virus. It would have got them off us, and got her out of the way."

"Well, I wish someone had told me that. It would have made things a lot easier. It took me ages to get her off my trail."

"I apologize for that. We weren't expecting you to be quite so . . . effective."

Carlos gave a depreciative shrug.

"I better debrief you properly before we send you through then," Hermandez said. "I'll take him from here, Herman."

"See you around, Carlos," the young orange-top said, letting go of his arm.

"This way," Hermandez said, leading Carlos outside. Carlos could hear the cry of birds in the distance and smell pine trees on the breeze. Unlike last time, and the mud and rain that had greeted him, the ground felt dry and firm under the thin leather soles of his moccasins.

They didn't have to walk far, only twenty steps or so, until Hermandez guided him over the doorstep.

"Stay here," Hermandez told him. "I'll be back in a couple of minutes. You can take the blindfold off and make yourself a cup of tea while you're waiting."

When Carlos heard the door close, he lifted the blindfold cautiously, to find himself in a small, metallic, half-cylindrical building, about sixteen feet wide and eighteen in length. The walls were made of corrugated iron that curved overhead before settling onto the room's pressed earth floor. The building reminded him of the Nissen huts developed by the English during the War of Prussian Succession against the Russians. It even had the clap-board walls which filled in the end of each cylinder.

The building had a single door and two windows built into each end. The windows were covered with blue and white checked curtains. The room itself was sparsely furnished with a sink, a small gas stove, and a formica table with four metal-legged chairs placed around it in the center of the room.

His eyes flicked over the windows, making sure the curtains were all closed, before he slid his watch off and turned it over. The five major zodiac signs engraved into the back of the case stared back him. Pressing them in the order ImpInt had drilled into him he was reassured by an almost inaudible buzz from the watch.

Mission accomplished, he thought as he slipped the watch back on. And in a couple of days, an assault team of ImpSec's finest would descend on the base with all the subtlety of a baseball bat.

With that out of the way he headed for the basin, and the small cupboard under it to make that cup of tea Hernandez had suggested. Instant milk, sugar, and a variety of teabags rewarded his search. The first teabag he pulled out was Earl Gray, and he remembered Jade telling him Bergamot made her sick. He found himself smiling inanely as he remembered Jade's promise of a night of unbridled debauchery if he didn't do anything that got him killed.

He frowned, surprised by the fact that he was still staring at the teabag – what? It took a moment to realize that the label was in English – which meant they'd got it from the Mainline. If it was from the Sultan line it would have been in Arabic, or maybe Mandarin, he'd heard the Han Empire was a significant player on the line.

There was a knock on the door, and Hernandez poked his head around it. "Carlos, I need to introduce you to someone. Bring your pack."

Carlos sighed and replaced the teabag in its container. As Hermandez hadn't said anything about the blindfold, he wasn't sure if that meant his security rating had improved, or it no longer mattered what he saw as they planned on killing him. 'Don't panic', he told himself, 'remember unbridled debauchery'. A memory of Jade burst from his memory, eyes flashing, her lips thinned as she rounded on him after discovering he had been an undercover agent for the Agence Nationale de la Sécurité (the French Secret Service). Given her temper, ending up dead would probably be the least of his problems – for some reason, that served to calm him.

"This is quite a setup," Carlos said, as he stepped outside and got his first look at the base proper.

Directly in front of him was a row of three buildings of the same size and construction as the one behind him. All the buildings were skinned in corrugated iron, which presumably had made it easier to bring through the portal. Flat pack housing.

"It is," Hermandez agreed. "Unfortunately, I can't take any responsibility for it. But if you come this way, I'll introduce you to the person who can."

"So where are we?" Carlos asked as they headed back toward the sandbagged bunker that he presumed housed the portals.

"I'm not sure," Hermandez admitted, as they detoured around the bunker. "But it's definitely not part of the C-T E. There's been no sign of any human activity on the river while I've been here. Come through here," he said, holding the door open to the building on the far side of the bunker.

"Sayyid ibn Ali," Hermandez said politely, as he knocked on the open door just off from the short corridor inside. "I'd like to introduce you to Carlos Babineaux."

A small dapper man with a thin mustache came to his feet and gave Carlos a short, perfectly measured bow of his head. Carlos was not surprised to see he was wearing the dark-blue, almost black uniform of a General in one of the Etehad Sho'mali's guard regiments.

"Sayyid," Carlos said, returning the bow deeply enough to bend from the waist.

"Mr. Babineaux, you will drink tea with us — no?"

"Thank you," Carlos said, taking the seat offered, as Hermandez took the chair next to him.

"Corporal, three teas please," the Sayyid called, before turning his attention back to Carlos. "Mr. Cortez has informed me you recovered some of our property. May I see it?"

"Of course," Carlos said, opening his pack and pulling out the package about the size of a small box of cigars. He placed the plain, brown-paper on the desk in front of the Sayyid.

"You have opened it?" the Sayyid picking the package up.

"Yes," Carlos said.

As the Sayyid carefully unwrapped the paper the corporal appeared with three cups of fine bone china.

"Thank you," Carlos said, as he took a sip. He almost giggled at the thought it wasn't Earl Grey.

The Sayyid opened the simple wooden case, and all three leaned forward to consider the two glass phials, carefully stopped, sealed, and cushioned in cotton wool inside the box. One of the seals was broken and carefully the Sayyid lifted the phial out of the box. "Its been opened," he said suspiciously.

Carlos nodded. "I think Jade, Miss Carvello, did it before I recovered it." In reality, ImpInt had done it to obtain a sample. He hadn't been told what they intended to do with the sample, and he hadn't asked.

The Sayyid nodded, and carefully replaced the phial in its bed of protective cotton wool.

"It is unfortunate that you obtained the virus, but I am impressed by the fact that you were able to do so. Mr. Cortez has informed me that given the situation in New York at the moment, it might be better if you didn't return immediately."

"Oh?" Carlos looked at Hermandez questioningly.

Hermandez shrugged. "There was an attempt to kidnap the daughter of Markus Ackov. It resulted in the death of two ImpSec officers and ImpSec have been breaking down doors and busting heads ever since. If you went back, you'd be in custody within twenty-four hours. And you're too useful to the cause for that."

Carlos tried to hide his relief that apparently he was getting promoted and not killed. "And the kidnapping. How did it turn out?" he asked, already knowing the answer.

Hermandez looked embarrassed. "The child was recovered by a joint ImpSec — Rucker Agency operation, about a week ago."

Carlos nodded. "So, what do you suggest?"

"We have need of an agent for an operation on our own line," the Sayyid said.

"On Sultan?" Carlos could not hide his surprise.

"On Sultan," the Sayyid confirmed.

Carlos raised an eyebrow. Sultan's cold war had turned hot about five years ago, in an orgy of mutual self-destruction between the two major military alliances. The consensus on the Mainline, until recently, had been that it had become a dead line. That view had recently changed, not least because of intelligence he'd provided. But it was reassuring to have that intelligence confirmed.

"Where precisely?" Carlos asked.

"I will need the permission of my superiors on Sultan before I can tell you, but I thought I should explain why you'll be staying here for a couple of days, so you didn't start to worry." The Sayyid checked his watch. "I am due to return to Sultan later today. I will inform you as soon as a decision has been made."

"Of course, and thank you for telling me," Carlos said, wondering how Jade was going to take his continued disappearance.

5

She's Awake

(Tuesday: Mainline, New York)

Margaret lay there, struggling to move, as her muscles continued to ignore her commands. Her thoughts floundered, circling and dissolving as she tried to remember what had happened. Gradually her thoughts coalesced into memory, and she recalled the decision to call it quits — taking the pills she'd been hoarding for months along with the vodka. Obviously, something had gone wrong, and she almost groaned at the thought she might have to do it all over again or, even worse, have to explain to others why she had done it. She must have made some sort of noise, because she heard a movement and felt someone lean over her.

"Margaret?"

The voice sounded familiar, but for the moment she couldn't place it.

"Mama," the voice called. "She's awake."

The voice helped her sit up, stroked her back, and she felt a glass pressed against her lips. Parched. She felt a trickle of water enter her mouth and tried to swallow, but the water went down the wrong way and she coughed explosively.

When she'd stopped coughing, she felt the press of the glass on her lips again and took a sip. A couple of sips was all she could manage before she shook her head and the voice helped her lie back down. Someone pressed their lips against her forehead, and she drifted off to sleep again.

She woke to the subdued glow of a gaslight. Turning her head cautiously, she saw the shadow of someone familiar sitting in the chair next to the bed.

"Mama?" she asked, puzzled, wondering what her mother was doing there.

Her mother looked round, startled. "Margaret?"

Suddenly Margaret remembered the pills and felt a surge of embarrassment. How was she going to face everyone?

"Louise!" her mother called as she bent over her to help her sit up, plumping the pillow up behind her before offering her some water from the glass on the bedside table.

Remembering what had happened last time, Margaret took a cautious sip.

There was the sound of running feet, and her sister appeared in the doorway. "Mama?"

"Margaret's awake again. Can you ask the nurse to step in?"

"How do you feel?" her mother asked as Louise disappeared.

"I've got a headache."

"Well, I'm not surprised. You've been unconscious for three days. You're dehydrated."

"Is Papa here?" Margaret asked, dreading the answer.

"No, he's back on Dontfrey. He's still not well enough to travel."

Margaret's embarrassment increased at the thought that it had been her actions which had made her mother leave her father at home.

"And don't you worry about that," her mother said, as though reading her mind. "Papa is fine. He sends you his love."

Louise reappeared, followed a moment later by the nurse.

The nurse looked across at Margaret, then made shooing gestures at Louise and their mother. "I will see the patient by myself."

Margaret wanted to argue, feeling there was safety in numbers, even if one of the numbers was her mother, but her family disappeared without complaint. Then she had to put up with ten minutes of getting prodded and poked as the nurse made sure that everything was working as it should. Satisfied at last, the nurse replaced her stethoscope in its case and surveyed her patient through narrowed eyes.

"I'll send a message round to let Doctor Castle know you're awake, and in my view he can see you tomorrow."

Margaret nodded.

"But I must ask. Why did you try to kill yourself?"

'Kill'? Margaret puzzled at the word. She hadn't really thought about it that way. To her, it had simply been a way to escape the relentless despair that had enveloped her. In the end, she simply shrugged. "I was tired," she said, aware that it didn't really cover the hopelessness she'd felt.

"Of what?"

"Of everything."

The nurse studied her. "Can I have your promise you won't try it again until Doctor Castle has spoken to you?"

Margaret eyed her exhaustedly. "I'm too tired to try anything," she admitted.

"I'll take that as a yes. You do realize I'll hold you to it."

If Margaret had had the energy, she'd have rolled her eyes. Just what did the nurse think she could do if Margaret tried to kill herself again?

But apparently after taking her non-response as agreement she left. Margaret struggled to keep her eyes open, but she must have lost the fight because the next thing she was aware of was a hand gently stroking her forehead and the soft sound of crying. Although her eyelids still seemed like lead, she forced them open to see Louise looking down at her, tears slowly coursing their way down her cheeks. One tear broke free, and Margaret flinched as it splashed onto her forehead.

She batted her sister's hand away. "You're making me wet."

"It's your fault for making me cry," Louise said, not backing down.

"And how did I do that?" Margaret asked.

Louise gestured helplessly, temporarily lost for words, which for her sister must have been a first, Margaret thought.

"Why?" Louise demanded finally.

"I'm tired."

"Tired!" Louise's voice rose hysterically.

"Yes, tired," Margaret said. "And yelling at me isn't helping."

"What am I supposed to do then? That doesn't make any sense."

Margaret remembered how tired she had been that morning when the uprising on Dontfrey had finally come to its final, bloody conclusion. She blinked, and once again she was staring down from the outer walls of the fort into the crater and the remains of the bodies that filled it.

Over the fresh stink of death, she could smell the reek of cordite, and the residue of the explosives that the defenders had used in that last gesture of defiance and despair. The stink clawed at her throat as she stared blankly down into the crater.

Finally, unable to face what she, and hers, had done, she turned her back on the scene and walked away down the hill. Behind her the soldiers continued to transfer the remains of what had once had been humans into the pit they'd dug.

There was a tightness in her chest, and she had to remind herself to breathe. Almost on autopilot, she undid the buttons to her shirt.

She could remember how tired she'd felt at that moment. So tired of the war, of the killing. Tired of just being unable to ever admit that she couldn't carry on.

"I've been tired for a very, long time," Margaret said finally.

Louise took a deep breath, then settled herself on the edge of the bed. "What happened to you during the war? Mama would never say."

Margaret shook her head. "I can't tell you."

"Why?"

"Because I can't remember!"

Louise looked at her, surprised.

"Honestly, I can't remember," Margaret told her tiredly. "Now, leave me so I can go to sleep."

#

The sun woke her the next morning, and she must have made some noise as the person who'd been dozing in the chair next to the bed jerked awake. It was her mother, who grimaced as she looked at the clock before climbing stiffly to her feet.

"Can I have some water?" Margaret asked.

"Of course," Mama said. She helped Margaret sit up and held a straw to her lips to allow her to take a sip.

After finishing half the cup, Margaret pushed the straw away.

As her mother replaced the cup on the side-stand, there was a soft knock on the open bedroom door.

"Miss Peric?" a young voice asked worriedly.

Margaret craned her head round to see Jessie's anxious face peering around the door.

"Hello Jessie," Margaret said.

"Daddy said you were sick. Are you going to die?"

Jessie was obviously worried, and Margaret looked at her mother uncertainly. Just what did one tell a seven-year-old in answer to a question like that?

"No," her mother told the young girl. "She is most definitely *not* going to die."

There was an edge to her mother's voice, but Jessie's worried face continued to watch her from around the edge of the door.

"No, Jessie. I'm not going to die," Margaret said.

"Jessie!" Markus's voice said from the top of the stairs.

Mama looked as if she wanted to slam the door on them both, but Margaret squeezed her hand, and when Mama looked down at her, Margaret shook her head.

"Come here, Jessie," Margaret said, giving the coverlet a pat.

Jessie uncertainly crossed the rug, as though with every step she expected Margaret to disappear.

When Jessie reached the bed, Margaret pulled the young girl against her. She smelled clean and fresh, so different from Margaret's own memories of the war. The shampoo in her hair had the odor of roses.

"Margaret, I'm sorry," Markus said embarrassed, from the doorway. "Jessie, I told you not to worry Miss Peric."

Out of the corner of her eye, Margaret saw her mother raise an immaculate eyebrow at the informality of Markus's address.

"It's all right Markus," Margaret said. "Come in," she told him, waving him in from where he still hovered uncertainly by the door. "I presume you've met my mother."

"Indeed," her mother said. "Good morning, *Markus.*"

Markus blanched. "Ma'am," he said.

"Oh, come now," Margaret's mother said. "Surely you can call me Isobel."

Just what did her mother think she was playing at, Margaret thought.

"I don't think I could do that," he said helplessly, looking at Margaret.

"Do you think you could give us some time alone, Mama?"

"Of course," her mother said.

Margaret patted the bed and Markus sat down doubtfully on the coverlet, lifting Jessie onto the bed beside him.

"How are you?" Markus asked uncertainly, as Margaret's mother closed the door behind her.

Margaret gave a small shrug. "Embarrassed."

"Why?"

"I don't know. . . ." She trailed off. "I just am. Perhaps because it feels as if I failed, and I'm not allowed to."

"Failed how?" he asked softly. "Because you tried to kill yourself, or because you weren't successful?"

"How should I know?" Margaret retorted angrily.

"Daddy," Jessie warned him.

"Sorry liebchen," he said, before turning back to Margaret. "If there's anything I can do . . ."

"I know."

"But you need to ask," he pointed out.

She gave him a small smile. "I know."

"I . . . we," he said, catching himself, "thought we'd lost you."

"Well, you haven't," she said, patting his hand.

Her eyes sagged, exhausted. When she opened them again, she found Markus watching her, a strange expression on his face and Jessie lying next to her.

"What?" she demanded.

Markus simply shook his head.

"How was your trip?" she asked, shifting her arm around Jessie to make herself more comfortable.

"A waste of time," he said. "But the First Leader's scientific staff wanted me to have a look at the gene sequencing equipment Iapura brought through the portal with him from Nayarit. See whether any of it still worked."

"And does it?"

"Of course not — it's over a hundred years old. Assuming it was even working when it came through. Which, given the situation at the time is highly unlikely."

Margaret gave him a wan smile. "I've no idea why you'd think that eighty years of total war would have had any effect at all on their ability to maintain any sort of technological infrastructure."

"Well, even if it was working then it clearly isn't now. And we just don't have the technology, or the knowledge to repair it."

There was a moment's silence as Margaret stroked Jessie's hair. "Any news on Jade?" she asked finally. Her friend had left for Sultan the day before her suicide attempt.

"Not yet, but it's still early days."

"And nothing on Carlos?" she asked, referring to Jade's boyfriend.

"Nothing since he triggered the medallion."

"Poor Jade," Margaret said, feeling for her friend. That relationship didn't look as though it was going to get any easier.

She was unable to resist a sigh, and Markus returned it with a small smile, understanding her concern.

"So," he said. "Has anyone brought you up to date on Lauren's love life yet?"

"No," Margaret said, brightening at the thought of a little harmless gossip concerning the second of the household's underhousemaids. Lauren had just started walking out with her first beau, an employee of the New York's Tram-line, and the entire household seemed intent on providing her with advice on how to handle the situation. It was all so much simpler than Jade's situation and her missing double agent, or even compared to her own non-existent love life she thought, catching Markus's eyes. "Has he asked her out again?"

"He has indeed," Markus said and immediately launched into a description of their second date, which apparently had involved pizza in the park, followed by roller skating on the rink.

When her mother looked in half an hour later, Jessie was lying next to her on the bed, her head sharing Margaret's pillow, as Markus continued an explanation of what he actually thought of his first airship ride.

6

Welcome To Sultan, Mr. Babineaux

(Monday: Sultan)

Carlos carefully lifted the blue and white checked curtain covering the room's back window to peer out into the darkness. He could just make out the dim glow from the sentry's cigarette in the distance, where he had paused for a moment by the edge of the fence. Carefully sliding the window open, Carlos silently lowered himself out. On the ground, he paused. The night air was damp with the hint of rain, and the low clouds that hid the moon gave him the best chance he'd had all week of getting rid of the watch. ImpInt had assured him that there was no need and it was virtually undetectable. but they weren't the ones surrounded by paranoid terrorists while wearing a tachyon pinger that had been used to let the Empire know the location of their secret base.

Sliding the window closed behind him, he wondered why he'd ever accepted his uncle's offer to join the Agence Nationale de la Sécurité. Admittedly, the hours were usually better than a pâtissier's, but the pay was rubbish, and the job could get you killed. The only thing he had going for him at the moment was that the base was still short staffed due to the flu.

As the sentry stubbed his cigarette out and moved away, Carlos worked his way further along the path that ran inside the high wire fence that ran round the base until he reached the grate covering the drain at the intersection of two buildings. Cautiously peering around the corner, he checked out the building on the far side of the path. Nothing.

He slowly lifted out the grate and placed it by the side of the hole. Sliding his watch off he wiped it clean with his handkerchief, then, still holding it by the handkerchief, pushed it as far down the drain as he could reach. Hopefully, the first proper rain would wash it down into the dry well.

He'd just replaced the grate when a door opened in the admin building and light spilled out onto the path. He froze as a woman with short, red hair stepped out of the building. Hermandez and a guard were with her, but it was plain she wasn't a prisoner as Hermandez shook her hand before the guard escorted her across the path to the bunker housing the portals.

For a moment Carlos wondered who the woman was, then thinking he'd probably already used up more than his quota of luck for the night, turned and carefully worked his way back to his room. Edging the window open again, he hoisted himself back into the room, where leaning back against the wall he let his breath out with a quavering sigh, relieved he'd finally got rid of the evidence. If anyone had found it on him, and worked out what it was, well goodbye Carlos.

The sudden clarion of an alarm slammed him upright as the glare of security lights outside flooded the site. For a moment, he was convinced they'd discovered him. A moment later, the sound of gunfire in the distance reassured him. Here comes the cavalry, he thought with a grimace. Now all he had to avoid was getting shot with the rest of the bad guys.

There was a knock on the door, and he opened it cautiously to find Hermandez standing outside.

"What's happening?" Carlos asked, already knowing the answer. Imperial Security had finally tracked the signal he'd sent back to its source. He offered a silent prayer of thanks to Saint Joshua, the patron saint of spies, that at least they'd left the attack until after he'd got rid of the watch.

"Don't know," Hermandez said. "Grab your bag."

"Why?"

"Just do it. Here, you might need this," Hermandez said, and tossed him something heavy.

Carlos swore and almost dropped it before he realized it was a revolver. He checked it was loaded, then slid it under the belt in the small of his back.

"Now move it."

As Carlos grabbed his bag from beside the bed, there was a sudden explosion in the distance and the power went out.

"Shit," Hermandez said. It was pitch black, with not even any emergency lighting to help. "OK, follow me," Hermandez said, turning right and heading down the side of the building.

Running his hand along the wall, Carlos followed the darker shadow of the anarchist in front of him. At the end of the building, Hermandez paused.

"Where are we going?" Carlos asked.

"Portal. OK, it looks clear," Hermandez said, and led them across the gap to the next building. He worked his way along the wall until he could see round the corner. He was peering around the corner when a shot spun him round, and a flood of blood stained his sleeve.

Stunned, Carlos watched him slide down the wall; the thump, thump, thump as his head hit each corrugation only ending when he reached the ground. Carlos reacted automatically, a flick of his wrist and the switchblade had locked into position. "Hold still," he told the unconscious Hermandez as he cut through the seam of Hermandez' shirt at the top of the arm. Slicing off a strip, he cut the rest of the sleeve in half and, placing half against the entry wound, he pressed the rest into the back of the shoulder and tied it into place. He tightened the strip around the two pads to hold them in place with a sharp tug that brought a gasp of protest from Hermandez.

"You're back with us," Carlos said brutally. "We need to get you a doctor."

"The Sultan portal," Hermandez hissed through clenched teeth. "It's the only one still with power."

Carlos nodded. For maximum security, the portal to Sultan would be controlled from that line. "Which one is it?" he asked.

"The closest."

The portal the woman had gone through less than half an hour before. Now it made sense, although it still didn't explain who she was. Lying down, Carlos wriggled forward to peer around the corner. It was dim, but he thought he could just make out four silhouetted figures in the heavy protective gear of ImpSec assault troops just outside the fence.

"Let's go," Carlos said, grabbing Hermandez and slinging his good arm over his shoulder to lift him. He rushed Hermandez across the gap, almost throwing him through the entrance to the bunker. Inside, the space was deserted, with just the shimmering soft glow of the portal to light the room.

The earth shook as a series of heavy mortar rounds walked their way across the base.

"What the hell's that?" Hermandez said.

"Closing time," Carlos suggested dryly.

Taking a fresh hold on Hermandez' belt, he hoisted him back up and pulled him forward at the run into the safety of the portal.

As the portal spat them out on Sultan, he came to an abrupt halt, and quickly releasing Hermandez raised his hands at the sight of the five assault rifles leveled at him. As he did, Hermandez slid slowly to the ground with a muffled groan.

"Carlos Babineaux and Hermandez Cortez. Hermandez needs a medic," he blurted.

There was a muttered order in Arabic and one of the soldiers handed his rifle to the other and came over to inspect Hermandez. Carlos carefully backed away to one side, still holding his arms up and aware of the weight of the revolver in the small of his back. Confirming the wound, the soldier helped Hermandez to his feet and the two disappeared through the door at the back of the room.

"Welcome to Sultan, Mr. Babineaux," an officer said, pushing through the group.

"Sayyid ibn Ali," Carlos said, recognizing the officer.

"What's happening?" the Sayyid demanded.

Carlos relaxed slightly. "I saw four heavily armed infantry at the perimeter fence just before we came through, but I don't know how many more there might be. The base is completely without power, and it sounded like they were using some sort of mortar."

The Sayyid winced. "Sergeant, take someone with you and check. If Mr. Babineaux is right about there being no power, activate the self-destruction charges and get back here."

The Sergeant nodded and with a jerk of his head to another soldier took off through the portal.

The self-destruction wasn't entirely unexpected but Carlos hoped ImpSec wouldn't lose too many officers. Unfortunately, there wasn't anything he could do to help.

"And we better get you out of here," the Sayyid told him. "You will find our accommodation a little crowded, but I hope you won't hold that against us. Please, this way," he said, gesturing Carlos toward the same door Hermandez had disappeared through.

The gun was a comforting weight in the small of his back, and Carlos started to calculate the odds of taking control of the control room. He'd need to hold the portal open until ImpSec could come through, which he doubted would be possible, still . . . The faint hope disappeared when one soldier let out an exclamation, and raised his rifle as Carlos followed the Sayyid.

The Sayyid turned. "Mr. Babineaux, your weapon please. Slowly," he added quickly.

Slowly, very slowly, Carlos removed the revolver and handed it over. The Sayyid looked at the gun and lifted an eyebrow.

"Hermandez gave it to me," Carlos explained.

"And we will certainly give it back to you when you leave our care," the Sayyid said. "But it would be safer for all concerned if you didn't carry it while here."

Well, there went that idea, Carlos thought dryly. He wasn't that disappointed. The whole idea had seemed pretty much a suicide run. At least this way, there was still a chance he would get to see Jade again.

Outside the room, he found himself in a narrow corridor. One way went approximately twenty feet before it ran up against a heavy airlock. The other toward what appeared a steep set of stairs. "Downstairs, first landing, then first on the left. Find a bed and wait. I'll catch up with you just as soon as we've finished up here," the Sayyid said.

"Of course," Carlos replied.

The steps were steep and Carlos had to proceed carefully to ensure he didn't slip. At the bottom of the first landing he paused, wondering what existed further down, but it was probably too dangerous at the moment to find out. Taking the first door on the left, as he'd been told, he found himself in a brightly lit room crowded with ten bunk beds. There was barely enough room to slip between the bunks. Whatever they were doing here, they didn't have much room for it.

"Are you looking for something?" a female voice asked and Carlos raised an eyebrow at the New York accent and grimaced when he realized he'd missed the fact that one of the beds was occupied.

"The Sayyid said to grab a bed."

"Well go ahead, there's enough of them," she told him.

Carlos dumped his satchel onto the closest upper bunk, then bent down to peer under it at the woman on the lower bunk at the far end of the room.

The woman, obviously the same one he'd seen going through the portal earlier, was lying on top of the covers reading a book.

"Carlos Babineaux," he said.

"Karen."

Carlos quickly controlled his anger as he recognized the name. Karen was the rogue agent from the Agency who'd tried to kill Jade, and when that had failed had planted the potato virus on her and tipped off Chikyù security. What made it worse was that Jade had considered Karen a friend. That betrayal was something that Carlos knew he would never forgive or forget. For now, though, he plastered a smile on his face.

"Pleased to meet you, Karen," he said. "How long have you been here?"

"About an hour," she said, not looking up from her book, and obviously trying to give the signal that she wished he'd stop talking to her. Well, if he couldn't arrest her, or shoot her, at least he could spoil her reading.

Lifting himself up, he allowed himself to fall back onto the mattress, before bouncing up and down a couple of times, making the springs creak. The bed sagged badly.

"You from the Mainline?" he asked.

"Hmm . . ." she said.

"It's just you sound like you're from New York."

She ignored him.

He bounced a couple more times.

"So have you seen outside? It's just this setup seems a little unusual," he said, not looking at her. "I mean, being underground and everything."

That seemed to have got through to her as he heard her sigh and close the book.

"No, I haven't been outside, and I'm not looking forward to having to do it."

"Why?"

"Radiation. This base is just on the edge of the radiation areas, but if the winds blow from the East, well . . ."

"What happened?"

"The Great War against the United Christian States is what happened. The entire confederation was destroyed — all thirty million people in a nuclear holocaust. Now, if I've answered your question, I would like to finish my book?"

"Of course," Carlos said. Thirty million people! Admittedly, that paled into insignificance when you looked at the number of those who died during the expansion of the C-T Empire. But the deaths caused by the Empire had generally been unintentional, simply the result of the diseases that followed in the wake of contact with the Empire. But to intend to kill all those people — that was completely different.

Lying back, he wondered how the attack on the base was going, how he could get a message back to the Mainline, and then, perhaps even more importantly, how was he going to get home. He had the feeling that if he wasn't around to keep an eye on Jade, she would get herself into trouble again. If he hadn't been around last time, she'd have been dead within twenty-four hours because of Karen's stitch-up. And wasn't that a great thought to try and get to sleep on, he thought.

To relax, he thought about the next motto he could suggest for Jade to adopt. Perhaps: *Nam solus honor,* 'For Honor Alone'. He thought about it, then shook his head. No, too serious. He'd need to remember it though, for when he'd given up trying to get a rise from her.

7

VIGNETTE:
A BRIEF INTRODUCTION TO SULTAN (2)

While Christian Missionaries on the Sultan Line accompanied Leif Erikson to North America in 999 to establish the first European colonies in America, it was not until 1252 that a Spanish fleet from the Southern Caliphate established the first colony in South America.

Islamic influence, backed by gunpowder and guns quickly expanded across South America. However, the arrival of the Black Death in Europe in 1348 disrupted all contact between Europe and the Americas for almost a hundred years. It was during this period that Husan bin Movak, born in the Mayan capital of Mayapan in 1350, declared he was the Mahdi, and had received revelations from Kukulcán, the Mayan's Feathered Serpent God. Merging Mayan and Islamic beliefs his followers were later declared zindiqs, or heretics by Ja'fari jurisprudence, but his faith still retains significant influence in both Central and Southern America.

CYCLOPEDIA OF THE CROSS-TEMPORAL EMPIRE
GAZETTEER

8

I Must Apologize For My Mother

(Thursday: Mainline, New York)

Margaret was sitting in the sunroom with her mother. Both of them were reading or, at least in Margaret's case, pretending to read. She couldn't concentrate. The words blurred across the paper in front of her, but if she wasn't reading her mother would be worried so she turned the pages and feigned an interest. There was a soft cough from the doorway, and she looked up to see Lauren, the underhousemaid, standing uncertainly by the door.

"Pardon me ma'am, there's a Doctor Helen Rubenstein for you. She says you have an appointment."

Margaret shook her head. "No," she said surprised. "I'm not aware of any appointment."

Her mother looked up from her reading. "That's fine, Lauren. Please show Doctor Rubenstein to the front room and ask her if she'd like tea."

"Of course, ma'am," Lauren said, pulling the door closed behind her.

"Mama!" Margaret protested.

"Now don't you Mama me!" her mother said. "Doctor Castles recommended her. I had to pull a lot of favors to get her to agree to see you here rather than at her rooms. Doctor Castles felt it was important though."

Great, Margaret thought. Now her mother was colluding with her doctor. Slamming her book closed she stood up. "I'd better see her then," she snapped.

"You do that dear," her mother said placidly, her eyes already back on her book.

Lauren was just pulling the door to the front room closed behind her as Margaret appeared.

"Is she in there?" Margaret asked.

"Yes, ma'am."

Opening the door Margaret walked in, causing the woman standing by the window to turn quickly.

Margaret hid her own surprise at how young the woman looked. Her brown hair was heavily coiffured, while the long string of pearls around her neck reached almost to her waist. She wore a beaded, flapper style dress, something that had already gone out of fashion before the war. With her heavy eyes and thin wrists, the dress suited her though.

"Doctor Rubenstein, I presume," Margaret said.

"Yes, and you are?"

"Margaret Peric." Margaret offered her hand. Doctor Rubenstein shook it firmly.

"Please," Margaret said, seating herself in one of the wing-backed chairs in front of the empty fireplace. "Is Lauren getting you anything to drink?" she asked.

"No. I didn't need anything."

"I must apologize for my mother."

"Oh?" Rubenstein looked genuinely surprised.

"For dragging you here."

"Your mother? Oh no it was the First Leader."

"Donald!" Just why was everyone conspiring against her? "What did he do?"

"He phoned me personally to stress the importance of ensuring your recovery. Apparently, he needs you to lead an embassy to Sultan."

Margaret raised an eyebrow.

Rubenstein gave a small smile at the gesture. "He also stressed his personal regard for your continued good health."

"And that persuaded to you make a house call?"

"No, it didn't. It was the offer to establish a clinic for returned soldiers and fully fund it for the next ten years." She gave Margaret a good-natured smile. "I've been operating on a shoestring for the last two years. The offer was simply too good to turn down."

"And so now you're here."

"And now I'm here," Rubenstein agreed. She pulled a notepad and pencil out of her briefcase.

"So, what happens now?" Margaret asked.

"You've never had any counseling?"

Margaret shook her head.

Rubenstein sighed. "Why am I not surprised. To give you some background — for the last two years I've specialized in treating the post-traumatic stress disorders of ex-soldiers. Generally, the approach I favor is called cognitive behavioral therapy. You could think of it as a talking therapy."

"And that works?" Margaret asked dubiously.

"Yes. Basically, it helps you notice how your thoughts and actions influence one another. The therapy aims to break overwhelming problems down into smaller parts to make them easier to cope with."

"Makes sense, I suppose," Margaret said doubtfully.

"I'm glad you agree," the doctor told her dryly. "So why don't you tell me a little about yourself. Your entry in 'Esquire's Who's Who' was so brief as to be almost useless."

"You'd know I'm thirty-two though. Single. I have one brother, and two sisters."

"And you're presently Secretary of the Department of Agriculture. Yes, that was all in your entry. But I understand you had a second brother — Nedo?"

"He died at the beginning of the uprising on Dontfrey."

> Suddenly Margaret found herself back on Dontfrey on that never to be forgotten, balmy October night almost eight years ago.
>
> The air in the room was close and sweat prickled her forehead from the humidity. Although the palace was built on a hill rising high over the Mississippi below, there was no wind, and with the number of officers crammed into the small room the atmosphere could only be described as 'close'.
>
> "Leader?"
>
> Margaret looked up from the map she was studying to find one of her father's aides standing uncomfortably in the small

room's doorway.

"Yes, Sergeant?"

"Your father needs to see you."

"Now?" She'd only got back with her Troop from the reconnaissance and still needed to finish preparing her report. Suddenly she felt a cold dagger of fear slide into her heart as she realized what the request meant. There had already been reports of atrocities being committed by the rebels and Nedo and Arnold had been missing since the uprising began earlier that morning. "Of course," she said. "I'll be back as soon as I can," she told her Troop Leader.

She'd been expecting the Sergeant to lead her to the command center but instead he turned left and led her into the garden that opened onto the back of the palace. As they emerged into the garden, she heard the rattle of small arms from the city on the far side of the river. Things were not going well, but all they needed to do was to hold onto the portal for another twenty-four hours until their promised reinforcements could arrive.

The garden was softly lit by lights powered by the small hydroelectricity generators situated on the Ohio, several miles upriver. Her reconnaissance had involved checking the turbines, but for the moment it appeared the rebels were concentrating on trying to seize the portal.

Her father sat bent over on a bench under an olive tree. Mama was sitting next to him, arm over his shoulder.

"Papa," she said softly.

When he looked up, she was shocked at how old he looked. He'd been crying and his eyes were red, the emotion raw on his face. Margaret's eyes flooded with tears.

"Nedo?"

Papa nodded. "He's dead."

"Oh Papa, I'm so sorry."

And then she was back again and looking into the concerned eyes of Doctor Rubenstein.

"Does that happen often?" Rubenstein asked.

"What?"

"Your flashbacks."

Margaret shrugged.

Rubenstein leaned forward. "All right, a couple of things: flashbacks can contain very painful material. The important thing is to take pride in your survival and your current safety."

Margaret pulled a face.

"One day that may actually mean something to you," Rubenstein said, "but for the moment, when you notice you're having a flashback you need to acknowledge your response. Whether you are responding to the past or the present, your emotions and reactions are real, and you have to recognize that. Sometimes simply naming the flashback reduces its intensity, but another way is to ground yourself."

"How?" Margaret asked, despite herself.

"Take a deep breath; stamp your feet; get up and get a drink of water. Anything that helps bring you back to the moment. You need to remind yourself that it ended. Whatever you are remembering, you survived it."

Margaret nodded thoughtfully, then gave Rubenstein a small smile. "I'll try to remember."

"Good." The doctor consulted her notes. "Your mother mentioned that you had a breakdown a couple of years ago?"

Margaret frowned. "Did she? I don't remember."

"Really?"

"Really," Margaret said. Flashbacks always left her feeling drained and raw. Deciding to take Rubenstein's advice she stood up and faced the sunlit window. She took a deep breath and let it out slowly.

feeling some of the stress disappear with it.

"Better?" Rubenstein asked.

"A little."

Rubenstein was still looking at her as though she was some sort of specimen.

"Louise, my sister, asked me that as well. What happened after the war?"

For a moment she could smell the shattered pine trees and the stink of cordite and burned flesh.

It's a memory, Margaret told herself, and just like that, it stopped.

"Another flashback?" Rubenstein asked.

"A memory of the last day of the war," Margaret said, naming it. "We'd cornered the rebels but rather than surrender they killed themselves, the children as well. I can remember that morning . . ."

She smelled the stench of cooked flesh and broke out in a sweat.

Finally, she shook her head. "But what happens after that is a complete blank."

Rubernstein watched her for a moment, her head slightly tilted to one side. "Do I have your permission to ask your mother what happened?" she asked. "I think it may be important."

When there was a gaping chasm in her memory, yes it was important. Margaret crossed to the fireplace and pressed the bell. "I think we should both ask her," she said. "Can you ask Mama to come in here please," she asked Lauren when the underhousemaid appeared.

Margaret stood at the window, pretending to ignore Rubenstein, who simply continued to watch her.

"What is it, Margaret?" her mother asked as she came into the room.

"Lauren, can you close the doors and make sure we're not disturbed?" Margaret asked.

As Lauren closed the door behind her Margaret turned to her mother. "You told Doctor Rubenstein I had a breakdown several years ago. I don't remember it."

"Oh." Her mother sat heavily, her normal control deserting her. Looking from one to the other she seemed to shrink into herself. "I presume you want me to tell you about it?"

Margaret and Rubenstein started to speak at the same time, then stopped. "Go on," Margaret told the doctor.

"I think that would be useful," Rubenstein said.

Her mother stared down at her hands. "It was just after the final mop-up on Dontfrey," she said finally. "Margaret's Battlegroup had cornered the last of rebels in a hill fort. They were the last of Jhansi's fanatics, the worst of the worst. We got the story from her Sergeant when he brought her home.

"The Sergeant said Margaret had planned to attack at dawn," she continued, still staring at her hands. "No one expected it would be easy.

They'd been fighting the rebels for nearly two years. They knew what to expect, or they thought they did. But they didn't expect what happened."

The smell of cordite, pine trees, and the stink of death.

Margaret swallowed uneasily at the memory. "They blew themselves up," she said. "Everyone: men, women, children. When we went in at sunrise there was just this massive crater in the center of the fort, and bits of bodies scattered over the grass."

A small hand, bleached white, lying at her feet.

She swallowed hard, trying not to retch.

"According to your Sergeant," her mother said, "you'd been watching the cleanup when you just dropped your revolver and started to walk away, stripping your uniform off as you went. By the time anyone realized what was happening you were already down to your underwear."

"Oh gods," Margaret said, burying her face in her hands at the embarrassment.

Her mother looked at her levelly. "You had a very loyal staff. I never thought we could keep it quiet, and yet not a single rumor. You've always attracted those who will give you their loyalty."

"You said the Sergeant brought her home?" Rubenstein asked, probing.

Margaret's mother nodded. "Apparently she didn't speak the entire trip. Only ate when she was told to. It was as if she'd withdrawn."

Margaret shook her head slowly, unable to believe what she was hearing, and yet why would her mother make something like that up?

"And how long did that last?" Rubenstein asked.

"Perhaps a couple of weeks after she came home," her mother continued. "Then suddenly one day she just woke up and it was as though nothing had happened, and we had our daughter back." She gave Margaret a small, tremulous smile.

"Oh Mama," Margaret said, suddenly understanding the pain her mother must have felt.

"And no counseling or psychiatric sessions?" Rubenstein asked.

"Not that I know of," Margaret said. She looked at her mother, who shook her head.

"No," she confirmed.

Rubenstein looked at her watch. "And that I think is probably enough for today," she announced. "I will be back tomorrow."

Margaret didn't know whether to feel pleased at the news, or terrified at what she might have to find out about herself.

"Thank you," her mother told the doctor. "Margaret," she prompted when Margaret gave no indication of saying anything.

Margaret sighed. "Thank you, Doctor," she parroted.

9

YOU BASTARD - DO YOU KNOW HOW WORRIED I'VE BEEN?

(Saturday: Sultan, Pesh)

Jade had decided to take the morning off and accept the offer from Darda, Emre's sister, to take her shopping. She'd never had a younger sister, or an older sister for that matter, and the experience proved quite different from whenever she'd gone shopping with her mother. Although, she privately conceded, that might be more the fact she'd never shopped anywhere other than in New York. And this was not only a different city, but on a line with a totally different history from her own. Darda's enthusiasm and butterfly interest as she flitted from display to display was exhausting to watch, let alone to participate in.

Jade still had difficulty understanding how such a minor change in Sultan's history in 735CE could have driven it down such a completely different path from that of the Mainline. According to Ferai, who had an interest in such things — perhaps because he'd come from another line — 735 marked the year the Franks lost the battle of Bourges. With the Franks crushed, the Arabs gained control over France up to the Rhine, and within ten years the only remaining countries still Christian were Ireland and

Scotland. In 1252 a Muslim fleet had reached South America and established the first Muslim colony there.

Regardless of the historical facts, according to Darda, Pesh had been the fashion capital of the world 'forever'. Given the variety and number of shops, as well as the range and price of goods on offer, Jade wasn't prepared to argue. By lunch time she found herself the possessor of two new pairs of boots, a belt, and some lingerie that she was looking forward to modeling for Carlos — *if* he ever turned up. While Darda had also acquired a new pair of shoes and a handbag, she had fortunately shown no interest in purchasing her own lingerie. That, given her age, was all to the good. Jade hadn't the foggiest how she'd have explained the purchase to Emre.

They were just about to enter a shop that Darda had promised sold the cutest leather covered notebooks when Jade felt the faint hint of a breath on her ear.

"Fancy meeting you here," Carlos whispered. His breath tickling the hairs on the back of her neck.

"You bastard!" she said, spinning round to face him. "Do you know how worried I've been?"

He grinned back at her unrepentantly, a small boy caught with his hand in the chocolate jar.

"What are you doing here?" she demanded, lowering her voice. "You're supposed to be back on the Mainline. I've been worried sick."

"Change of plans," he said.

"Change of plans!" She thumped him hard enough on his arm to cause him to wince.

"Jade?" It was Darda, and Jade realized they'd been speaking English.

"Sorry," Jade said, quickly swapping back into Arabic. "This is my . . . partner." She paused for a moment, uncertain how to describe her boyfriend to Darda. The Ottoman Empire was a trifle conservative about some things.

Darda looked significantly at the bag containing the lingerie, and Jade felt a flush stain her face.

"Come on," Jade said, grabbing Carlos by his arm and pulling him across the street to the coffee shop she'd noticed opposite. Darda followed uncertainly.

Inside the shop Jade took a table at the back of the shop. "Sit," she ordered him.

"Have I told you how much I like a take-charge woman?" Carlos said, still grinning.

Jade ignored him. "Three coffees," she said, when the waiter came across to take their order.

"So," she said, when the waiter had retreated out of earshot. "What are you doing here, and why the hell didn't you let me know you were OK?"

"I'm sorry Jade," he said sincerely, obviously now aware of how thin the ice he was skating on was. "I honestly didn't know how. The portal was knocked out before I could get back and they've had me working with Karen to build links with the local expatriate Angevin community in Pesh."

"Karen?"

"Yes, your former friend and fellow Rucker's agent, now on ImpSec's most wanted list."

Jade's eyes slitted. "What's she doing here?"

"The same as I am, whatever that is. You need to be careful though," Carlos told her. "If Karen knew you were here, she'd probably arrange to have you killed."

"I'd like to see her try," Jade spat.

"Yes, well let's not give her the chance."

Jade took a deep breath and let it out slowly. "Darda," she said. "Please call for a taxi. We need to get my *partner* back to the base."

Carlos held up a hand. "I can't, Jade. We don't have anything yet. And if I break my cover, we lose our best chance to find out what's actually going on."

"So have you got anything I can pass onto ImpSec that might actually be useful?" she asked, frustrated. "Like who's running the show?"

Carlos shook his head. "I wish. Initially I thought it was the Etehad Sho'mali, but I'm not so sure now. Whoever it is seems to be operating on a shoestring. Technically I'm on the staff of the Angevin Embassy here in Pesh."

"Angevin?" Jade asked.

"The Empire of Great Britain and France."

Darda's eyes went wide. "My brother must know of this," she said.

"Brother?" Carlos said, looking puzzled.

"Emre Kaymakam, Commander of the Janissaries," Jade explained.

"Ah." Carlos sounded impressed. He drained the last of his coffee. "I need to go," he said regretfully. "I have come up with another motto for you to consider though."

"What?" she asked suspiciously. Ever since she'd received the Order of Saint Vladimir for saving the life of the First Leader's cousin Carlos had been joking about her needing a motto, now she was a member of the nobility. His first suggestion had been *ego sum vestrum semper* which had translated as 'I am always right'. She suspected this was going to be along the same lines.

"*Pertinax est a culpa.*"

"Which means?"

"Stubborn to a fault," he told her with a grin.

"I prefer *Armatum periculosum* — Armed and dangerous," she said, smiling sweetly.

Carlos held up his hands quickly, in mock surrender. "Just trying to help."

"Of course you are. Here," Jade said, writing down the phone number Emre had given her. "My cell. If I'm on Sultan, you can reach me on this."

He looked blank.

"My cellular telephone."

He still looked blank.

Rolling her eyes, she rummaged in her handbag for the small phone Emre had given her.

"Ah," he said. "A 'mobile'." Reaching into his jacket pocket he produced his own. "The Embassy gave me one when I arrived."

"Then you shouldn't use it," Darda piped up. "I know my brother has ways of extracting information from a cellular phone if he needs to. It would be dangerous to assume the Angevins can't do the same."

Carlos nodded. "Thanks."

"We may be returning to the Mainline in the next couple of days," Jade told him. "I'll leave the phone with Darda if you need to contact me."

"Understood," Carlos said, standing up. "I need to get a move on before I'm missed. I'll see you soon."

"Make sure you do."

"Oh, you will," he said. Bending, he placed his lips to Jade's ears. "I still have to collect on the night of unbridled passion you promised me."

Jade colored, reminded of the lingerie in it's bag under the table. Carlos smirked at her reaction and started to lean over further for a kiss but catching Darda's look of startled concern he straightened up.

He touched a finger to his forehead, then turned and left.

"Perhaps we should head back," Jade suggested, tearing her gaze away from his retreating back.

Darda nodded.

When Emre had invited the two of them to stay at his house on the base Jade hadn't expected to be invited into a 500-year-old, stone building, last renovated over 100 years before. She could still remember her surprise when she'd found the maid vacuuming the slate floor for the first time, and heard the click, click, click of the slate tiles as they were lifted off the ground by the head of the vacuum cleaner. Luckily that last renovation had included inside toilets and the addition of en suite bathrooms for all the main upstairs bedrooms. That was still a hundred years ago, however, and the white, walled tiles in her own bathroom were cracked and uneven in place from subsidence, while the grout between the floor's blue and white tessellated tiles was black with age. To make up for that the room contained a massive enameled claw-foot bath that she was still trying to work out how, if she could persuade Emre to sell it to her, she would be able to get it back to Mainline New York.

"We're back," Jade called as she and Darda entered the large, central atrium around which the house was built.

"In here," Colonel Ferai called from the living room.

Jade found Ferai lying down on the couch watching *The Brave and the Beautiful.* Jade didn't know what Ferai saw in the daytime dramas, but he had quickly become addicted to them despite the overacting and corny scripts. At least his Arabic was improving as a result.

"Carlos is here," Jade said without preamble, sliding the cheap chintz curtains back from the window to let some light into the room. She slipped off her shoes before stepping onto the thick Persian rug that covered the center of the room. It was one of the few genuine exotic features in the house, and according to Darda had been a present from her grandmother.

"Who?" Ferai asked, not taking his eyes off the screen.

"Carlos Babineaux, my . . . partner." She stuttered over the term again. This stage of a relationship always seemed fraught with definitional difficulties. "The French Secret Service agent."

"The Agence Nationale de la Sécurité?"

Jade rolled her eyes. What was it with guys that they always needed to correct her with the name — there wasn't all that much difference. "That one," she confirmed. "Apparently he's working out of the Angevin embassy here in Pesh."

"I've called my brother," Darda told them, as she entered the room. "He said he'd be here as soon as he could."

Ferai nodded and patted the arm of the sofa behind his head. "Make yourself comfortable until he arrives," he said. "Nurray is going to expose Karli's relationship with their second cousin."

Jade shook her head. "No thanks. I need to pack these away." She waved the bags she was carrying to demonstrate. "From what Emre said yesterday we might be heading home tomorrow."

"You can't stay longer?" Darda asked surprised. "I was hoping . . ."

"Not this time," Jade said, startled at the dismay on Darda's face. "We should be back in a couple of weeks though, if your brother has the news we're hoping for."

Darda nodded, mollified.

It was actually two hours before Emre arrived accompanied by the Vizier, the Caliph's chief adviser, who had been conducting the negotiations. A tall, thin man, the Vizier wore both a Van Dyke goatee and the manner of a professional politician with equal aplomb. More importantly he seemed genuinely intent on helping to establish the new embassy.

"The Caliph has agreed to the terms we discussed yesterday," he said, handing Jade a heavily embossed envelope. "And I can confirm the Old Madrasa will be available for occupation within the week."

"Oh good," Jade said, and Ferai nodded his agreement. The Old Madrasa, or Islamic college, had been built around 1350 and had been derelict for the last thirty years or so. While its massive stone walls would provide a significant degree of physical security, more importantly it occupied the same site as an old monastery on the Mainline which the First Leader had already appropriated in anticipation it might be able to be used for the portal.

"When do you think the first group will arrive?" Emre asked.

Jade looked at Ferai.

"I understand it may take up to a month before the Ambassador can get here," he said. "But the Deputy Ambassador should be here within a week."

Jade nodded again. She'd never met Deputy Ambassador Cardinal Lincoln Abbott, but from his bio in *Who's Who* he didn't seem like someone who'd let anything slow him down. Although trained as a Catholic priest he'd never been ordained, instead being appointed a Cardinal when he'd accepted the role of the Holy See's representative to Naisre. Jade wasn't sure of the sense of appointing a representative of the Christian church to the new embassy on an Islamic line, but she reassured herself that surely someone *must* know what they were doing.

"Good," the Vizier said. "Now concerning this other matter?" He looked at Emre.

"Darda told me that two of your agents are presently on the staff of the Angevin embassy," Emre said, looking at Ferai.

Jade sighed. She'd noticed that while most of the time Emre was quite aware of the need to involve Jade in discussions, at times he couldn't stop himself regressing to the paternalistic attitudes of the vast majority of Ottoman men.

"Not our agents," Jade pointed out. "Well at least Carlos is, but he's a double agent for the anarchists. That's a group who believe in the overthrow of the state."

"And yet despite that they have, as I understand it, allied themselves with the Etehad Shomali." Emre raised an eyebrow. "Who would not generally appear supportive of such an attitude."

"No one ever said extremists made any sense," Ferai said.

"Do you have any idea what they're doing here?" Emre asked Jade.

Jade shook her head. "Carlos didn't know. All he said was that the mission involved establishing communications with the expat community in Pesh. Beyond that . . . ." She shrugged.

"Do you wish me to take immediate action, Excellence?" Emre asked the Vizier. "I could arrange to have them picked up."

The Vizier tapped his chin thoughtfully. "If not for this Carlos, perhaps. But surely it would be better to have someone on the inside, at least until we know precisely what they intend?"

"Then I will merely arrange to increase our monitoring of the Embassy and its staff. Do you have a way of contacting Carlos?" he asked, turning to Jade.

"No, but he does have my . . . number," she finished. "I told him I'd leave my cellular with Darda in case he needs to contact someone."

"Thank you," Emre said. "Excellency?"

"I think that finishes our work for today then," the Vizier said. "I look forward to meeting you again on your return Miss Carvello, Colonel Ferai," and with a bow he ushered himself out.

"Will you be returning tomorrow?" Emre asked.

Jade looked at the envelope on the table and nodded. "I think we'd better."

"I will of course supply a vehicle," Emre said. "What time do you wish to leave?"

"Earlyish, say eight o'clock?"

"I'll arrange for the vehicle then."

Jade noticed Darda still looked unhappy. "I'll be back," she promised.

Darda nodded but didn't look convinced.

"Shall I order in?" Emre asked. "I can get Dim Sum dumplings?"

"Oh please," Darda said, brightening at the thought.

10

I Heard You Were Born In England

(Tuesday: Sultan, Pesh)

"Is this it?" Carlos asked looking up at the four-story, brown-brick apartment building on the far side of the street. Most of the top floor was missing, while the broken windows on the remaining floors were covered by sheets of plywood, already stained and peeling.

Karen checked the slip of paper she was holding. "This is it."

Carlos looked uncomfortably up at the building. "Third floor?" he asked, worriedly. The whole building looked likely to collapse at any moment.

"Don't be such a baby," Karen said, leading the way into the foyer. "It hasn't fallen down yet."

"Which doesn't necessarily fill me with confidence," Carlos said. "So what do you think is going on?"

She shrugged. "I don't think. We're being paid to get a driver, beyond that . . . ." She paused in front of the elevator which had a sign in Arabic stuck on its door. Carlos guessed it said something along the lines of 'Broken — do not enter'. They looked at each other, then Karen headed for the stairs. Giving a sigh Carlos followed her.

The stairs were steep, dimly lit by the light that leaked in around the fire doors, which had been propped open on each floor by bricks. The pungent odor of urine filled the stairwell, and Carlos tried to breathe through his mouth. As they climbed he kept one hand on the handrail, and tried not to think about what he might be stepping into.

At the third floor Carlos paused to catch his breath but Karen headed down the corridor, forcing Carlos to follow. About halfway down the hallway she stopped, and as Carlos took up position out of sight of anyone in the apartment, she banged on the door.

Carlos heard movement from the apartment and the door was opened. "Yes?" someone said.

"Charlie Stephenson?" Karen asked.

"Why?" The speaker was a small, heavily muscled man with a short scruffy beard, and a faint cockney accent. He must be one of the many English expatriates who had made their exile in Pesh following the democratic student uprising two decades before.

"I have a message from your mother. Can I come in?"

"I suppose so." He stepped back to allow Karen to enter and as he did Carlos pushed past.

"Hold on, who are you?" Charlie demanded.

"A friend," Karen said. Their 'driver' was about Carlos's height, but Carlos strong-armed him into the room, kicking the door closed behind them.

The apartment looked like a single bedroom apartment. Faint light filtered in from around the plywood that blocked the windows.

"Is there anyone else here?" Karen asked.

"No, my wife is due home with our child soon though." He glanced at the television in the corner of the room which was covered with small photographs of a smiling woman and child. Karen picked up one of the frames and placed it on the table.

"Then we'll make this short," she said, and gave him a shove that caught him off guard, sending him stumbling back into an armchair. "We want you to go to Venice."

"Why would I want to go to there?"

"That doesn't matter. Here's a picture of your mom. She wants you to go to Venice." She pulled out a photograph and placed it on the table.

"What?" the driver said uncertainly.

"Your mother, taken three weeks ago," Karen said.

He reached forward and picked it up carefully. "How did you get this?" he demanded. "My mother lives in London." The photo showed an old woman, wearing a thick felt coat holding up a newspaper under her face.

"That's not important," Karen said. "What is important is that you understand that her continued wellbeing is dependent on you fulfilling the instructions you will be given."

The driver started to protest but in a quick movement Karen pulled out her extendable baton, flicked it out and slammed it down across the driver's upper arm. He screamed. Carlos started to protest but subsided at a warning look from her.

Resting the tip of the baton in the hollow of the driver's throat Karen glared down at him. Carlos felt the hair on the back of his neck rise.

"You will listen very carefully to what I am about to say," Karen said, slowly and distinctly. "I understand you have an enclosed four-ton truck."

He started to say something. "No, don't say anything," Karen said warningly. "Just nod."

He nodded, looking strained.

"Good. Our clients wish to procure your services. You are to pick up a package from Venice in ten days' time in your truck. It is a large package and is arriving by ship. Here is the address. You are not to tell anyone where you are going. You understand?"

This was the first time Carlos had actually started to get some idea of what the driver was needed for.

The driver nodded, still looking strained.

"Excellent. It would be a shame if something happened to your wife or child," Karen said, flicking her baton out and sending the photograph of the woman and child tumbling to the ground where the frame shattered on the hard tile floor. Before the driver could even start to complain Karen had straightened up and placed an envelope on the table.

"Your expenses," she said. Then with a jerk of her head to Carlos toward the door she turned and led the way out of the room. As she opened the door she slammed the bottom of the baton against the door frame, collapsing the baton back into its handle.

"That went well," Carlos said.

She grunted.

They passed the woman and child in the photograph on the stairwell, and both stood back to allow them to pass.

"Any idea what the package is?" Carlos asked conversationally as they resumed their descent. "It must be quite important."

"Don't know, don't care," Karen said without looking round. "So long as I get paid."

Figured, Carlos thought. "So, what's next?"

"We need a warehouse."

"And I presume you have one in mind?"

"Our clients do. It's on the outskirts of the city so we'll need to take the bus. It's owned by an agent of theirs."

#

The warehouse was actually well beyond the outer reaches of the city, in an area that echoed the disintegration and decay of the city. The warehouse must have been built shortly before the war. It sat, a squat prefabricated building on a deserted industrial block.

The doors were all locked and after walking around the building Carlos looked at Karen. "I thought someone would have been expecting us."

Karen checked her watch. "We're early. They'll get here soon." She settled herself on the doorstep in the sun. She had barely done that when a small scooter turned in off the road, the sound of its engine tinny across the open sand.

"That might be her," Karen said, standing up and dusting off her trousers.

The scooter pulled up beside them, and removing her helmet the rider was revealed as a slight woman with delicate, elfin features.

"Borhala Russel?" Karen asked in English.

Borhala stiffened, looking around nervously to make sure they were alone. "Yes?"

"I heard you were born in England," Karen said. "Did you ever visit Liverpool? My aunt lives there."

"Not Liverpool, but I did get to Edinburgh one summer," Borhala replied.

Carlos noted the relief that both Karen and Borhala showed, so obviously the passphrase had been given and accepted.

"After the war I didn't think I'd ever actually hear that phrase," Borhala said.

"Our bosses have decided to activate you," Karen told her.

"Then I take it you don't actually want to rent the warehouse?" Borhala sounded disappointed.

"Not rent, but we do need to use it."

Borhala nodded dispiritedly. "Come on in," she said, pulling the scooter back onto its stand and opening the door to the office for them. "How long do you need it for?"

"A couple of weeks. We have a package we need to store out of sight for a while."

"As you can see, there isn't anyone around here to see it," Borhala said bitterly.

"How many people can you provide?" Karen asked.

"For what? You do need to be a little more precise."

"Security."

Borhala considered the matter for a moment. "Five or six," she suggested. "All shooters. But I'll need to pay them, and frankly I'm suffering a certain shortage of cash . . ." She shrugged helplessly.

Karen nodded. "Give me an estimate and we'll transfer the money. We'll need your bank details though."

Carlos could feel the skin on the back of his neck starting to tighten. He was getting a very bad feeling about all this. All he could do was hope that Jade would be there when he phoned. He had never felt so alone before.

He watched Borhala scrawl down her bank details for Karen, then as Karen stepped back outside, he followed her, eyes sweeping their surroundings for any danger. Unfortunately, no one was watching; if they had been it might have made things much easier by removing any choice.

The trip back to the city was made in silence, but as they stepped off the bus Karen cleared her throat.

"Are you doing anything tonight?" she asked.

"I haven't got anything planned. Why?" he asked, carefully.

"It's just that I thought we could have dinner together, then maybe head out and make a night of it."

Oh hell, Carlos thought. He had enough experience, way more than enough experience actually, to know a come-on line when he heard one. "Not tonight. Dinner's fine but I need an early night. I still haven't got over my jet-lag, and when I'm this tired the only thing I can do is sleep, otherwise I'll have a splitting migraine tomorrow."

Karen looked disappointed. "Dinner it is then. Six o'clock?"

He nodded, checking his watch. It was just coming up to five. "Six o'clock," he agreed. "I'll see you back at the embassy."

"See you then," she said.

Carlos was disappointed she had given up so quickly, although more rational thought reminded him that he didn't want to be in a position that he pissed either Jade *or* Karen off. Either would be dangerous to his health, although for different reasons. He smiled, remembering his girlfriend's competitive streak and quick temper.

The embassy was only a short distance from the river and, deciding to enjoy the remainder of the day's fine weather, he headed down to the embankments. There the broad walkways were already starting to fill up with those participating in the afternoon's promenade along the river's shaded banks. Despite the damage wrought by the war, the people of Pesh seemed intent in maintaining at least a veneer of normalcy. Following the curve of the river Carlos found a small café and settled down on the terrace to order a short black.

As he waited, he pulled out the small mobile phone his new employers had provided him with and looked at it moodily. It was too risky to use, but it did offer him another opportunity, and when the waiter returned with his coffee, he held up his mobile.

"Telephone?" he asked. "*Mein ist kaput.*"

The waiter pointed inside. "Fifty kurus," he said.

Taking his coffee with him Carlos followed the waiter inside. At the desk he dropped a lira note on the counter. "No change," he said.

Reaching behind the desk the waiter produced a telephone connected to a cable and plumped it down on the counter.

Carlos watched him move back to the other end of the counter to serve someone else before he picked the handpiece up and dialed the number he'd memorized.

"Hello," a young girl said, when the phone was answered.

"Who's this?" Carlos asked. It certainly wasn't Jade.

"Who are you?" the girl asked.

"Is this Darta?" he asked uncertainly, trying to remember the name of Jade's young companion.

"Darda," she corrected him.

"Darda, this is Carlos. I was hoping to speak to Jade."

"Ah, hello Carlos." She giggled. "Jade's not here."

Carlos frowned, wondering what Jade had been telling her. "Do you know when she'll be back?" he asked, hoping it was going to be only a couple of minutes.

"Emre said she'd probably be back in two weeks."

"Damn," he said. Well, there went that bright idea.

"Jade did say you might want to speak to Emre, if you phoned," she told him.

"Oh?"

She giggled again. "Jade said that was going to be your reaction. She said I was to ask you what you thought about *precium tribulationis* as her new motto?"

Carlos couldn't help a snort. 'Worth the trouble,' indeed. That sounded like Jade though. "When you see her, you can tell her I prefer *ac primum, dein cogitat.*

"'Acts first, thinks afterward'," he offered after a moment of silence.

"Oh," she said uncertainly.

"You have to know her as I do," he said. "Look, I don't suppose Emre is around?"

"No, but I can give you his cell-number."

"Hold on," he said grabbing a napkin and a pen. "Shoot."

She recited a number.

"Thank you," he said and hung up. He pulled out another one lire note, placed it on the counter and called the number Darda had given him.

The phone was picked up on the first ring. "Emre."

"I'm Carlos. I'm Jade's friend."

"Carlos," Emre said. "Jade said you might call. What can I do for you?"

Carlos brought him up to date concerning the day's activities.

"And what do you suggest I do with this information?" Emre asked when Carlos had finished. "I can certainly have both these individuals arrested."

"That would be a bit unfair on the driver," Carlos suggested. He could almost hear Emre's shrug through the end of the phone. "Can you put them under observation? If you arrest everyone you wouldn't necessarily stop whatever they're planning."

"I'm concerned at this 'package' they've moving, though."

"So am I," Carlos admitted.

"But I agree, if we act now, we may not actually stop whatever they intend from happening. All right," Emre said decisively. "We'll leave them running free for the moment, but I'll put them under observation. Now, how can I contact you?"

"I do have a 'cell' number, but if you use it it's likely to blow my cover. And you need to keep the number to yourself. Otherwise, I will try and contact you on this number within a week."

"I understand," Emre said.

Carlos gave him the cell-number and hung up. Now all he had to do was to get through dinner with Karen.

11

SULTAN: A COMPLEX WEB OF ALLIANCES

The network of alliances that bound the nations of Sultan into two competing camps before contact with the C-T E traces back to the rapid expansion of the Ottoman Empire and its absorption of the Northern Caliphate under Sheik Abdul Moris in the 1850s C.E. One consequence was the abdication of the French King, replaced by his son Francis IV, who within ten years merged the Kingdoms of England, Ireland, and France to create the Angevin Empire—later the kernel of the Western Caliphate.

While the Muslim world on Sultan united during the Great War against the United Christian States (1896–1899), disagreements between Ottomans and Angevins soon splintered the alliance. In 1936 the Western Caliphate, concerned by Ottoman influence in South America, signed a Mutual Aid Treaty with Peru and the Southern Caliphate, creating the Etehad Sho'mali.

In response, Mexico allied with the Ottomans, creating the Etehad Junoobil. By the 'One Week War' in 1984, the Etehad Sho'mali included Peru, the Western Caliphate (centered on the Angevin Empire), the Southern Caliphate (Africa and the Middle East), and the United Tribes of America's Great Plains. Against it, the Junoobil comprised Mexico, the Northern Caliphate (centered on the Ottoman Empire), and central European states.

CYCLOPEDIA OF THE CROSS-TEMPORAL EMPIRE:

12

APOLOGIZING TO A SEVEN-YEAR-OLD SHOULD BE EASY

(Saturday: Mainline, New York)

Markus was reading a file, a further stack on the small coffee table beside him, when Margaret stalked into the drawing room and sat down heavily on the sofa facing him.

"Louise is doing it again," she announced.

"What's she doing now?" he asked calmly, looking up from the file.

"Leaving me to deal with Mama. She always does it."

Markus looked puzzled. "She is working."

"And I'm not?"

"I didn't say that," Markus said defensively. "But your mother is here to see you, not Louise."

"I don't see why that excuses her."

"Margaret," Markus said patiently. "You're not being very reasonable."

Margaret straightened, hurt. "Reasonable. What's not reasonable is that you're defending her. But then why should you be different from everyone else? Everyone defends poor little Louise. Even during the war. Too young, too . . . too . . ." she struggled for the word. " . . . too girly!" she ended explosively.

She saw Markus struggling to contain a smile and fumed. Of all people, she thought she could trust him. But then why should he be any different? Everyone just wanted something from her. Take, take, take. It was time she stood up for herself. "And you!" she said, pointing a finger at him. "It's time you and your daughter found your own place. You've been living off my good graces long enough."

For a moment Markus simply stared at her, his face completely emotionless, then lowering his eyes he closed the file he'd been reading and calmly replaced it on top of the other files on the table beside him.

The loss she saw in his eyes shredded her fury, and awkwardly, unable to face him she wrapped her tattered anger round her and headed for the door. She hesitated for a moment in the doorway. They were actually in her house, well in so far as she was the one actually renting it, and if anyone should leave the room it was Markus, but to turn round now would spoil a perfectly good exit. More importantly, perhaps, it might mean admitting she was probably in the wrong and was behaving irrationally. With that uncomfortable thought she continued out of the room and across the foyer to the outside greenhouse. That was where her mother found her when she came looking for her half an hour later.

"They're not going to grow if you treat them like that," her mother said, her perfectly made-up face displaying not a flicker of emotion as Margaret jammed another cutting that she had just dunked in a hormone solution into a pot.

Margaret ignored her.

Her mother took a breath. "You need to apologize."

"To whom?" Margaret asked, not looking up.

"To Mr. Ackov — Markus," her mother continued. "You've upset him, and you've upset Jessie. She's in her bedroom crying, and I won't have it. I know you're unwell, but that does not excuse bad manners."

"And you automatically jump to his defense without knowing what he did?" Margaret said angrily. "What did he say?"

"That you had asked him to move out."

"And has he said why I asked him to move out?"

"No, he hasn't said anything."

Margaret could sense her mother's eyes on her. She started to pick the pot up then watched as it slid out of her fingers and smashed on the ground.

"Well?" her mother asked, her gaze not leaving her daughter's face.

"Well, what?" Margaret demanded, looking around for the dustpan and brush. Why did it always going missing when she needed it?

"Are you going to tell me what he did that justified you telling him to leave?"

"It doesn't matter, Mama." Margaret sighed, starting to pick up the pieces of the pot up and place them on the bench. "I told him to move out. Nothing I can say will change that."

"You can still apologize," her mother said implacably.

Margaret looked up at her mother who returned her gaze levelly, arms folded.

"Why?" Margaret asked, looking away.

"Because you're in the wrong, and you know it. I reared you better than that."

"And how do you know I'm in the wrong?" Margaret asked snidely.

"Because you're avoiding my eyes. You always do that when you're in the wrong. Even when you were a child."

Margaret rolled her eyes, and her mother lifted one immaculate eyebrow.

Margaret sighed. "I don't think I can, Mama. I went too far." It hurt to admit it. She didn't know why she'd lost her temper. Well, she did — it was Louise. She paused. Or perhaps not. Not that it mattered now.

"Margaret Chantelle Peric," her mother said. "You will immediately apologize to both of them."

"And if I don't?"

Her mother simply stared at her.

"Oh, very well," Margaret said, slamming the remains of the pot she was holding down on the bench and nicking her finger as she did so. "Damn!" she said, sucking at the finger. "Now look what you made me do."

Her mother continued to look at her pitilessly.

Still sucking her finger Margaret started for the door. "Where is he?"

"In his bedroom."

Margaret paused at the top of the stairs uncertainly. She could hear Jessie sniffling in her room, while the door to Markus's room was closed. Taking a breath, she gave a short knock.

"Come in," Markus called.

She opened the door to find Markus sorting piles of clothing on the bed. An open suitcase sat beside him. He looked up, surprised to see her.

"I've come to apologize," Margaret said, closing the door behind her. "I was wrong. I don't know why I told you to leave, but I don't want you to go."

Markus resumed his sorting. "It's time Jessie and I had our own place again."

"No, it's not," Margaret said. "Jessie's crying."

"And whose fault is that?" Markus demanded, finally meeting her eyes.

"Mine," Margaret admitted.

He simply shrugged and returned to his packing, and she felt a prickle of unease that suddenly exploded into full-on panic.

> The stink of gunpowder, and of smoldering, damp wood. On the other side of the sandbagged room that was serving as their temporary hospital her aide-de-camp lay on a stretcher, jerking erratically as the medic struggled to intubate her. They'd gone through so much together. Klington, Mutter's Ford, but one wrong bullet and her aide's face was a mangled mess, the entire left side of her face exposed to the bone.
>
> "We're losing her!"

"Margaret?"

She blinked.

"Margaret!" A hand touched her shoulder and she flinched.

'Name the emotion, accept the memory.' She remembered Doctor Rubenstein's words and recalled the fear of death and the loneliness she had felt that day.

She blinked as Markus's worried face filled her view.

"Are you all right?" he asked.

"No," she admitted. "I'm not."

She allowed him to guide her to the bed, and to sit next to her on it. Suddenly she knew why she had told him to go.

"I know," she said surprised.

"Know what?"

"Why I told you to leave." She held up a hand to forestall his response. "But I doubt it's the reason you think."

"Oh?" he asked uncertainly.

She took a deep breath. "I missed you when I went to Naisre," she said. "And then when Jessie was kidnapped . . . I'd been trying to hold myself together for months before that, but what I felt then . . ." She paused. "I didn't want to have to go through that again," she admitted.

He frowned doubtfully.

"The world is full of gray that sucks the warmth out of everything I touch. But you and Jessie, you bring color back into my life. Without you"—she paused to control the sob that threatened to break free. "Without you," she tried again, and was suddenly crying, great, jerking sobs that tried to rip her very heart out of her chest.

She felt Markus put his arm around her uncertainly, and she turned into his embrace, burying her face in his chest. Finally, drained, she looked up at him to find Markus watching her with a strange look on his face. Margaret felt exposed, naked. She started to get up, but Markus held up a hand to stay her. "You know," he said, handing her a tissue. "I was probably more hurt than I would have been if I didn't feel the way I do about you. You're the first person since Adriana died that I have felt anything for. You have taken Jessie and me into your house and I have never understood why."

"Because you and Jessie are the best thing that's ever happened to me," she said. She shrugged self-deprecatingly. "I've really only been just been holding on for the past couple of years. Flashbacks, depression . . . I've been a wreck. But you two helped me to keep myself together. Gave me a reason for living. And that frightened me."

He frowned and started to open his mouth to say something, but she reached up a finger and touched his lips.

"You might have noticed that I have relationship issues. I tend to try and keep a distance from anyone. I used to do it before the war, but it's even worse now. Doctor Rubenstein feels it's a coping strategy, to make sure I don't feel loss. But she's also been trying to get me to admit that it's a strategy that means I can't gain anything either."

She paused then shrugged wryly. "But you and Jessie, you broke through that, and you've given me so much that I was frightened of losing it."

"So, you pushed me away?"

She nodded. "I'm sure that's what Doctor Rubenstein would say . . ." She paused again, not quite sure where she was going with the thought. "What I do know is that you and Jessie have brightened my days and made it a little easier to face the morning. Without you, well . . . ." She shrugged.

"But I'm not sure where this, us, can go," he said.

"It can go wherever we want it to," she said. "And whatever you or I may think, it appears my mother approves."

"How do you know that?"

She evaded the question. Admitting that her mother had commanded her to apologize would probably take something away from her own apology.

"Markus, I'm thirty-two. My mother and father have all but given up on me ever marrying. Our parents never expected either me, or my brothers or sisters to marry for political reasons. This is something I chose to do for myself." She paused and gave another wry smile. "And given the makeup of the Council, and Donald's attempts to align himself with the general populace, having a cousin marrying outside the Families would probably gain his enthusiastic support. But—" She held up a hand to forestall him. "This is just us. This may not exactly be a declaration of love, but you give me reason to keep on living."

Markus shook his head, but there was an ironic smile on his face. "So, no pressure."

"No pressure," she said. "All you have to do is be yourself and stay."

He stared at her, then nodded slowly. "I'll need some time to think about everything but . . ."

"You'll stay?"

"I'll stay. But . . ."

"What?" she asked nervously.

"You have to explain to Jessie that you've changed your mind."

That wasn't what she was expecting. "Can't you?" she asked, aware that she was whining.

"Nope." It seemed obvious to Margaret that he was enjoying his revenge a little bit too much. "You caused this, you need to sort it out. Besides, if you apologized to me, apologizing to a seven-year-old should be easy."

"All right," she said, reluctantly getting to her feet. It seemed unfair though: she'd apologized to him, the least he could do was explain it to Jessie for her. She paused at the door. "Markus, please be aware that I may . . . probably will lose my temper again while Doctor Rubenstein and I are working our way through my . . . issues. It's nothing I have control over . In fact, shouting at you might actually be good for me, but . . ."

He looked at her and shrugged. "Now I know where we stand, I can take it."

"Just be aware that it doesn't actually reflect how I feel about you."

He nodded, and she felt his eyes on her back until she pulled the door closed behind her.

She paused a moment, listening to Jessie's muffled sobs in the next room. Straightening her shoulders, she gave a soft tap on the door.

"Go away," came the voice from the bedroom.

Lifting an eyebrow, she opened the door. Jessie was lying on her bed, her face cradled into a pillow. Beside her Mrs. Mack was sitting on the bed. The diminutive housekeeper was gently stroking Jessie's shoulder.

"Miss Peric," Mrs. Mack said, a note of accusation in her voice.

"Mrs. Mack, I need a couple of minutes with Jessie, please."

Mrs. Mack gave Jessie's shoulder a gentle pat and stood up giving Margaret a baleful look. Margaret shook her head and stared her down.

As the door closed behind the housekeeper Margaret sat down on the bed and placed a hand on Jessie's shoulder. Jessie shrugged it away. No, Jessie wasn't going to make this easy for her. Like father like daughter.

"You're staying," Margaret told her.

Jessie just tried to shrug her hand off her shoulder again, and Margaret placed both her hands in her lap. "I've apologized to your father, but I need to apologize to you now."

Margaret could feel Jessie listening to her now. Perhaps the idea of an adult apologizing to her had overridden the hurt she felt, at least temporarily. She decided to keep it simple.

"I've been sick," she said. "It makes me very sad and tired at times, and then I get angry. But losing my temper was no excuse for telling you and your father to leave, and I'm sorry. I've spoken to your father and you're both staying."

Jessie's face appeared around the edge of the pillow. Her eyes were red from weeping, her cheeks stained with tears. "We can stay?" she asked uncertainly, and Margaret's heart crumpled.

She nodded. "Yes."

Jessie considered the matter seriously. "Are you going to die like Mama?" she asked finally.

"No sweetheart," Margaret said, hoping it was a promise she could keep. "I'll need your help though, and your father's. And Doctor Rubenstein is helping. But it's not going to be easy. And if you have any questions, you can ask your father."

This time when Margaret rested her hand on Jessie's shoulder she didn't resist, and leaning forward Margaret dropped a kiss on her forehead. "I am really glad you're staying," Margaret said.

Jessie nodded, just as there was a quiet knock on the door.

"Come in," Margaret called softly.

The door opened a little and Markus poked his head round the edge. "Everything all right?" he asked.

Margaret nodded and patted the edge of bed next to her.

As Markus settled himself Margaret leaned back against him. There was a pause, then she felt his arms carefully reach around her, and a moment later Jessie wriggled over to include herself in the hug.

13

You Look Like Death Warmed Up

(Wednesday: Mainline New York)

At least Jade now knew why Margaret always looked so tired after flying — it was exhausting. The flight from Budapest had taken almost four days, which included a twenty-four hour stopover in London because she'd missed her connecting flight due to the headwinds they'd battled across Europe. At least the stopover had allowed her to have a hot bath, and to catch up on her sleep uninterrupted by the steady drone of the engines and the constant flexing of the airship around her.

And now here she was disembarking in New York only two hours before midnight, and in just a couple of days she had to get on another airship and do it in reverse. She shook her head, wondering how she had become so quickly tired of international travel.

She was looking around for her luggage when she noticed someone holding up a sign with her name on it.

"Jade Carvello?" he asked when she approached him.

"Yes."

He handed her an envelope. "Cardinal Abbot has asked you to phone him as soon as you can."

She opened the envelope to find a number, with an unfamiliar country code. With a sigh she headed for the bank of phones in the center of the

77

lounge, only to discover she wasn't carrying any CoA currency. She sighed, already missing Sultan's cell-phones, and headed over to the bank counter to cash a travelers' check.

By the time she'd manage to cash the check she'd decided she disliked the man. She knew the feeling was irrational, and part of it was probably because she was already prejudiced because he was a priest in the Catholic church, and a 'Cardinal' at that. Jade had been reared an agnostic. Her father had been one and while her mother had followed the faith of her people, it had been more of a matter of acknowledging it as part of her Nayarit culture than having a genuine belief in its religious teachings. Besides, as no priests had come through that first gate with Iapura the practicality of the faith was moot.

The other reason for her prejudice was an instinctive defense of Margaret, and the implication was that by naming Cardinal Abott as the mission's Deputy, the First Leader didn't feel Margaret was actually good enough to run the mission. She was aware of how unfair that was given that she had been in the room when Margaret herself had pointed out her lack of diplomatic experience. But prejudices were never exactly rational.

When she'd phoned the number she'd been given it proved to be ImpSec's local office in Hungary, and she was put through to the Cardinal almost immediately.

"Thank you for phoning, Miss Carvello," the Cardinal said. "I have a meeting with Emre Kaymakam in a couple of hours and was hoping to pick your brain. I've already spoken to Colonel Ferai, who has proved helpful, but your input would be most appreciated."

"Of course." Jade paused. "I'm sorry, sir, but I'm not really sure how to address you."

He laughed. "It is a question of too many titles, isn't it. And the matter of precedence is complicated in your case by your own recent ennoblement."

Jade flinched. She hadn't even considered that.

"Technically a Cardinal ranks as a 'Prince of the Church'," he continued, "but your own title outranks that of a simple 'Deputy Ambassador'. Can I suggest that we don't bother with the 'Cardinal' and you only use 'Deputy Ambassador' on formal occasions when use of my title is necessary. Otherwise, I'm Lindsay. We'll be working in close proximity for some time."

"Of course, sir."

"Lindsay," he reminded her.

"Lindsay, then, I'm Jade."

"Well Jade, as I was saying I appreciate the call. I was in Rome when I was given my summons and I haven't even had the opportunity to speak to Lady Peric yet, although the First Leader has assured me that she will fully brief me when she arrives."

"How can I help?"

"As I said, I've, spoken to Colonel Ferai, who quite impressed me."

Jade nodded, happy that the Cardinal recognized the Colonel's worth. She hoped that boded well for the Cardinal's abilities.

"And I do have a couple of questions he suggested I put to you."

"Oh?" Jade said doubtfully.

"Oh, nothing significant," the Cardinal hurried to assure her. "He just felt it would be better if I got a second opinion."

"Of course, sir." She flinched as she realized she'd done it again.

"I understand from Colonel Ferai that both of the two military alliances, the Etehad Junoobil and the Etehad Sho'mali, appear to have all but collapsed."

"That's correct."

"And what do you believe of the Northern Caliphate's military and economic capability?"

Jade considered the matter carefully. The Northern Caliphate made up most of central Europe, stretching east across the Russian steppes and including a number of member states. It had been the major power in the Etehad Junoobil. "While the Caliphate only exists in name at the moment, the Ottoman Empire appears viable, and its forces provided the core of the Caliphate, and through them the Etehad Junoobil. It certainly escaped the significant damage suffered by many other countries."

"And their willingness to negotiate with us in good faith?"

"I can't really comment about the Caliph, as we've been working through his Vizier, Said Halim. But the Vizier does appear to be negotiating in good faith, although that might simply be political expediency. In my view Emre Kaymakam is genuine, and his background in the military does create a certain directness. Besides," she couldn't help adding, "I liked his sister."

There was a moment's considered silence from the other end of the line. "Thank you, Jade. That accords with Colonel Ferai's view. I look forward to meeting you in the flesh on your return."

"Thank you, sir. Lindsay," she quickly corrected herself.

# # #

She'd been expecting to take a taxi back to her own apartment and drop by at the house to see Margaret first thing in the morning. She was surprised to find Margaret's Rolls double-parked in the taxi rank opposite the main doors.

"Evening, Rolf," she said greeting the chauffeur as he held the door open for her while the porter lifted her luggage into the boot.

"Welcome home, Miss Cavello. Miss Peric asked me to pick you up. She was hoping you'd stay at the house until you returned to Budapest."

"Of course," Jade said, perfectly willing to accept the offer of a proper bath and warm sheets over the tiny shower at her own apartment. And, despite changing the sheets before she left, her bed certainly didn't compare to the one she had when she was staying at Margaret's house. "How's everything at the house?" she asked as Rolf slid into the driving seat and started the engine.

There was an uneasy silence, and Jade looked at the chauffeur curiously. "Rolf?"

The chauffeur looked uncomfortable. "You'll probably find out when you get there," he said nervously.

"Find out what?" she asked as Rolf glanced in the side mirror and pulled out into the traffic.

"Miss Peric tried to commit suicide."

"Suicide! Is she all right?"

"Yes ma'am. Luckily Miss Louise found her in time."

"When did this happen?" Jade asked, trying to make sense of the news. What had Margaret been thinking?

"About ten days ago. Her mother's at the house at the moment."

"Her mother?" Jade was startled, knowing what Margaret thought of her mother.

Rolf smiled at her tone.

"But she's all right now?" Jade demanded.

"Yes ma'am, it appears so," Rolf assured her.

Jade spent the rest of the trip to the house trying to come to grips with what she'd been told and wondering if there was anything she could have done to have prevented it. She simply hadn't known Margaret was that depressed.

Only the night maid was still up to take her bag and run the bath for her when they arrived and Jade quickly retired to bed, although her concern about Margaret meant her sleep was restless.

It was after nine the next morning when she followed the smell of bacon to the breakfast room see what was left. She found Margaret sitting at the table in her dressing gown, back to the door, sipping on a cup of tea with a plate of cold toast in front of her. At the sideboard Jade poured herself a cup of coffee before turning and getting a good look at Margaret. It was the first time she'd seen Margaret without makeup, and she paused, horrified. Her employer's face was puffy, and there were dark shadows under her eyes.

"You look like death warmed up," Jade said, then clapped her hand to her mouth, mortified at her indiscretion. "I'm sorry. I shouldn't have said that."

Margaret waved off her apology. "I take it you've heard about my . . . problem."

Jade nodded, still embarrassed at her gaffe.

Margaret shrugged. "I'm not sleeping well at the moment. Doctor Rubenstein, my psychiatrist, is trying me on a new drug. She warned me I'd feel worse before I felt any better. But I wasn't quite expecting how bad, worse was going to be." Suddenly she smiled, one of her rare, brilliant smiles. "But if you think I look bad now you should have seen me when Louise found me. Apparently, that *was* 'death warmed up'."

Jade nodded uncomfortably as Margaret doubtfully prodded at the cold piece of toast on her plate. Mrs. Mack, the housekeeper, appeared and replaced the plate with another containing a fresh piece of toast already buttered and still steaming gently from the toaster.

"Thank you, Mrs. Mack," Margaret said dryly.

Mrs. Mack glared at her. "Doctor Rubenstein left strict instructions that you were to eat something at each meal."

Margaret took a bite. "Satisfied?" she asked.

Mrs. Mack looked at Jade. "I trust you will ensure she finishes the toast at least. And no breaking it up and giving it to the dog," she warned Margaret sternly.

Margaret waited until Mrs. Mack had gone and offered the toast to Jade.

"Sorry Margaret. I'm not prepared to face Mrs. Mack's wrath."

"Coward," Margaret said, and took a second bite, giving all the appearance of swallowing poison. "How was the trip?" she asked, replacing the toast on its plate.

"Awful," Jade said, happy to shift to a more comfortable subject. "The winds were abominable, and I was sharing a tiny cabin with a young woman taking her first trip to New York with her parents, who couldn't stop talking about it."

Margaret covered her mouth to hide a smile.

"That wasn't even the worst of it," Jade continued. "The only time she stopped talking was when she was asleep, and that was only so she could snore."

Margaret snorted.

"The good news is that Sultan has started to analyze the potato virus we gave them to see if they can identify the source. And I spoke to Cardinal Abbott by telephone when I was in London. He was charming enough on the phone, but he seemed to be trying too hard."

"You might worry him."

"Me! Why?" Jade said startled. "He's the flipping Cardinal."

"And you're the recently ennobled young woman who has the ear of the First Leader, and the personal friendship of his new boss. Of course he's going to treat you with kid gloves."

"Oh," Jade said, and blinked uncertainly.

"So," Margaret said with a smile at Jade's reaction, starting to push her toast around its plate again. "Have you heard anything about Carlos? It's been what— ten days?"

Jade froze, remembering she hadn't told Imp Sec. She grimaced at the reaction she was going to get telling them that she'd seen their missing agent five days after the event.

"Are you all right?" Margaret asked worriedly.

"Fine," she said, lying through her teeth. "He's on Sultan. Apparently, he's got himself attached to the staff of the Angevin embassy in Pesh. The Angevin Empire pretty much covers the Mainline equivalents of England, Scotland, Wales and France."

"He's well?" Margaret asked.

Jade started to say he'd looked good then stopped, remembering his appearance. "He looked stressed, but he's alive. Apparently, Karen's there as well."

Margaret raised an eyebrow. "The agent who went rogue and tried to get you arrested on Chikyù?"

Jade nodded, still wondering why Karen had done it. They'd been friends ever since they'd attended the Agency's training academy.

There was a quiet tap on the door and Markus poked his head in. "I'm off," he told Margaret. Seeing Jade, he came into the room. "Welcome back, how was the trip?"

"Long," Jade said dryly.

"But successful?"

"Very," she assured him.

"I should be back in about an hour," he told Margaret, as he dropped a hand onto her shoulder.

"I'll see you then," she said, her eyes fixed on his face. Jade watched mesmerized as Margaret placed her hand on top of his.

Markus gave Jade a nod, and with a gentle squeeze on Margaret's shoulder headed off.

"So, what's with you and Markus?" Jade asked, as she watched the door swing closed behind him.

Her eyes widened as Margaret suddenly blushed bright red. "Oh my god! You and Markus!"

Margaret made shushing movements with her hand.

"So, when did this happen?" Jade demanded, pulling her chair closer.

Margaret blushed again. "Yesterday," she admitted. "We had an argument. Well . . ." she said and paused to think about it for a moment. "I had an argument. And I told him that he and Jessie had to leave."

Jade frowned, not understanding. "And how did that get you two together?"

"I apologized."

"And?"

"And we're going to see what happens."

"Margaret," Jade protested. "What does that mean? You can't leave me just hanging with a statement like that."

Margaret lifted an eyebrow.

"Didn't I tell you everything about my relationship with Carlos?" Jade said.

"Ye-es," Margaret said slowly. "And sometimes it was way more information than I wanted."

"Then I'll tell you when you've told me too much."

Margaret shook her head at her friend. "Look," she said. "Both Markus and I would prefer to have a private love life, unlike a certain girlfriend I have, who insists on telling me everything."

Jade gave a gasp. "You've done it! Already!"

Margaret gave her a push. "No."

"Then what?"

"It's complicated."

Jade gave her a look of pure exasperation.

"All right, maybe it's not complicated, but it certainly feels like it at the moment. But if it's any consolation my mother approves."

"Your mother?" Jade had never met Margaret's mother, but from the way Margaret and Louise, her sister, always spoke about her she had seemed a regular harridan and a snob; definitely not someone who would approve of a match between her eldest daughter and a penniless scientist.

"My mother, and yes, it surprised me too."

Jade looked at her friend. "What are you doing this morning?"

"My psych has me walking for an hour each morning. But no, nothing after that."

"Then we're going shopping."

"Why?"

"To get you some proper lingerie."

"Jade!" Margaret protested.

"Don't you Jade me. I've seen your lingerie drawer. Practical and boring are the only two words that spring to mind. We're going to 'Victorian Secrets'."

"Jade," Margaret protested again, but her protest only seemed halfhearted this time.

Cheered up by the thought of helping her friend get some decent underthings, Jade stood up. "Now," she said, lifting up the cover on one of the warming plates. "What's left for breakfast."

14

VIGNETTE:
VICTORIAN SECRETS

'Victorian Secrets' is a New York based lingerie, clothing, and beauty retailer. It is known for its innovative re-imagining of the lingerie worn during the time of the two Victorias. Victoria I (Alexandrina Victoria; 1849 – 1884) was Empress of the British Empire from 1868 until her death in 1884. Victoria II (Vickie Victoria; 1870 – 1901) succeeded her mother to the throne during a time of significant turmoil following the arrival of the Nayarit. Unlike her mother, who had had several quietly hushed up affairs, Victoria II became an icon for strict standards of personal morality.

Despite, or perhaps because of this, Victorian Secrets' advertising focuses on salacious marketing of what those living in that time might have worn under their outer wear. A strategy that has made Victorian Secrets the largest retailer of lingerie on the Mainline.

ALAN RAYMOND.
UNDERCOVER IN THE UNDERWEAR TRADE.
NEW YORK: BIG BOOKS.

15

AND NOW THE GAME BEGINS

(Wednesday: Sultan, Pesh)

"But Jade did," Darda said.

That seemed all Emre had heard for the last week. "Jade does this, Jade would do that." He bit back his automatic retort, knowing that losing his temper was not the way to win this particular argument.

"Jade is at least twice your age," Emre pointed out. And an infidel to boot, he wanted to add. But, given the way Darda idolized her, if he tried to run that particular argument Darda would try to convert just to spite him.

"You can start your driving lessons when you're eighteen, and not before," he said. "Look, Darda, I'm sorry, I really am, but the law is quite clear that you can't get your learners permit until you're eighteen."

"But I don't want to drive on the road," Darda pointed out. "And what happens if there's another war? I'll need to know how to drive then."

"There's not going to be another war," he snapped, and shuddered at the thought of Darda driving one of the regiment's Jeeps around the barracks.

"It would make me a better driver when I do get my learner's permit," she pointed out.

"It probably would. But I can't make an exception for you. That sort of favoritism can stick in the craw of any soldier. And we're talking about Janissaries here, who have even higher expectations of their CO."

"Then run a course for everyone," she said. "Mutazz and Nasir both think it's a good idea."

"Of course, run courses for everyone," he said sarcastically. "Why didn't I think of that?" He paused — actually it wasn't that bad an idea.

He held up a hand to forestall her next comment. "I'll think about it," he promised.

Darda seemed to realize she'd pushed it as far as she could for the moment, but from the look in her eyes this was not something she would let him drag his feet on. "And Mutazz and Nasir, who are they?" he asked.

"Two of the boys I know at school."

He frowned. With the war he'd decided it would be better to pull her out of the all-girls' school she'd been attending on the other side of the city, and to have her schooled with the rest of the regiment's children on the base. Now he wasn't so sure.

Darda stared at him unflinchingly.

"Details?" he prompted.

Darda sighed dramatically. "And by that I take it to mean are they suitable friends for their CO's younger sister?"

"I didn't say that," Emre protested.

"But you thought it."

Not something he could argue with. "Well?" he prompted when it appeared that she wasn't going to say anything.

She gave another deep, theatrically approved sigh. "Mutazz' father is Sergeant Sayegh of the Deep Penetration Wing. And Nasir's father was killed in the war, Trooper Al Din Sarkis. He was awarded the Triple-star posthumously, although that's cold comfort for Nasir."

He nodded, acknowledging the pain in her voice for Nasir's loss.

Neither of the two were exactly suitable companions for Darda, though if he were honest with himself, he doubted there was anyone he would consider a suitable companion for his sister. And knowing what he now did of the behavior of some of the Ottoman Empire's elite, having her mix with her own 'class' would probably be even riskier for his peace of mind — drugs being the least of his problems.

"Fine," he said. "I'll think about it."

Darda leaned across the desk and gave him a quick hug, that left him wondering if he'd been outmaneuvered.

He picked up the next report from his in-tray but he'd barely got halfway through the first page when he hit his forehead with his palm in exasperation. "Idiots," he said, reaching for the phone.

"Director Bedreddin's office, please," he told his receptionist, then had to wait impatiently to be put through.

Finally, he heard the female Director of Counter-Intelligence's amiable voice. "Emre, what can I do for you?"

"You could tell your staff to stop being such idiots and to pull their bugs out of the C-T E's embassy," Emre said tersely.

There was a moment of stony silence. "I'm not sure this is something we should be discussing over an open-phone," the Director said coldly.

"Fine." Emre checked his watch. "I'll be there in half an hour," he said and hung up before she could tell him otherwise.

The offices of Counter-Intelligence occupied several of the old Treasury buildings in the center of the city. They'd moved there only recently, their old facilities having been destroyed during the war when it had been hit by a Kinetic Orbital Weapon.

The Director met him as he stepped out of his vehicle. "Kaymakam," she said, giving him her hand. "I have an appointment with the Vizier in fifteen minutes that I'm already late for. I thought we could talk in my car, and my driver can then drop you back at your barracks."

"Thank you," Emre said, allowing her to guide him toward her vehicle pulled up in the no-parking zone just in front of his.

"So what's got you all riled up?" the Director asked as they settled themselves into the back of the armored limousine. The vehicle was built like a brick, and Emre's view was that it handled like one as well, though you couldn't fault the interior. It had leather seats, there was a vid-screen built into the dividing wall and, he'd been shocked to discover, even a small bar.

Emre took a deep breath. "It doesn't make sense," he said, trying to remain calm. "If the C-T E want to discuss anything of any import they'll simply head through the portal to the doppelganger of their embassy on their own Line. And then when they discover our bugs, and they will—" Emre held up his hand to stop the Director's protest. "We provided them with enough of our technology when we were allies during the war. And when they *do* discover the bugs, it will be seen as a lack of faith on our part."

The Director shrugged. "I might agree with you, but my advisers won't allow me to do nothing."

"So what, you simply do what you're told?"

The Director waggled her finger at Emre. "Unlike you, Emre, I am a political appointee. And one who is severely constrained by the political environment in which I operate. Unlike the military."

Emre restrained himself from saying what he thought of that particular piece of horseshit. Perhaps as a mere Binbasi he had avoided much of the politics but as a Kaymakam he was only too aware of the degree of politics within the military's senior hierarchy.

"Then how about we attempt to bug the doppelganger building on the Mainline?" he suggested. He wasn't comfortable about describing the line as 'the Mainline', the Etehad Junoobil had called it 'Balkan Renaissance - One' during the war, but in anticipation of the establishment of the new Embassy he had started to use their own term for the line. "That will be less expected, and if the bugs are ever discovered it will certainly be easier to deny. I mean, who would try to bug the monastery when there is an embassy?"

The Director smiled at the suggestion. "It would be difficult."

"But probably not that much more difficult that bugging the actual Embassy. Particularly as they already have their security on site."

The Director tapped her chin as she considered the suggestion. "Unfortunately, I don't have the authority to collect intelligence off-line."

"But I do," Emre pointed out. In fact, the Janissaries intelligence activities were generally unconstrained by any sort of limits, other than they weren't to be caught — a limit that the 5th Corps was very good at adhering to.

"And you'll agree to share what you have."

"Of course," Emre said, mentally crossing his fingers.

The Director squinted at him suspiciously, then nodded. "I'll tell my Department to back off."

"Thank you, Director," Emre said, as the limousine pulled into the underground garage under the government's central offices.

He watched the Director climb out of the limousine, then leaned back into his seat as the driver headed back to the barracks.

# # #

Half an hour after returning to his office there was a knock on his door.

"Kaymakam?"

Emre looked up from the staffing report he'd just been checking. Even with the end of the world threatening at any moment the Janissaries still needed their pay. That was the contract between the Caliph and his Janissaries. Without that the end of the world *would* occur.

"Yes Lieutenant?" he said, pushing his spectacles back up his nose.

The earnest young Lieutenant who was presently acting as his executive assistant handed him an envelope. "The preliminary report on the DNA analysis you requested, sir."

"Thank you, Lieutenant," Emre said, wondering if he'd ever been that young, and if he had, how he had ever survived it. Picking the envelope up he slid the report out. "I take it you've read it."

"Yes, sir."

"Then summarize it for me."

"The blight does appear to have been artificially created. The lab was quite impressed by its abilities. There were a number of safeguards built in, and apparently it is highly susceptible to benomyl, a common fungicide. Significantly, the lab was not able to track it back to any particular laboratory operating on Sultan. This is not to say it wasn't but they're reasonably confident that it's foreign to the line."

"Oh," Emre said, surprised. "How confident?"

"98 percent."

"That is . . . confident. How can they be so sure?"

"Apparently the non-coding DNA —"

"The 'junk' DNA?"

"Yes, Kaymakam. They've found some code in it that matched something already on file. Of course, I queried the results with the lab, but they assured me they had double checked the results."

Emre looked up from the report he'd been scanning while listening. "Enlighten me, Lieutenant. What caused you to query the results?"

The Lieutenant looked worried. "While not precisely the same, there is a match in the header and footer markers of the code with an individual we have on file."

"Who?"

"Donald Clemhorn."

"The C-T E's First Leader?" Emre said, surprised.

"Yes Kaymakam."

Emre shook his head. *That* was going to set the cat among the pigeons. "And just how do we happen to have his genetic material on record?"

"When he was here for his operation several years ago, Kaymakam. They took samples of his DNA to ensure maximum compatibility for the donated kidney; to minimize the amount of manipulation required of the donated kidney's own DNA. It's a standard process."

Emre looked at the report, then carefully slid it back into its envelope. "I think, Lieutenant, we might go slow on this. At least until we have worked out why the esteemed First Leader is sharing artificial DNA markers with a particularly virulent potato virus."

The Lieutenant looked uncertain, and with a small sigh Emre gestured for him to take a seat. "Lieutenant, this sort of information could have all sorts of political repercussions we are not aware of. So before firing the gun we need to know where the bullet will go and what the damage will be."

The Lieutenant nodded uncertainly. No, Emre thought. He had never been that young.

"Right," Emre said, "the first thing we need to do is to try and identify others with the same genetic marker. We can start with the Embassy staff when they arrive. I'll work up some excuse. But we need a broader sample from the Mainline. I am therefore putting you in charge of obtaining enough samples."

The Lieutenant gulped. "How many samples will be enough, Kaymakam?"

"A thousand to start with. Or at least enough for us to start looking for patterns."

"But how?"

"That is why I'm giving you the job," Emre said, "so I don't have to think of everything. Pull together a task group and get a plan to me within a week. Speak to Stepanian *Miralay* about accommodation and let him know what staff you need." The Miralay was the Janissary equivalent of Colonel Ferai. "I'll phone him and let him know you're on your way as soon as you leave."

The Lieutenant nodded, but Emre was pleased to see that his brain seemed to have started to engage. It wasn't that much a surprise. The Lieutenant had been the top of his graduating year, and had already been tagged for accelerated advancement. So, let's give him the chance to start advancing, Emre thought. "That's all Lieutenant. Dismissed."

"Thank you, Kaymakam." The Lieutenant jumped to his feet, almost tipping his chair over in his haste to leave.

Emre looked at the envelope. Perhaps they couldn't tell the Ambassador everything they'd found, but the susceptibility to benomyl was something they could share as a measure of good faith immediately. But just why did the First Leader share DNA markers with a potato blight?

Before he forgot, he picked up the phone to let Miralay Stepanian know that the Lieutenant was on his way. He had barely put the handset down when there was another knock on the door. It was the Lieutenant again.

"Yes?" Emre said.

"Your pardon Kaymakam, but I just received word that Colonel Ferai and the new C-T E Deputy Ambassador have arrived on the line."

"Here?"

"No Kaymakam, at the Madrassa."

"Thank you, Lieutenant," Emre said curtly, dismissing him with a nod. And now the game begins, he thought, turning his attention back to the staffing report.

16

MY 'ASSETS' ARE CONSIDERABLY LARGER THAN YOURS

(Friday: Mainline, New York)

Margaret stared at the itinerary in front of her, knowing with cold dread that she couldn't get on that flight in three days' time. She wasn't ready yet. Doctor Rubenstein seemed convinced she was, but Margaret could feel the darkness pressing in on her. She knew with a dreadful certainty, that if she did leave, she would be back to looking into the same bottomless pit that had driven her to attempt suicide less than a month before.

And yet the alternative was to admit to Donald that she couldn't do the job; and she couldn't do that either. The one thing she had clung to over the past seventeen years was that her depression had never once impacted on her ability to do her job. But if it did now, then those seventeen years of pain and effort would have been for nothing. And where would that leave her?

"Margaret?" It was Markus. "What's wrong?"

Margaret waved silently at the papers laid out on the desk in front of her. "I can't do it," she said, tears welling up in her eyes.

"Can't do what, liebchen?" Markus asked gently, his left hand resting on her shoulder as he leaned over her to read the papers spread out in front of her.

"This," she said, gesturing helplessly at the papers.

"The ambassadorship? I thought you'd talked it over with Doctor Rubenstein and you'd decided you could handle it."

She shook her head as tears ran silently down her cheeks.

"Oh, liebchen," he said taking a hand and turning her around to face him. "What can't you do?"

"Any of it," she said, frustrated with her inability to explain.

"I doubt that very much. You are one of the most capable people I know. But if you can't do it just tell Donald."

"I can't, because if I do that then I've failed, and I can't! It's just waiting to drag me down again."

"Oh — so you're between the rock and a hard place." He thought for a moment. "All right, so what specifically is frightening you about going to Sultan?"

She thought about it, trying to be honest with herself, and with Markus. "I'm scared of how I'm going to cope without you, without you and Jessie," she finally admitted.

Markus shrugged. "So, what if we came with you?"

Margaret looked at him, horrified.

"Oh, I didn't mean to Sultan. Although I can't see your cousin sending you if there was much of a risk. But what about to Budapest? From what you've been saying the gate is getting established in an old monastery. Is there anything that says you actually have to live on Sultan? Couldn't you just commute through the gate from Budapest on a daily basis?"

"Would you, I mean, could you? How would you get leave?"

"Margaret. Technically I work for your Department. I'm just on loan to the Comptroller-General."

"Oh," Margaret said, embarrassed that she hadn't thought about that.

"And why not ask Doctor Rubenstein if she could come with you until you're a little more settled. Given how much you told me your cousin is bribing her with surely she could give you a couple of weeks until you're settled and can find someone else to provide that support."

"I suppose so," she said doubtfully.

"Just let me see if I can't arrange something," he offered. He produced a handkerchief and gave it to her. "Here."

She gave him a tremulous smile. "You see why I need you."

# # #

Later that day Margaret was studying the report on the new Embassy's staff when she looked up to find Jade shaking her head disapprovingly at her from the doorway.

"What?" Margaret demanded.

"What is your problem?" Jade asked, looking her up and down.

"What problem?" she asked uncertainly.

"What is the sense in wearing sexy lingerie for your man if you don't give him the opportunity to see it?"

Margaret looked down at the blouse she was wearing. "What's wrong with this?" she asked worriedly. She'd chosen the peach silk blouse thinking it actually made her look softer.

"Nothing's actually *wrong* with it," Jade said. "But it's not exactly showing off your assets."

"Assets?" Margaret said puzzled.

Jade cupped her own breasts. "Hello, assets," she said pointedly.

Margaret raised an eyebrow. "Jade, in case you haven't noticed my 'assets' are considerably larger than yours, and I have no doubt Markus is well aware of them."

"Oh, really?"

Margaret realized what she had just said. "I meant . . ." She trailed off, blushing.

"Margaret, there is a significant difference between being aware, and being *aware*. Here," she said as she came over and undid the top two buttons of the blouse, "try this."

Margaret looked down at the lace now showing over the top of the blouse, and the depth of cleavage it revealed. "I can't wear it like this," she protested, and started to do it back up.

"Margaret," Jade pleaded. "Just have a look. This is quite proper."

Margaret paused, then stood up to consider herself in the mantelpiece mirror. Despite what Jade had said, the mirror did show a significant amount of cleavage. Certainly, there was no missing the smooth curve of the top of her breasts, nor the hint of lace showing.

Margaret shook her head. "It's not really me," she objected.

"Wearing sexy lingerie wasn't you last weekend," Jade pointed out.

97

Margaret acknowledged that with a small shrug and pulled the front of her blouse closed. Jade rolled her eyes at her as Margaret defiantly did one of the buttons back up.

"Anyway, I presume you didn't come in here to critique my clothes?"

"No, I was just going to check that it was all right if I headed back to my flat. I need to make sure everything's set for an extended departure."

"Are you playing tomorrow?" Margaret asked, referring to Jade's netball competition.

Jade shook her head. "The competition runs Sundays. But I have to speak to the team captain to give my apologies for the rest of the season."

Margaret nodded, feeling guilty at having to take Jade away. "How's the team doing without you?" she asked.

"Not as well, but we're still on track to win the competition."

"Good. And no, I don't need you for the moment."

"Then I'll see you Saturday night," Jade said, and with a jaunty half-salute disappeared out the door.

Margaret adjusted the blouse to try and minimize the amount of skin that was showing and returned to the settee, picking up the report she'd been working through before Jade had interrupted her.

She had just turned the last page when she became aware of Markus watching her from the doorway.

"What?" she asked.

"Nothing," Markus said, crossing over to sit down facing her. "I've just confirmed I've been transferred to your staff, so Jessie and I will be accompanying you to Sultan. Or at least to Budapest. We'll be leaving a couple of days after you."

As he'd been speaking his eyes had seemed drawn to her chest, and looking down she was amused to find that while she'd been working the button she'd done up had worked its way open again. Instinctively she started reach up to do it up before stopping herself.

"Aherm," she said.

Startled he looked up and Margaret gave him a small smile, realizing that Jade was right and there was a real difference between being 'aware' and *aware*.

"I spoke to your mother," he continued. "And she spoke to the First Leader, who spoke to Doctor Rubenstein, who will now be accompanying you to Sultan for as long as you need her."

She blinked at him, amazed. "My mother?" she repeated.

He nodded, looking like the cat who'd got the cream. Well, she'd cure that she thought, leaning forward. As she did that his eyes flicked down to the smooth curve of her breasts, then her lips touched his and suddenly she had his full, and instantaneous attention.

He tasted of peppermint, and she gently ran her tongue over his lips, causing him to groan. She deepened the kiss and his breathing roughened satisfactorily. She smiled, pleased at the effect she had had on it, then his tongue pushed against hers and coherent thought became impossible as she lost herself in the sensations he aroused. When she finally pulled away, she was amused to find his eyes unfocused.

"Well, that was nice," he said.

"Only nice?" she asked, raising an eyebrow.

"By nice, I meant mind-blowingly fantastic," he said quickly.

"Much better," she said.

"But perhaps I need another one just to make sure I remember it properly."

"Later," she said, swatting him.

He nodded and reluctantly moved toward the door. "Oh," he said turning back. "I've also arranged for Mrs. Mack to accompany us."

"How did you do that?" she demanded. She had wanted to keep Mrs. Mack but had been so sure she would never be able to steal her away from the house she hadn't even bothered to try.

"I asked," Markus said, giving her a satisfied smile, then suddenly gave her a little cheeky-boy grin. "And I had Jessie with me when I asked. You should have heard her. 'Please Mrs. Mack, pleeeaaaase!'"

"Oh, that was so cheating," she said, laughing.

"It was for a good cause," he said seriously.

Margaret was suddenly flustered and turned her gaze back to the report. When she looked up Markus was back and leaning over to drop a quick kiss on her lips.

"I need to start packing," he said.

17

WELL THAT WAS FUN

(Wednesday: Budapest, Mainline)

It was late evening as Jade stepped down onto the cracked concrete pavement of Mainline's Budapest Airfield and waited for the ground to stop moving beneath her feet. To her left a few massive airships squatted uneasily, clinging to the ground with the help of their air-cushion landing systems, while a large puddle of water on the grass to her left marked where ballast had been dumped from the last airship to take off. Behind her she could hear the gurgle of water as they pumped ballast into the airship that had brought them direct from London, causing the craft to settle itself firmly onto the ground.

She looked around, wrinkling her nose at the heavy stink of diesel on the air and wondered why she felt so . . . disappointed. It took her a moment to realize she'd been hoping that Carlos would have been there to meet her. OK, so that was irrational, she thought. Carlos was in deep cover and couldn't just take the portal through to meet them, but she *missed* him. When they'd been on the run across Chikyù together she had got used to being able to rely on him, and now there seemed a very large Carlos-shaped hole in her life. At least the odds of actually seeing him again had improved. Yes, Pesh had a population of over three million, and he was still operating under cover so she couldn't just look him up, but at least they were going to be in the same city, rather than being on different lines and separated by half the globe.

As Jade pulled her jacket tighter against the piercing wind Margaret stepped down from the stairwell behind her and paused to re-tie her scarf to protect her hair.

"I am *so* looking forward to a bath," Margaret said, and headed straight for the arrivals' building.

Jade hitched her bag higher onto her shoulder and waited politely for Mrs. Mack to join her on the ground before leading the diminutive housekeeper in pursuit of the new Ambassador.

"It's cold," Mrs. Mack complained.

"Colder than last time," Jade admitted. "Apparently it can get quite cold in winter."

"How cold?" Mrs. Mack asked.

"The Danube actually froze last winter."

"The Danube?"

"It's the main river through the city. Apparently, it happens every five or six years."

Mrs. Mack looked worried and pulled her knee-length camel hair coat tighter around her small frame.

"We've still got a couple of months," Jade said reassuringly, "and I'm sure the house we've got has central heating."

Mrs. Mack sniffed, making it clear what she thought about the adequacy of central heating in any city other than New York. Jade, who had grown up in the tenements of Brooklyn, had a great deal of sympathy for that view, although she had to admit Budapest was certainly prettier.

It was warmer inside the building and Jade found Margaret talking to Colonel Ferai just inside the entrance. Despite Margaret's height she looked almost short next to the one-eyed, former Mmbuto é Imperial Marine.

"Colonel," Jade said, pleased to see him again.

"Miss Carvello," Ferai replied with a broad grin, the intricate white tattoos that covered his face a dazzling contrast to his dark, almost blue-black skin.

"Can I introduce Mrs. Mack, Colonel," Margaret said. "Mrs. Mack is our housekeeper. Mrs. Mack, this is Colonel Ferai, presently on loan from the First Leader's personal guard. He's just been telling me that he'll be responsible for the security of the Embassy, and our own house."

"I hope the decision to set up house on the Mainline and commute to the Embassy has not created any problems," Jade said, unable to suppress her professional concerns.

The Colonel shook his head. "We exist merely to serve," he assured them, winking at Mrs. Mack as he did so. "Besides the actual arrangements have been coordinated through the Governor's office. And until Mrs. Mack and I have assured ourselves of the adequacy of the facilities, the Governor has arranged for everyone to stay at the Gresham Palace Hotel."

Jade sucked in her breath. She and the Colonel had walked past the five-star hotel that overlooked the Danube the last time she was here, joking about the skin-flinted bureaucrats who had booked the two of them into the two-star Railway Hotel. It seemed someone had finally prized the Imperial purse open. And the Gresham Hotel was definitely something worth spending it on. Built just over a hundred years ago, shortly before the Decimation had wiped out two-thirds of the Mainline's population, it had been constructed by the Gresham Life Assurance Company for office space, and as a residence for senior staff of the company. Its exterior had been constructed in the Art Nouveau style to reinforce the impression of power and influence that the then expansionist British company had wanted to portray. Of course, the Decimation had quickly put paid to that particular aspiration. Over the following ten years the building had been deserted and risked becoming derelict until the city had bought it for social housing. It had been converted to a hotel about thirty years ago with its developers seeking to restore the building to its former glory.

Margaret simply nodded at the news, however, as though it was her right. And perhaps it was. Sometimes you forgot just how privileged Margaret's upbringing had been. Not that she was envious of Margaret. You only had to look at the emotional and mental mess she was in at the moment, but having some of the money Margaret was used to would have been nice while she'd been growing up. At least it seemed she was going to experience a little of it for the next couple of days.

The ride to the hotel was taken in the hotel's Rolls-Royce Phantom IV. It was so luxurious that it put Margaret's own Silver Shadow in the shade. Even Margaret was impressed by the size of the bar built into the dividing wall, and by the time they arrived at the hotel both Jade and Margaret were giggling like schoolgirls having pressed, prodded, and tested every asset that had been built into the limousine's Dionysian interior. Mrs. Mack's frown indicated what she had thought of their behavior.

Inside, the lobby was furbished with brightly polished bronze fittings, while the massive stained-glass windows set high into the tall walls overlooking the hotel's reception glowed in bright shards of blue, green, orange, red, and yellow light. Chandeliers hung from the decorated high ceiling, and the two small bars on either side of the check-in desk were still serving a late high tea.

Each of the party had been provided with a suite, even Mrs. Mack who looked for a moment as though she might refuse the honor before giving a small shrug and gesturing to the porter where she wanted her chest placed.

With the door shut behind her, and temporarily alone in her room, Jade peered through the curtains to find that her suite overlooked the river. She could just see the lights of the promenade reflecting off the dark waters of the river below. When she'd walked past the hotel with the Colonel, gazing up at it and wondering what it was like inside, she would have seen this very window. And now here she was, she thought, sliding her shoes off and walking across the thick piled carpet to throw herself on the bed, before sitting up and bouncing on it a couple of times. She could definitely get to like this sort of life, she thought happily, noticing the massive oval bath that she could just see around the corner of the bathroom door. Despite the bath's size, it was dwarfed by the bathroom itself. She really had to see if she could get Carlos here to try out some of the facilities with her. In the meantime, she had, when she checked her watch, precisely fifty-six minutes to get ready for dinner.

After starting the bath running and pouring in the bubble mixture she returned to the bed, picked up the telephone on the side-stand and dialed her mother's number in Boston. When her mother answered, Jade threw herself back onto the pillow.

"Hi Mom," she said.

"Hi sweetheart. I presume you arrived in Budapest all right?"

"Yep. I haven't got long; dinner's in an hour and I'm running the bath. But you should see the suite they've given me — it's enormous!"

The conversation was finally cut short when she began to worry about the bath overflowing. Dinner proved every bit the gourmet experience she had been anticipating, and it was close to midnight before she returned to her room. She paused before turning the key in the lock hoping that when she opened the door she would find Carlos there, but the suite was empty. To her surprise, however, someone had turned the bed down and slippers had been placed next to the bed while a luxurious dressing gown of deep purple was laid out on top of the coverlet. After a quick cleanup she retired to bed, to be up and running around the bridges shortly after seven the next day. She got back to the hotel at eight-thirty pleased with her workout and feeling more relaxed than she had been for some time to find a note slipped under the door.

Puzzled, she unfolded it to find it was from Margaret.

> I knocked but you didn't seem to be in. If you're running, don't forget we have breakfast with the Cardinal at eight for a progress report on setting the Embassy up. See you in the dining room. Margaret.

She swore, angry with herself for forgetting. She stripped off as she headed for the bathroom, leaving a trail of clothes behind her. Twenty minutes later, with her hair still damp from the shower, the maître d' showed her to the table occupied by Margaret and a stranger with a balding head and sharp, beady eyes who stood politely as the maître d' pulled her chair out for her.

"Ms. Carvello, I presume," he said.

"Cardinal Abbott," she said, recognizing the voice from the telephone call a week or so ago. "I apologize for being late.

"That's quite all right. But it's Lindsay, remember."

"Lindsay," she acknowledged with a smile. It was just so difficult to remember to call him by his first name. "Just a latte and some scrambled eggs on toast, please," she told the waitress who had arrived to take her order.

"Lindsay was just bringing me up to date on the embassy's remodeling," Margaret told her as Jade turned back to the table.

"Yes," the Cardinal said. "We've been working on both sites simultaneously. The old Madrasa on Sultan is requiring minimal changes and ImpSec took over security on the site just under a week ago. We're about halfway through the fit out and should be finished in another week or so. The monastery on the Mainline is proving more problematic. But the portal is fully functional, and Colonel Ferai is happy with security."

Jade nodded politely.

"I'm looking forward to being shown around," Margaret told him.

Lindsay checked his watch. "Which reminds me. I really should head off to make sure everything is ready for your visit. Or at least as ready as that madhouse can be. I presume you still want to have a look at the Madras."

"I think we should," Margaret said.

Jade started to rise as Lindsay got to his feet, but Margaret gave her a subtle shake of her head and she dropped back into her seat, feeling the heat of embarrassment on her face. This ennoblement was a real pain in the proverbial. She was so used to standing for those senior to her, and now she had to remember not to, being a 'lady' now rather than one of the hired help.

"I take it you were out for a run?" Margaret said.

Jade nodded as she reached for the carafe of orange juice. "Yes, the weather's perfect. And I needed to get the creases out after three days in the airship."

"Budapest certainly looks pretty from what I've seen of it. How does it compare to its Sultan equivalent?"

Jade rocked her head uncertainly. "It's hard to tell. Pesh is larger, and it seems to come across as more cosmopolitan. But Budapest is definitely cleaner, and prettier."

"Maybe that's the result of Pesh being the capital city of both the Ottoman Empire, and the Northern Caliphate."

"Maybe? There are a lot more mosques, and a lot less traffic, but I don't know if that's the result of planning, or a shortage of gas. On the downside the city's more damaged, both physically and emotionally."

Margaret nodded and took a careful sip of her tea. Jade considered the empty plate in front of Margaret which showed clear signs of once having housed tomatoes, bacon and eggs.

Margaret caught sight of the glance and gave her a small smile. "Even Mrs. Mack would have been happy with my breakfast."

"Speaking of whom?" Jade said, looking around for their diminutive housekeeper.

"Colonel Ferai took her off to have a look at the house the Governor's arranged before breakfast. Then they have an appointment with a recruitment agency at ten. If they get the right people Mrs. Mack thinks they could have the house ready for Markus and Jessie's arrival."

Jade thought that was probably going to be a bit of a hard ask. "You can tell her she doesn't need to hurry on my account." She gestured around. "I could live here for years." She almost knocked the plate the waitress was carrying out of her hand with the gesture and apologized quickly.

"That's all right ma'am," the waitress said, as she placed the plate containing her requested scrambled eggs in front of her.

"Thank you," Jade told her sincerely.

"I think I might leave you to it," Margaret said.

Jade waved her away with her fork, her mouth full of egg.

They met up in the foyer at ten where an aide from the embassy had arrived to drive them. Uncertain on how much longer she would be entitled to wear the Agency's uniform, given Margaret's offer to have her join her personal staff, Jade had opted to wear the scarlet uniform, with its distinctive brownfelt campaign hat. She stroked the tunic a little sadly, then, giving herself a shake, buckled on the belt and checked that the revolver in its holster was sitting comfortably on her hip, with the expandable baton on her other hip next to the handcuffs. She finished by attaching the small red and black enameled cross to her collar. It was still difficult to believe that she, Jade Carvello of Brooklyn, was now a noble of the Empire thanks to the Order of Saint Vladimir (second class) which hung from her neck.

Margaret had also dressed up and was wearing the black and silver uniform of a Dontfrey Battle Group Leader, her chest almost covered in ribbons.

"Well don't we look smart," Margaret said dryly, raising an eyebrow.

Jade gave her a small, uncertain smile.

"Leaders," their driver said, gesturing them toward the vehicle waiting for them outside.

The monastery turned out to be in a quiet backwater of the city surrounded by a series of narrow one-way streets. Its high stone walls gave it the appearance of some medieval fortress. A large gate pierced the wall and after the driver showed his pass to the two ImpSec officers in heavy body-armor guarding the entry, the vehicle was allowed to drive through into the small, crowded, car park.

As he held the sedan's door open for them their driver pointed out their surroundings. "The monastery used to have two cloisters — this one, as you can see, has been turned into a car park. The second one is still a garden and is through there." He pointed to a large, arched, gateway. "That's the church," he said, pointing to the building on their left. "The dormitory and Chapter house are built around the larger cloister."

Jade gazed doubtfully at the church, a squat, stone building that possessed the patina of extreme age.

"It's what, thirteenth century Romanesque?" Margaret said.

"I believe so," their driver replied.

No, there was certainly nothing like it in Brooklyn, Jade thought.

"And which building is the portal in?" Margaret asked.

"In the old kitchen. You have to go through the dormitory to get there though. If you'd like to come this way, I'll take you through."

They followed him through the gateway and into the dormitory beyond. Unable to hear their driver's spiel over the whine of a nearby electric saw, and the thud, thud, thud of several nail guns, Jade lagged behind. She sped up when she realized Margaret had reached the entrance to the old kitchen. As she did so, someone pushed past her, causing her to stumble. She turned, angry at being jostled, then paused, convinced that during the collision she'd felt, just for a moment, the unmistakable hardness of a concealed weapon in a shoulder holster. The person who'd so rudely pushed past her was wearing overalls identifying him as an electrician. Since when did an electrician carry a concealed weapon?

Instinctively her hand went for her own gun. "Stop!" she called, her voice cutting through the din, but he kept walking as though he hadn't heard.

"Damn," she swore, pulling her gun free. "Freeze," she called, her finger poised on the trigger, but he simply kept walking, and a moment later had disappeared through the same door as Margaret.

She swore again and took off after him. What was wrong with her? Why hadn't she fired? She had a sudden flashback to the first time she'd shot at someone, and the blood and the shock on the target's face as she'd hit him.

As she ran through the doorway, she was already aware that she'd made a mistake. It was likely to be her last because her target was waiting for her, his gun tracking her even as she dove frantically for cover.

She heard the sharp bark of a gun and feverishly tried to bring her own revolver to bear. But where was he? All she could see was Margaret standing, feet apart in the approved two-handed firing stance — automatic in her hand.

Cautiously she raised her head. "Margaret?" she asked uncertainly.

"It's OK,"Margaret told her as ImpSec officers piled into the room.

Jade carefully released her revolver and lay very still.

Half an hour later Jade was sitting, her second cup of sweet tea clasped between her hands, while Margaret finished briefing the ImpSec Lieutenant.

"Well, that was fun," Margaret said, joining her.

Jade looked at her unbelievingly.

"What?" Margaret asked, raising an elegant eyebrow.

"Fun!"

"How would you describe it?"

"I don't know. Not 'fun', though."

Margaret shook her head. "No one on our side died. That's got to be fun."

"You're mad," Jade told her.

"Tell me something I don't know," Margaret said.

"How can you be so calm? My hands are still shaking."

Margaret held a hand out and inspected it thoughtfully. It was rock steady. "Perhaps now, but later . . ." Her eyes suddenly glazed.

"Margaret?" Jade said, concerned.

"Sorry," Margaret said, and took a deep breath. "Just remembering something."

"I can't believe you shot him," Jade said, for what must have been the tenth time.

Margaret tapped the medals on her chest. "Excuse me — soldier. Still, none of that would have been any good if you hadn't spotted him."

"Do we know what he was doing here yet?"

"ImpSec found a bug concealed under fresh cement. They'd never have been able to find it in another couple of hours." She shook her head regretfully. "This is a major breach of good faith on the part of the Ottomans. It's not exactly getting us off on the right foot."

Jade shook her head. "I'm not sure it was them."

"Oh?"

Jade considered the mug she was holding, hoping it would give her the answer she needed. "There was something about the way he looked," she said uncertainly. "He reminded me of someone, but I'm not sure . . . . Besides, if it was the Ottomans, why did he try to shoot me? Placing a bug is one thing, actually shooting one of the staff is another level of pain."

Margaret nodded thoughtfully. "We've probably wasted enough time for the moment. Did you want to stay here, or come through to Sultan?"

"I'm fine," Jade said, taking a swallow of the tea and placing it back on the table. As she did that, she found herself remembering that moment when she had frozen. She frowned. She was going to be useless to Margaret if she couldn't look after her. Burying that thought for the moment, she stood up. "Let's go."

18

THE SULTAN IS ARRANGING FOR A BALL

(Wednesday: Sultan, Pesh)

Margaret breathed out as she stepped into the portal. There was the familiar blur, and an explosion of dots across her vision, then she was stepping out into the old Madrassa's courtyard on Sultan. In front of her a small fountain fed water into four rills that guided it across the marbled stones lining the courtyard into the long ponds that separated the courtyard from the high cloistered halls that surrounded it.

A young man in an orange silk uniform and Cossack style cap waiting beside the Cardinal started when he saw her step through the portal. He began to say something, but whatever it was caught in his throat, and he had to adjust his pince-nez to recover. "Ambassador," he finally managed.

"Kaymakam," Margaret said politely, ignoring Emre's reaction as the Cardinal looked amused. It didn't bother her and was something she'd learned to ignore ever since she'd started to develop breasts.

"Cardinal," she said. "It seems like only fifteen minutes ago we were speaking."

"Ambassador," the Cardinal said dryly, as after all it had been only fifteen minutes ago.

Emre's gaze suddenly focused behind her and she turned to see Jade had followed her through the portal.

"Emre," Jade said, with a broad smile.

"Miss Carvello."

Jade snorted, and Emre grinned back at her.

"I hope you had a good trip?" he asked.

"Lousy," she said cheerfully. "How's Darda?"

"Learning to drive," he said sourly.

"Good for her. How did she manage to convince you to let her start learning?"

"She just mentioned your name several times. Jade did it. Jade would do it. In the end I just got all Jaded out." Then, seeming to recollect where he was, Emre turned back to Margaret. "The Deputy Ambassador has just informed me that you detected someone trying to place a bug in the Embassy."

Margaret raised an eyebrow at the Cardinal, disappointed that she hadn't been the one to tell Emre. She really would have liked to have seen his reaction.

"We did," she confirmed dryly. "And I was just about to convey our concerns."

Emre grimaced. "And of course you would be perfectly entitled to do so if we had been involved. But I can assure you that in this case the Ottoman Empire was not."

"Really?" Margaret said disbelievingly.

"Really," he assured her. "I can understand your reluctance to take my word for it, particularly given that it had been our intention to do exactly what we are now accused of doing."

Margaret considered him suspiciously. "So, what you are saying is that while you *were* going to bug the embassy, this attempt was not yours."

Emre shrugged. "Difficult to believe, but it is the truth."

"But if it wasn't you, then who was it?"

"There could be any number of potential parties. The Angevins spring immediately to mind. Obviously, we could provide forensic assistance to determine the culprits. Our knowledge of the Mainline techniques from during the war indicates that our abilities would exceed yours."

"Thank you, I will take that offer under consideration."

Emre did not appear surprised by her response. "Then perhaps a sample of his DNA? We could run some tests to identify his genetic background?"

Margaret considered him doubtfully. "It would be useful for one of our scientists to be walked through the process you use . . ."

"I can't see a problem with that. But it would improve the accuracy of our database if we were provided with samples of the DNA of all those at the Embassy."

"We will need to consider that," Margaret said, looking at the Cardinal, who gave a small nod. Looking back at Emre she wondered why he looked so pleased. He'd obviously got something he wanted, and she wondered what it was, or rather why. She suspected he'd been angling for the DNA samples all along, but what could he do with them? She wished Markus were there to advise her. "But perhaps we could start our tour, now."

"Of course, Ambassador," Emre said. "But before I forget . . . the Sultan is arranging for a ball to acknowledge the establishment of the Embassy and to formally welcome you to the Line. You and all your staff will receive formal invitations tomorrow, but I thought I'd better confirm your availability."

"And the date for the ball?" Margaret asked, trying to remember if she'd packed a formal gown, or whether she'd have time to get something made up that adhered to local mores. From what Jade had been saying they were considerably more relaxed than Muslim cultures on the Mainline, but it was always better to consider local sensibilities.

"Tuesday, next week."

Just under a week, Margaret thought. And Markus and Jessie were due to arrive the day before. At least she'd have someone to accompany her. "Thank you, that will be fine. And now, Cardinal," she said, gesturing him to lead the way.

19

Mottos Materiae

(Monday: Mainline, Budapest)

Jade knocked tentatively on Margaret's hotel room door. "Margaret?" she called quietly.

It was almost eleven and Margaret hadn't appeared for breakfast. Worriedly Jade tried the door, to find it locked. She waited a minute or so, before knocking again. "Margaret? Rise and shine."

When there was still no reply, she pulled the keys she'd had cut a couple of days ago from her pocket and hefted them consideringly. She'd heard what Margaret had done when she taken that overdose, and there'd been a certain flatness to Margaret's manner for the last couple of days that had worried her, hence the copied keys.

Slipping the key into the lock she was relieved to find the door opened easily under her hand. Peering around the door she found the curtains still closed and the suite in darkness. She crossed to the living room curtains and jerked them open, flooding the room with light before turning to the bedroom. The bedroom door was open, and with light now pouring in through the window behind her Jade could make out the shape of someone in the bed.

"Margaret?"

"Go away," Margaret muttered, turning over and pulling the bedclothes up over her head

Thank the gods, Jade thought in relief. Unfortunately, with Markus, Jessie, and Margaret's psychiatrist not due to arrive for another couple of days she was going to have to get Margaret up. Carefully Jade sat on the edge of the bed, to avoid sitting on Margaret's arms. "Come on," she said, the bed sinking under her weight. "It's past eleven o'clock and you still haven't had any breakfast."

"Go away," Margaret repeated. "I'm not getting up today."

"Why not?"

"I don't want to. I don't want to do anything. Just go away and leave me alone." She gave a sob.

"Nope," Jade said. "It's a beautiful day, and you need to get up."

"It's not, and I don't," Margaret retorted.

Jade couldn't help a small sigh. She got up, went across to the bedroom curtains and flung them open. Behind her she heard Margaret groan and hid a smile. She might be doing this for the best of reasons, but that didn't mean she couldn't enjoy being the boss for a change.

"It *is* a beautiful day," Jade said, peering out through the sheer curtains at the river scintillating in the sunlight below.

"I'm still not getting up," Margaret said.

Jade crossed to the bed, and looked down at her employer who now had the blankets over her head as well. "Fine. But you need to have a shower."

There was a stillness under the blankets then Margaret's face slowly appeared. "Just a shower?" she asked.

"To start with," Jade said.

Margaret considered the matter. "All right," she agreed reluctantly.

Jade waited until she heard Margaret's gasp of shock as the water hit her, before remaking the bed. She had just finished when Margaret reappeared in a thick dressing gown, a towel wrapped around her hair.

Jade considered her. "You're looking a bit better," she said.

"I don't feel it," Margaret said.

"At least you're upright."

"Yeah," Margaret said, giving a hollow laugh. "Depressed, but upright. Doesn't seem that much of an improvement."

Actually, Jade considered it a significant improvement. "You can't go back to bed until your hair's dry, so let's go and get some brunch."

Margaret looked her up and down. "You're one hell of a slave driver."

"Whatever it takes," Jade said. "Now, are you going to get dressed, or are you coming downstairs dressed like that?"

Margaret looked down at her robe. "I'm good."

"Margaret," Jade said warningly.

"I'll get dressed."

"Good choice."

At the hotel restaurant Jade guided them outside to one of the tables on the patio overlooking the river.

"What do you want?" Jade asked, as Margaret glanced at the menu.

"Just a coffee."

"Do you want me to get Mrs. Mack down here?" Jade threatened.

"Fine." She sighed. "I'll have a kid's pancake stack."

Jade motioned a waitress over to take their order. "All right, are you going to survive until your doctor gets here?" when the waitress had disappeared.

Margaret shrugged.

Jade stared at her.

"Probably. Yes. Look, I'm not suicidal, just depressed."

"There's a difference?" Jade was surprised.

"Take it from someone who's been both, there is."

"So why are you depressed?"

"How should I know?" Margaret snapped.

"No, I meant aren't the tablets supposed to fix that?"

"The psych warned me that it may take time to get the medication amount right."

"Well, shouldn't you increase it, or something?" Jade asked.

Margaret shook her head. "I am not going to increase the dose until I'm told I have to. I'd much rather sort this out without drugs."

Jade looked at her, and Margaret raised an eyebrow at her enquiringly.

"All right," Jade conceded. "But you have to promise to tell me if you start having suicidal thoughts."

"Fine, mother."

"Now that's an idea," Jade said.

"No, you are *not* going to call my mother."

"Then promise."

"I already have," Margaret pointed out.

"Good."

They looked at one another, then both simultaneously broke out into smiles.

Margaret's smile turned into a scowl, and she looked up into the cloudless sky which was a faultless, pale, washed-out blue. "It's still not a beautiful day."

"On that I think we'll have to disagree."

"At least it appears you succeeded in getting me up," Margaret told her.

"We aim to please," Jade told her with a careful smile, hoping that Margaret had been telling her the truth, and wishing it was already Wednesday. She hadn't the foggiest what she was doing, and there wasn't anyone she could speak to until the airship got here.

The airship was due in at ten in the morning, and Margaret, Jade, and Colonel Ferai were waiting in the arrival's terminal as the vehicle maneuvered across the grass toward its allocated berth. Margaret had shown some minor improvement since Monday, although Jade still had to wake her up and coax her out of bed. They'd found that if they concentrated on fifteen-minute blocks Margaret was able to get up and work her way through the day. She'd even been able to get to the embassy yesterday, although she did seem very reliant on Jade. And Jade was looking forward to handing that responsibility over to someone else.

Jessie was holding her father's hand as they came through the door and seeing Margaret she let go of the hand and made a beeline to her. Margaret knelt down and wrapped her arms around her, burying her nose in her hair as though clutching a life saver.

As Markus arrived Margaret got to her feet, and Jade could swear there were actually tears in her eyes. For a moment Markus and Margaret simply stared at each other.

"Oh, for goodness' sake," Jade muttered and bumped her hip against Margaret, sending her friend stumbling forward into Markus.

Margaret cast a warning glance at Jade, but Jade noticed she didn't pull back.

Jessie was staring up at Colonel Ferai. "Who are you?" she demanded.

The massive former Mmbuto é marine knelt down to put himself at her level. "Sirom Ferai," he said, holding a hand out to her. "I'm setting up the security of your new house."

Jessie shook his hand solemnly. "I am pleased to meet you, Mr. Ferai."
She looked up at Margaret. "Where is Mrs. Mack?"

"She's at the house, making sure everything is ready for your arrival,"
Margaret told her with a smile. "Shall we go and see it?"

Jessie nodded enthusiastically.

Jade shook her head unbelievingly as she watched them. She'd wondered
about Ferai's first name ever since she'd met him. And that's all she'd had
to do — ask. She watched Margaret lead Markus and Jessie off to the
luggage area, *Sirom* Ferai keeping a watchful gaze over his three wards,
leaving Jade to wait for the rest of the party.

Doctor Rubenstein, Margaret's psychiatrist, was one of the last to
disembark, and she seemed a little unsteady as she came through the door.
She was wearing a soft gray pants suit, and her long hair, heavily coiffured
the last time Jade had seen her, had been pulled back into a ponytail.

"Doctor Rubenstein," Jade said, moving quickly to intercept her.

"Miss Carvello," the psychiatrist said, obviously relieved to recognize
someone.

"You had a good trip?" Jade asked, relieving her of the small case she
was carrying.

"Too long, I'm dying for a fag."

"I don't think you can smoke on the airfield," Jade said worriedly.

"Hmph," the psych said.

"Doctor, if I could speak to you for a moment," Jade said, guiding her
along the window, away from the door. "It's about Margaret."

"You do know I can't talk to you about her," the psych warned her.

"Oh, I know that. No, I just need to tell you that her depression seems
to have got worse. On Monday I only just managed to get her out of bed
at eleven."

"Oh," the psych said, looking in Margaret's direction. "Any threats of
suicide?"

"No. And she assures me no thoughts of suicide either."

Doctor Rubenstein acknowledged that news with a thoughtful nod.
"That's good. How was she today?"

"Better, sort of. She's been . . . brittle for the last couple of days though."

"Thank you. I will make sure I speak to her later."

"So, how long are you here for?" Jade asked as she led the way after the
other party.

"Four weeks. It was all the time I could take away from my patients."

"And is this your first time in Europe?"

"Oh no. I toured Europe before the war. This is the first time I've been as far east as Hungary though."

Jade felt a surge of envy at the dismissive way someone could simply refer to touring Europe. It seemed so unfair. And yet, until she'd started working for Margaret she wouldn't have even considered traveling outside of New York, let alone overseas or cross-line. And now look at what she'd done in the last three months! Been pursued the length and breadth of Chikyù Line's Mississippi and gone shopping for lingerie in Sultan's Pesh. The gods knew what she'd be doing next month, because she certainly didn't.

"I think you'll enjoy Budapest."

"I'm actually hoping to be able to visit Sultan," Doctor Rubenstein confided quietly. "Some of their psychiatric techniques are significantly more advanced than our own."

"I'm sure that can be arranged," Jade said, wondering who she should speak to to arrange it. Possibly the Cardinal?

The party took two cars, their luggage following in a small van. The house that the Governor had arranged for them was between the Danube and Gellert Hill. It was not so much a house as a small palace, built for one of the Pállfy family in the late 18th century it had been constructed in the Baroque style. Unusually it was surrounded by a large garden which had retained many of the splendors of the original construction, including an enormous fountain in the shape of a reclining Neptune being pulled by five seahorses in the middle of an enormous oval pond. In Jade's opinion it was so far over the top that it was almost worthwhile keeping. The entire property was surrounded by a high brick wall, that now (thanks to Ferai's work) boasted the very latest in microwave and sound detection systems.

Mrs. Mack and the ten staff she and Colonel Ferai had managed to recruit were waiting to greet them on the steps outside the palace.

"Mrs. Mack!" Jessie exclaimed, running up the steps to embrace the housekeeper.

"Miss Ackov," the housekeeper said, returning the hug, a broad smile creasing her face.

Once inside Jade couldn't hide her surprise at what had been achieved in less than two days. When she had seen it last the furniture had still been covered with sheets, and with the windows heavily curtained since the previous winter, the house had been cold and musty. Now the wooden floors gleamed in a new coat of bees wax polish, light streamed in through spotless windows, while scent sticks in all the rooms sent the perfume of lavender wafting through the house.

"You have done a marvelous job, Mrs. Mack," Margaret said, and Jade nodded her agreement.

Upstairs the bedrooms had all been aired, the thick cotton mattresses freshly turned, and the sheets replaced. Jade's chest had already been moved from the hotel and its contents unpacked. She was just going through the drawers to see where everything had been put when Mrs. Mack poked her head around the corner.

"Miss Carvello, there is a phone call from the Embassy for you."

"For me?" Jade said, surprised.

"Yes ma'am."

"Thank you. Oh Mrs. Mack," she said quickly as the housekeeper started to withdraw. "Where's the telephone?"

"At the top of the stairs, and there's another in the foyer."

Jade nodded her thanks. The phone was off the hook, and she picked it up curiously. "Jade Carvello speaking."

"Jade, it's Lindsay," the Deputy Ambassador said. "I just got a message from your partner. He's asked to meet with you."

"Did he give a time?"

"No, he just said he'd phone again tomorrow. And he also said to tell you *mottos materiae*. Does that make sense?"

'Mottos matter'. She grinned, though disappointed that she'd missed speaking to him. "It means it's him. Can you get my phone from Emre Kaymakam?"

"Already done. Someone will bring it around to the Embassy first thing tomorrow."

"Then I'll drop by around eight," she said, wondering what was so important that Carlos had to speak to her personally. While she might privately hope it was the attraction they felt for each other the reality was Carlos was too much of the professional to risk breaking cover for a purely personal matter.

20

Until I Met You I'd Never Killed Anyone

(Tuesday: Sultan, Pesh, C-T E Embassy)

Jade checked the time — eleven! She stared accusingly at the cell-phone lying on the table in front of her. Where was he?

"He'll phone," Darda said encouragingly. She'd accompanied her brother when he'd brought the phone round at seven, then announced that she'd keep Jade company until Carlos phoned.

"I wish he'd get on and do it then," Jade snapped irritably. "Just what is keeping the man? He didn't say *when* he was going to phone did he?" she demanded from Darda, who shook her head.

Surely Carlos wouldn't have broken cover unless something was seriously wrong. But if it turned out that she was going through all this worrying for nothing, and he simply wanted to talk to her she was going to kill him.

"You're muttering," Darda warned her.

She looked around the bare office the embassy had loaned her in the hope it might provide some explanation as to why he called, but the pad of lined paper and pen next to the phone on the desk remained silent. The bookcase on the far wall was equally bare, and the plain, stone walls, grimy with age, didn't offer any suggestions either.

Jade reached out to pick the phone up but just as her finger touched the case it began to ring. She jumped and stared at it accusingly.

"Well, answer it," Darda said.

Jade picked it up, trying to remember how you were supposed to answer it. She had to swipe her finger across the screen three times before the ringing stopped.

"Jade Carvello," she said uncertainly.

"*Solus enim honor,*" came Carlos' voice, his french accent wrapping itself arround her down the line. "Meet me at the coffee shop in half an hour. Make sure you're not followed." And with that he hung up.

She stared at the phone. '*Solus enim honor*' for honor alone, she translated.

"What did he say?" Darda demanded.

"To meet him in the coffee shop in half an hour. Aarr, he can be so infuriating."

"What coffee shop?"

"How should I know," Jade retorted. "Oh gods!" She checked her watch. Five past eleven. That left her only twenty-five minutes. And of course there was really only the one coffee shop it could be, the one across the street from the handcrafted leather covered notebooks she and Darda had been looking at when Carlos had found her last time. She swore again. There was no way she was going to get there in time, especially if she had to lose a tail.

She grabbed her wallet and her phone and was halfway to the door when she realized Darda was following her.

"Where do you think you're going?" Jade demanded.

"With you," Darda announced.

"Oh no you're not."

"You need me," Darda said calmly. "What happens if someone tails you there? You may need me to muddy the trail."

Jade considered her for a moment. Darda was about her height, but her hair was darker than Jade's muddy blond, and they certainly weren't wearing clothes that had any similarity. "Fine. You have your cell?"

Darda held up her phone to show her.

"Money?"

Wordlessly Darda held up her bag.

"We need something to cover our hair," Jade said. She looked around hopefully but couldn't see anything that might serve.

Darda rummaged in her bag and pulled out a knitted beret. "Any good?"

"Perfect," Jade said taking it and pulling it on over her hair. "Darda, Is the car that brought you still here?"

"It should be."

"We'll take that then. Once it drops me off, it can take you back to the barracks."

Darda's car was still there, and waving off the offer of an escort Jade slid into the backseat, pulling Darda into the car after her. Giving the driver the address she settled back into her seat and pulled her mirror out of her handbag to check her face.

"Damn," she said, as she caught sight of the taxi that had been in the rank in front of the embassy pulling out to follow them.

"What?" Darda asked nervously.

"We've got a tail."

"What do you want me do?" Darda started to turn to look out of the back window.

"Don't look round," Jade snapped.

Darda nodded and shrank into her seat.

"In about five minutes I'll get out of the vehicle," Jade told her quietly. "I'll leave you with my hat, and jacket. All you need to do is drive around for ten minutes, then tell the driver to take you back to the Barracks. Is that all right?" The sooner Darda was safely back at the Janissary barracks the better.

Darda nodded. "Sure," she said, trying to look confident, but still looking very young.

"Good."

They were passing through the old Christian quarter now, the streets narrow and twisty, the buildings on either side leaning in to cut out the sun.

"OK," Jade said, shrugging out of her jacket and giving Darda the beret. As Darda started to swap her jacket the vehicle slowed down to squeeze around a narrow corner and Jade was out of the car, slamming the door shut behind her, even as she heard Darda order the driver to keep going.

Jade had emerged next to a narrow alleyway, and she darted down it and around the corner. Peering back around the edge of the wall she watched the taxi follow the embassy's vehicle down the street. She waited another minute to make sure they didn't have follow up, then headed north. There was a tourist shop on the next corner so she purchased a Cossack cap with the Janissary logo on it and jammed her hair into it. She picked up a large slushie at a food shop then strolled north toward the main shopping precinct. She was going to be late, she thought, checking her watch, but in this case it was definitely better to be safe than sorry.

It was close to twelve when she entered the coffee shop. In the shop's dim light, it took a moment to see Carlos sitting at the back table, back to the wall.

He gave her the merest of nods, and, immeasurably happier at the sight of him, she slid into the seat next to him.

"You're late," he said, his eyes dancing.

"You didn't give me enough time," she replied lightly. "And I was being tailed."

He looked worriedly up at the door.

"I lost them," she assured him. He looked tired; his face thinner than a month ago.

He nodded, and, holding up two fingers to attract the attention of the waiter, he mimed for two coffees.

"So what did you want to see me about?" she asked. "Not that I'm not pleased to see you," she added hurriedly. "But . . ." she trailed off uncertainly.

He nodded, his eyes pausing a moment from their endless scanning of the street outside to rest on her face. "I'm starting to get worried about what our bosses have Karen and me doing. I'd feel happier if I had back up. but I'm fairly sure Ottoman security has been compromised, and I think whoever's running Karen and me has at least one mole in the Angevin Embassy." He smiled up at the waiter who delivered their coffee before his eyes resumed their ceaseless scanning of the traffic outside.

"So, *what* have you been doing?" Jade asked.

"Arranging transport of some highly sensitive cargo through Venice to Pesh. Everything seemed to be going well but suddenly the plan's been changed and now they're routing it through Genoa. So now the truck has to drive across most of Italy." He shook his head. "Given the way it's being handled the cargo *has* to be one of the big three."

"What — nuke, chem, or bio?"

"Yeah."

"If its nuclear the Ottomans are going to go off their heads," she said. "You know how they feel about nuclear weapons as a result of the Great War against the United Christian States."

He nodded. Thirty million people had died in the nuclear holocaust that destroyed the UCS. "Merde," he said suddenly.

"What?"

"It has to be nuclear," he said, lowering his voice. "The portal I came through to Sultan is in the Pittsburgh area, which is within what used to be the former United Christian States. It's outside the most heavily contaminated areas, but I presume the UCS had nuclear weapons, and if they did and the people I'm working for located a military base. . . ."

"You said they're bringing it into a port..."

"Yeah," he said unhappily. "And you're going to love this. Karen and I have been tasked with escorting the cargo across from Genoa. We're leaving tomorrow."

"Oh Carlos."

He shrugged. "I'd say stuff it, and evacuate our embassy, but I can't see it's going to be a good look if our prospective allies get the shit bombed out of them just as they start talking to us."

"No." Jade took a sip of her coffee, trying to ignore her building headache, and the tightness in her shoulders. "Maybe we should get the Ottomans to just pick everyone up."

He shook his head. "Karen's developed a relationship with the intelligence officer at the Angevin Embassy, and she's getting a whole heap of information from him that she shouldn't know about. More importantly it's stuff he shouldn't know about either."

"Oh?"

"I suspect we heard about the discovery of that attempt to plant the bug in the embassy before the First Leader." He gave her a cheeky grin. "You should have heard Karen swear when she found out you were responsible for that."

"I wasn't," she said, looking down at the table, unable to meet his eyes. "I spotted him, but I froze. It was Margaret who nailed him."

Carlos frowned, surprised. "You froze?"

"All I could see was the person I killed on the barge on Chikyù." She looked up uneasily. "Does it ever get easier?"

"Jade, I'm the last person to answer a question like that. Until I met you, I'd never killed anyone."

"But. . . ."

"I might give the impression of being some sort of topnotch secret agent. But in reality, I'm just a pâtissier."

"With some rather specialized additional training."

"With *three* months rather specialized additional training. But if it's any consolation, my uncle told me that if it ever starts to get easy you need to get a new job."

"What do we do about the leak then?" she asked, returning the conversation to the real reason for their meeting.

Carlos sighed. "Update Emre, but he's going to have to locate the leak before he can do anything. And he's going to have to compartmentalize his counter terrorism activities."

"And Margaret?"

"Let Margaret know but tell her to keep it under her hat."

"Oh, did you know that Markus and Jessie are here as well?" she asked.

"On Sultan?" he asked surprised.

"No, on the Mainline. Margaret will be commuting from there."

"Jessie!"

"What?"

"You remember they had to create a joint force of ImpSec and Agency officers when they recovered Jessie from her kidnappers?"

"Because the Anarchists had a mole in ImpSec?"

He nodded.

"And who told them that?" she asked dryly.

He tried to look humble, without much success. Too much Gallic in him she thought fondly. Carlos could never look humble.

"Anyway," he continued. "You might want to get your boss to consider something like that here."

"OK," she said. "Here, you'd better have these." She pulled up the numbers of both Margaret and Lindsay from her phone.

Thanks," Carlos said, taking a moment to memorize the numbers. "And how are you traveling otherwise?" he asked as he handed the phone back to her.

Jade wondered if the exhaustion she'd been trying to hide from him was leaking out.

"Missing you," she admitted. "And I haven't been sleeping well."

"Snap! Let's hope this will all be over soon." He checked his watch. "I need to head back," he said, downing the last of his coffee in a single swallow.

She nodded sadly, wanting to reach out, to touch him. "Take care."

He gave her a tired smile. "Of course."

She watched him walk to the door, and then without a glance backward disappear into the traffic outside. For a moment she stared after him, then looking down at her coffee, she pushed it away decisively and stood up. There was too much to do. She had to tell Margaret, and then they had to arrange to speak to Emre without anyone noticing. Perhaps they could do it at the ball that night — that might work.

21

I Have The Pleasure Of Introducing The New Ambassador

(Saturday: Sultan, Pesh)

"Stop fidgeting," Margaret told Markus as they waited at the top of the stairs to be announced. Below them the ballroom thronged with people dressed in the formal attire of the Ottoman court.

"I can't help it," he muttered. "My collar's too tight."

"Then you should have said something at the fitting."

"I did, but you said it suited me."

"It does," she said, looking at him out of the corner of her eyes. He was wearing the new Peric uniform. Now her brother was the World Leader of Notway he'd adopted the previous World Leader's colors as his own, and the dark, Lincoln-green uniform with its red facings quite suited Markus. Given her time in the army, she knew exactly how uncomfortable his collar was, however. That was one advantage of the dress, no collar, although the cinching in at the waist did make it a little impractical at times.

"It's not going to make dancing pleasurable," he said.

Margaret raised an eyebrow. "That is *not* the type of thing you're supposed to say to your dance partner."

"That wasn't what I meant," Markus said quickly.

She gave him a smile. "Better."

They'd been able to sandwich in an afternoon of dance practice between meetings. Most of the local dances seemed to resemble the Mainline's polka. That was not entirely unexpected, Margaret thought, given that the polka had originally come from Bohemia, which couldn't be more than 300 miles away. There were differences, however . . . And speaking of that, the drone of someone tuning their bagpipes drew Margaret's attention to the small orchestra just taking their place on a raised dais to the left of the staircase.

"You know the Caliph can't take his eyes off you," Markus whispered in her ear, giving a small jerk of his head in the direction of the throne on the far side of the room, occupied by a thin, ascetic man with a long white beard and wearing a simple black fez and a long black tunic that reached to his feet. Even as she watched, the Grand Vizier bent over to say something in the Caliph's ear. The ruler smiled and said something back without taking his gaze off them.

"It must be my magnetic personality," Margaret said lightly.

"Or your gown. It does show a significant amount of skin."

"Really?" she asked, pleased he'd noticed. She'd fallen in love with the gown as soon as she saw it in the shop four days before. The gown was a glorious light blue, with a corset style off-the-shoulder bodice, a Basque waistline, and a two-toned layered tulle skirt. There was no doubt the gown emphasized her 'assets', as Jade described them.

"Margaret," Jade prompted. She was standing at Margaret's other shoulder. Unlike Margaret, Jade *was* in uniform, and wore the Agency's high collared scarlet uniform, but with Agency's red dress beret rather than the forage hat she normally wore. Margaret had tried to get her to wear a gown, but Jade had insisted on the uniform, and on the basis that she was Margaret's bodyguard tonight had won the argument. The uniform certainly made her stand out, almost as much as Margaret's gown.

"I see him," Margaret said. Emre had taken his place at the foot of the stairs, and the majordomo stationed at the top of the stairs was now motioning them forward.

"The Ambassador and representative of the Cross-Temporal Empire, Hraffekwi Margaret Peric," the majordomo announced in a loud voice. There was a sudden lull in the conversation from the floor of the ballroom below as she stepped forward, the bottom of her gown swirling out around her.

"Her partner Doctor Markus Ackov," the majordomo continued into the sudden stillness. "And the Ambassador's companion Dame Jade Carvello, OSV."

"Arm," Margaret hissed out of the corner of her mouth to Markus, who immediately offered her his arm.

"OSV?" Markus asked Jade quietly.

"Order of Saint Vladimir," Jade whispered back.

"Given the Ottomans are so fixated on their titles the Cardinal felt it was important we title up," Margaret said. She gave Markus a nudge and they started slowly down the steps.

"You will pardon my ignorance, but Hraffekwi?" Markus said. "I don't think I've heard the term before."

"I'd be surprised if you had. Jade and I cooked it up yesterday."

She caught him looking askance at her and gave him a wry smile. "Unfortunately, the rank of World Leader, or Continental Leader is too new to have been 'nobilized'. That might change one day. I mean, Baron is derived from the Latin word for soldier or mercenary. It was only after a couple of hundred years that it became the rank of a noble."

"So power, but no honor?"

She gave him a dazzling smile. "Exactly. But really, we haven't needed anything else. There are only fifty-four World Leaders, and maybe another two-hundred-and-fifty or so Continental Leaders. It's a small enough group that everyone knows everyone else. But we really need some sort of title that we could give those in the family not directly holding the position."

"And Hraffekwi?" Markus asked.

"It's from 'Hraffor'," Jade explained.

Markus looked just as confused. "That doesn't help."

"Hraffor is a Nayarit term. It translates as 'Soldiers of the Empire'. It's a little like the Spanish 'conquistador'," Margaret explained. "It used to pretty popular about fifty years ago but seems to have fallen into disuse. I thought it might be time to dust it off again."

"And Hraffekwi, roughly translates as family of the Hraffor," Jade explained, "at least as far as I remember my Nayarit."

"It does have a sort of nobility to it. I think I need to speak to Donald about confirming it," Margaret said.

"My lady," Emre said, giving the group a deep bow as they reached the foot of the stairs. "And what do you need to speak to the First Leader about?"

"About formally recognizing the title of Hraffor," Margaret said, acknowledging the bow with a precisely measured one of her own that was perhaps half as deep.

Emre nodded, though it was obvious he didn't have the foggiest what she was talking about.

"I'll explain when we have a spare half an hour," Margaret told him with a smile.

"That is not now," he admitted. "My instructions are to convey you directly to the Caliph. Obviously, he wishes to formally accept your credentials, but apparently, he also needs to ask you where you got your gown from. He intends to buy one for his senior wife."

"Of course," Margaret said, as Markus gave her a knowing look. "There is something we need to talk to you about first though."

"Oh," he said, casting a worried glance toward the Caliph on the far side of the room.

"It is important," Margaret assured him.

"My Lady," he said reluctantly, and led them into a small room next to the stairs.

"Jade," Margaret said, prompting her.

"You heard I met with Carlos today?"

Emre nodded.

"He is convinced the package his 'employers' are trying to bring in is some sort of nuclear weapon."

"He's sure?"

"Yes."

"Crap!"

Margaret nodded. "A succinct, and accurate summary of the situation."

"And Carlos also told me to warn you that you've got a leak," Jade said. "Apparently the Angevin are getting too much information that could only be coming from a source within the Janissaries. He said they've already rerouted the cargo they were bringing in via Venice through Genoa, and that you're going to have to compartmentalize your counter terrorism activities until you've located the leak."

Emre shook his head. "It doesn't have to be from the Janissaries; we have been sharing information with Counter-Intelligence." He held up a hand to forestall Jade's protest. "I'm not saying it isn't from the Corps, and I'll start compartmentalizing, but that's not going to make things easy."

"If I could make a suggestion?" Margaret said.

"Of course, My Lady — suggest away."

"We had a similar situation a couple of months ago when Imperial Security were dealing with a kidnapping by a terrorist group. Unfortunately, that group had penetrated ImpSec. You've heard of the North-Western Police Agency?"

"Yes, the Rucker's Agency." He gave a nod at Jade's uniform. "A private police force, an unusual concept."

"We created a joint strike team, pairing each ImpSec officer with a Rucker's officer. The two agencies do not necessarily like each other . . ."

"ImpSec officers all being overbearing thugs," Jade cut in.

"While ImpSec considers Rucker's agents as amateurs of the worst kind," Margaret responded with a smile. "Neither of which is true. More importantly they proved they could work with each other."

"And the operation was successful?"

"Very!" Margaret remembered the dark night when the strike team had gone in, and she had waited an apparent eternity until that female Agency officer finally appeared in the doorway holding Jessie's hand. An ImpSec officer looming protectively over them both.

"I will bear that in mind," Emre said, and Margaret nodded, knowing that she had taken it as far as she could. "For the moment I do need to introduce you to the Caliph."

"Emre, any word on the results of the DNA testing on staff at the Embassy?" Jade asked as they started to work their way across the dance floor.

"Not as yet," Emre said. "But we do have some news on the potato blight you gave us the sample of. It appears to have been an artificial creation, although we haven't confirmed the designer as yet. The good news is that the lab has confirmed that it appears to be highly susceptible to *mantar ilacı*, a common fungicide."

Markus looked interested. "You've tested it?"

"Yes."

"Mantar ilacıl?" Margaret asked Markus.

"Similiar to your Fungadice?" Emre said.

Markus pulled a face.

"What?" Margaret asked him.

"Fungadice is effective, but it's not the safest of fungacides, there's been some reports it can affect the liver."

Margaret considered the matter for a moment. "All right, let's just pass the information onto Sylvia and let her worry about it."

"The lab mentioned it also appears it has a kill switch, but they're still trying to identify what the trigger is. As soon as we have something we'll let you know."

Markus grimaced. "Not quite the news we were hoping for. Have you —"

"It can wait," Margaret told him, tightening her hand on his arm and flicking her eyes toward the waiting Caliph.

"Of course," he said.

"Ambassador," the Vizier said, with an enormous smile as they reached the dais. A tall man, he was dressed in a red split silkgown, with a black, fur-lined jacket. His white turban was twice as large as his head.

"Vizier," Margaret said politely. She and the Cardinal had already had one meeting with the Vizier, and they had both separately formed the view that the Vizier would not be a man to trifle with. "My credentials," she said, handing him the parchment envelope containing the letter.

The Vizier broke the seal on the envelope and quickly scanned the contents of the letter, having already been provided with a facsimile.

"My Lord," the Vizier said, turning to the Caliph. "I have the pleasure of introducing the Cross-Temporal Empire's new Ambassador, Hraffekwi Margaret Peric.

"I am pleased to welcome you, Ambassador," the Caliph said slowly in clear, accented English. "It is my hope that this will signal the start of a new relationship between our respective Empires."

"As it is ours,"Margaret replied in equally careful Arabic.

The Caliph smiled and leaned forward. "And now to a matter of some importance," he said, reverting to Arabic. "I really must ask you where you got your gown? I would like to order one for my first wife."

"Certainly. From a designer in Budapest, on the other side of the portal. I could ask the designer to see her at the palace, or alternatively I would be happy to accompany your wife to the Mainline."

"Excellent," he said beaming. "I will speak to her to find which she would prefer."

Margaret was startled by the sound of a ringing phone and gave Jade a reproving stare as she pulled away to answer the call. She became aware that Emre had also backed away and had his phone pressed against his ear.

"What?" Margaret demanded, suddenly worried as Jade's expression turned to shock. But Jade simply shook her head and pressed the phone closer to her mouth, speaking in a low voice.

"My Lord," Emre said, putting his own phone away. "I must apologize but something has come up that requires my immediate attention."

Emre turned to leave but stopped at Jade's hand on his arm. "The embassy?" she asked.

He nodded.

"What?" Margaret demanded again.

Jade looked worried. "Could I speak to you privately?"

"My Lord, if I could have a couple of minutes?" Margaret said.

"Of course, Ambassador."

The Vizier had stopped Emre, and they were discussing something urgently as Margaret pulled back just enough to give their own conversation a little privacy. "Well?"

"That was the Cardinal," Jade said. "Somebody bombed the embassy."

"Was anyone hurt?" Margaret asked, worrying about Jessie who had been left in Budapest, on the other side of the portal.

"At least two confirmed dead."

Margaret swore. "Right, call for our car. I'll make our apologies to the Caliph."

"My Lord," Margaret said, returning to the Caliph. "My apologies. Apparently, there's been a bomb attack at the embassy. My Deputy has confirmed there are at least two dead." She noticed the Vizier look up from his conversation with Emre at that.

"I take it you would like to return to the embassy?" the Caliph said. "I'm sure we can come up with some polite fiction to explain your disappearance." He looked at the Vizier who clicked his fingers to attract the attention of one of his aides.

22

How Could We Be So Stupid?

(Saturday: Sultan, Pesh)

The night air was refreshing after the warmth of the ballroom, and as they paused for a moment at the top of the steps Jade took the opportunity to undo the buttons on her collar.

"I just need to speak to Emre," Markus said, spotting him talking on the phone a short distance away. "I won't be a minute. I'll see you at the car. I want to ask him a question about the riboswitch. We might be able to start running some tests on Chikyù. It's not as if we could make anything worse . . ."

"Anything more from the embassy?" Margaret asked Jade quietly as Markus headed off. Jessie should be safe on the Mainline, but until they knew what had happened . . .

"Nothing," Jade replied.

The ImpSec officer standing next to their car opened the door for them. Jade gave him a nod, then frowned as she slid across the seat to the far side of the car, wondering when they'd swapped the escort. As she settled back into the seat a scent tugged at the edge of her memory.

"Ma'am, we have to go," the ImpSec officer said as Margaret paused to look around for Markus. Without giving her time to respond he placed a hand on the back of her head, pushing her down and into the car as he swung in behind her, slamming the door behind them. "Go," he told the driver.

"What?" Jade said, as the car pulled away.

She was reaching for her holster when there was a quiet, "I wouldn't do that," from the front seat, and she froze as she noticed the pistol trained on her over the top of the seat.

Her gaze rose higher, and she gave a startled "Karen!" as she recognized the Agency's renegade agent, and her former friend, holding the gun. Now she knew what the scent had been. 'Floral Rose', Karen's favourite. It was a little late to make any use of the information though.

"Good girl," Karen said as Jade froze. "Now very carefully unfasten your holster and pass me the gun. Slowly!" she said as Jade reached for the strap of the holster.

Carefully Jade slid the catch open and removed her revolver, handing it to Karen who took it from her without taking her eyes off Jade, and placed it on the seat next to her.

When Karen's hand reappeared, it held two handcuffs. "Put these on," she said. "One for your Principal, then put a pair on yourself."

Jade considered assaulting Karen, but even if she could temporarily overpower her, it would undoubtedly cost her own life.

Margaret gave her a small shrug and held out her hands, leaving Jade no choice. Handcuffed and fuming, Jade turned and looked out of the window. They'd turned off the main road and were pulling into a parking space behind a small delivery van.

"Right," Karen said. "You are to get into the back of the van. No heroics. I would prefer not to have to shoot anyone, but I am perfectly willing to if anyone gives me any problems."

The driver climbed out of the car and after opening the back of the van returned to open Jade's door. It was difficult to get out of the car with her hands in cuffs, but not as difficult as it would have been if her arms had been behind her back.

Jade hesitated, waiting for Margaret to leave the vehicle, but the driver gave her a shove and she stumbled forward.

"In," he said.

The windows of the van had been given what looked like a coat of black paint, and the smooth floor of the back of the van gave little in the way of purchase. Jade wriggled her way across the floor, then watched as Margaret had to maneuver her way into the van in her gown. As she settled herself next to Jade the doors were slammed shut and Jade heard the click of a padlock being fitted to the outside of the door. Jade looked around but there didn't seem to be any microphones or cameras.

"Any ideas?" Margaret asked as the van pulled away, and they were forced to brace their feet against the door to ensure they didn't end up sliding across the floor.

"Afraid not, unless you can unlock these?" Jade held up her hands to show the handcuffs.

"Nope."

Jade shook her head. "Crap!"

"It is a little like that," Margaret said, trying to simultaneously wriggle the gown up, and down.

"I should have recognized Karen's perfume," Jade said, furious with herself.

"Don't beat yourself up," Margaret told her. "I don't think anyone would have guessed they were going to try something like this."

There was a sudden explosion from behind them, but the blacked-out window prevented them from seeing anything.

"That was probably the car," Jade said. "Burning the evidence."

"Probably," Margaret agreed.

There was a moment's silence. "I should have known though," Jade said finally. "Carlos warned me. We knew they'd penetrated the Ottoman's security apparatus. Oh —"

"What?"

"Carlos." Worry began to gnaw at her stomach. Had his cover been blown, and if so, what had happened to him? Damn! She slammed the handcuffs against the wall.

"Try and relax," Margaret told her. "Getting angry isn't going to help anyone."

"It would help me if I was alone with Karen for a couple of minutes."

"I doubt they'll give you that opportunity," Margaret said.

"Probably not," Jade said, allowing her head to fall back against the wall. Closing her eyes, she tried to take Margaret's advice. It wasn't easy — there was a lot of history between her and Karen.

Fifteen minutes later the van pulled to a stop, and they heard the screech as a metal roll-door was pulled closed behind them. A moment later the van's back doors were swung open.

"Wakey, wakey," Karen said, pulling back as they crawled out.

They found themselves in a large, open concrete-walled warehouse. There were empty shelves against one wall and what looked like an office built into one corner. The office walls had been reinforced recently with corrugated metal, and a small washroom built up against it. Beside the office was a small open kitchen consisting of a sink, fridge, and a microwave on a small bench. Two beds had been set up outside the office but otherwise the warehouse was bare.

"In you go," Karen said, waving them toward the office.

"Why?" Jade demanded.

"Why what?" Karen asked.

"Why set me up on Chikyù? I thought we were friends."

"It was purely business. Nothing personal."

"Business!"

Karen shrugged. "If you'd done what was expected the Agency would have got you out. But I had a contract. A little something on the side. Everyone at the Agency does it."

"I don't," Jade said quietly. And she wasn't convinced the Agency would have been able to get her out. Sure, they'd have tried but by the time they found out she'd been picked up it would have been too late. Carlos had been right, the Chikyù authorities would have had her hanged by morning.

"Probably not," Karen admitted. "Little Miss Perfect doesn't live in the real world."

Jade shook her head, wondering how she had ever considered Karen a friend.

"And don't expect Carlos to get you out of this one," Karen said.

Jade tried to keep her shock hidden, but something must have shown on her face as Karen sniggered. "You thought we didn't know. He's been useful to date, but his usefulness came to an end . . ." She checked her watch. "Half an hour ago."

They'd reached the office now and Karen gestured them inside. Two mattresses were propped up against the sidewall with a blanket on the floor next to each. A chemical toilet occupied one corner.

The door slammed behind them, and Jade heard the lock click into place.

23

I Seem To Have Set A Petrol Station On Fire

(Saturday: Sultan, Genoa)

The truck's brakes hissed as it jerked to a halt, and Carlos was jolted awake.

"What's the time?" he asked Charlie, who'd been driving, rubbing his eyes.

"Just after three," Charlie replied, his cockney accent stronger than normal because of his own tiredness.

"So where are we?" Carlos asked.

The trip should have taken eleven hours but it had been closer to sixteen because of what had seemed like a continuous series of roadworks ever since leaving Venice. That, coupled with the drizzle that had bedeviled their last fifty miles, had turned the trip into an unplanned marathon. It had not been made any better for Carlos by Charlie's chain-smoking, and his constant chatter about his wife, his daughter, and his mother still in England. That was not something Carlos really wanted to be reminded about given it had been Carlos who had forced Charlie into making this pickup by threatening his family. And as the radio had worked only intermittently, it had felt like a very long trip. He wondered what had happened to Karen, who was supposed to have been making this trip instead of him.

"We've arrived," Charlie said indicating their surroundings and the large white '4' painted onto the concrete in front of them.

Carlos peered out through the window. On their left he could just make out the dark waters of the Mediterranean, and the even darker shadow of the ship that presumably they'd been sent to pick up the 'package' from. On their right, under the glare of security lights, was a stack of containers. A white sedan was parked beside the containers, blocking the rails that ran down the middle of the wharf.

"It's stopped raining," Charlie said. "I'll see if our contacts are still here." He opened the driver's door, and as he swung himself down a rush of cold air filled the cab, clearing out the tobacco fug that had filled the cabin.

Carlos leaned back in the seat and stretched, trying to work out some of the kinks.

As Charlie approached the sedan its doors opened, and four men got out. They wore long, leather jackets, and one of the four cradled a shotgun in his arms, Carlos frowned as Charlie came to an uncertain halt. One of the men said something and Charlie waved in the direction of the truck. The man carrying the shotgun swung it round, there was a crack, and Charlie collapsed in a tangle of limbs.

"Shit!" Carlos muttered as he reached for his gun, still in its shoulder holster. He was going to be seriously outgunned here. He slid across the seat to the driver's position, checking for the keys as he did so. Luckily Charlie had left them in the ignition.

The four had already started toward the truck, the one carrying the shotgun pausing to put another shot into Charlie's head as he passed.

At least the truck was an automatic, Carlos thought. He couldn't have handled a manual. He turned on the engine, slammed the stick into drive and floored the accelerator. The truck took off, the cigarette lighter Charlie had left on the dash landing on the seat next to him. He narrowly avoided putting the truck into the drink and as he swerved away from the edge of the wharf he twisted the wheel, hoping to side-swipe the sedan.

As he straightened the vehicle the first shotgun blast peppered the side of the truck. He flinched and crouched lower, knowing the truck didn't offer much in the way of protection. At the last moment he veered to the other side of the sedan, putting it between him and the gunmen. As he accelerated past, he slammed the truck into the side of the sedan. The truck lurched and he prayed he hadn't killed the engine, but then with a tearing of metal the truck scraped past and with the accelerator still pressed flat to the floor it accelerated away as the gunmen let loose with everything they had.

He crashed through the simple drop-bar blocking the exit, and with the engine howling and the truck seeming on the verge of turning over, swerved onto the road leading away from the port. In the rear mirror he could see the security guard on duty reaching for the phone as he broke through the bar. Behind him the sedan was already in pursuit, although it looked as though he'd been able to smash at least one of the vehicle's headlights.

He wished he knew what had gone wrong because something definitely had. He could understand why some people might want him dead if they had doubts about his loyalty, but why Charlie? That he could never forgive — a young father with a wife and child. The only reason he could think of for that was that they believed he had already told counter-intelligence about Charlie so they had opted to remove all loose links that might lead the authorities to them. But if that was the case — oh gods. He reached for his phone and dialed Jade's number from memory.

"Pick up, pick up," he muttered as the phone rang.

"Hello," a voice said. He hit the disconnect and dropped the phone back onto the seat. Karen! That was not good. If Karen had Jade's phone, they probably had her.

He checked the mirror again. The sedan was catching up with him and it was obvious he wasn't going to be able to outrun it. He checked his speed, sixty-five mph, damn. Charlie had said something about a governor which restricted the truck's top speed. He doubted the sedan had the same restriction. At least the road was empty, so the only one likely to end up dead was one Carlos Babineaux. Why did things like this have to happen to him? He was a pâtissier for goodness' sake! Well that and an agent for the Agence Nationale de la Sécurité, the French Secret Service. But that hardly counted, four years to become a pâtissier, and all of three months training in covert and undercover surveillance to become a spy. The French might no longer control the world, well they probably never had, but they controlled even less than what they might once have done. He stopped his thoughts when he realized he was starting to panic.

He checked the mirror again, then pulled the speed back slowly to sixty. Maybe his training hadn't actually covered the situation of being pursued by four killers while driving a truck. Nevertheless, he had been given a week's advanced driver training, and his instructors had been clear that when something snafued as badly as this had the only thing one could do was the unexpected. So that's exactly what he was going to do.

He checked the mirror, and as the sedan came up fast on the outside lane, he floored the accelerator. The sudden speed surprised whoever was driving the sedan and he swung the wheel hard to the left, smashing into the front wing of the sedan and sending it careering off the road, over the median strip, and onto the opposite lane. It appeared he'd got the other headlight but unfortunately, he hadn't damaged anything else, and the vehicle was pulling level with him again. He weaved as a passenger in the back seat fired two blasts into the back of the truck. He veered back into the far lane then seeing a petrol station on top of the small rise by the side of the road slammed on the brakes and yanked the truck up the off ramp, flooring the accelerator again.

The petrol station was lit up, though deserted except for the petrol tanker making its deliveries. He lost control as he briefly became airborne, roaring out of the ramp and onto the station's concrete apron. The tanker was directly in front of him, and he yanked the wheel hard to the right. Unfortunately, the concrete was slick with rain and the truck failed to respond as quickly as it should have.

Everything seemed to happen in slow motion. He saw the tanker driver look up and throw himself out of the way as the truck scraped the side of the tanker, ripping the pipes free from the side of the truck and spewing petrol everywhere. Carlos slammed forward against the harness as the truck bounced off a pylon, then as though gathering itself, it launched itself at the pylon again before hiccuping to a halt, just as the airbag exploded out of the steering wheel and slammed into his face and chest.

As the airbag collapsed again Carlos stared through the cracked windscreen at the devastation that surrounded him. Automatically releasing his seatbelt, he reached across the seat and picked up his phone. He was just sliding out of the vehicle when he smelled petrol and noticed the petrol still pouring out of the tanker's valves. There was the squeal of wheels from the direction of the highway and the sedan appeared, sliding into the ramp and accelerating up it in his direction. Carlos's eyes followed the flow of petrol down the hill and with a smile he reached back into the seat for Charlie's lighter.

"Charlie," he muttered, "here's your chance for revenge." Pulling out his handkerchief he flicked the lighter, igniting one corner. He moved clear of the petrol already pooling on the concrete apron, dropped the handkerchief into the petrol and dove over the low brick wall that marked the edge of the concrete.

When there was no explosion, he cautiously peered over the edge of the wall. A blue flame was dancing over the top of the petrol as it flowed down the ramp. Beside him the flames were licking at the tanker's tires, and the pipes seemed to be burning. He watched the sedan slide to a halt in the center of the dancing flames. Bad move, he thought.

The driver must have had the same thought because the car lurched forward, then stalled. Flames were leaping up the side of the tires and Carlos suspected the rubber had started to melt. The doors sprang open, and the four goons appeared. Carlos took aim at the closest and fired quickly. His target dropped, flames licking up over his body but before he could shift his aim he had to dodge down as the other three returned fire. He wriggled sideways and when he popped his head back up, he could see only one, who was busy trying to put out the flames working their way up his trousers. Carlos started to take aim but his attention was drawn to the tanker again. Its tires were well on fire and flames were now issuing from the valves. Puzzled, he stared at it, until he realized that the flames were coming from *inside* the tanker, which meant the petrol within the tank must now be on fire.

He swung his attention back to the shooter whose trousers had been on fire and who now seemed to be trying to put the flames out by rolling in the petrol. His gaze shifted back to the tanker. A short distance away the tanker's driver had also seen what he was looking at and with a wild yell started running down the hill, away from the station. One of the shooters must have thought it was Carlos because two shotgun blasts rang out and the driver collapsed in a windmilling mess of arms and legs. Carlos had located the shooter, standing beyond the flames, and he quickly fired five bullets in his direction.

Carlos had just ducked down again when he felt the whoosh of air and heard the tanker explode. Blue and red flames balled into the sky, setting the station's roof on fire. He tried to raise his head, but the heat was too much so he dropped back down and started to crawl down the hill. In the distance he could already hear the wail of police sirens, probably called by the security officer at the port. There was no way they could be responding to this particular event quite so quickly otherwise. At the foot of the hill, he opened his phone and dialed Emre's number.

Despite the hour, the phone was answered after only one ring, and there was no hint that Emre had been asleep with his: "yes."

"Emre?" Carlos asked uncertainly.

"Yes, who's this? I'm in the middle of something at the moment."

"Carlos, Jade's partner. If it involves Jade, then I'm in the same mess."

"Where are you?"

"Genoa. Four shooters tried to kill me. I got two but I seem to have set a petrol station on fire and I'm about to be picked up by the local police."

"How — no, that can wait. I'll arrange for someone to come and get you. I take it you are seeking extraction?"

"Please."

"Leave it with me, then," and Emre was gone.

Carlos looked at the phone. Leave it with him? No, he didn't think so. He concentrated for a moment then dialed another number.

The phone had barely rung when it was picked up.

"Hello? Deputy Ambassador Abbot speaking." The Cardinal sounded harassed and Carlos grimaced, wondering just what had happened there.

"It's Carlos Babineaux; what's happening?"

"There was a bomb attack on the embassy and the Ambassador and Miss Carvello appear to have been kidnapped."

Short and sweet. Carlos shook his head. "I've just spoken with Emre and requested extraction. My cover's blown. I thought I should tell you just in case . . ."

"I understand, I'll arrange for immediate liaison with the Kaymakam's office."

"Thank you. I didn't want to simply disappear."

"Understood. Can I ask where you are at the moment?"

"Genoa."

"Hands up!"

Carlos froze, "I need to go," he said. He turned his head slowly to see the worried stare of a police officer with what looked like some sort of sub-machine gun nervously trained on him. The barrel wavered, and Carlos's eyes widened as he noticed the sweat on the officer's forehead. He dropped his pistol and raised his hands carefully.

"I have diplomatic immunity," he said distinctly. "Emre Kaymakam of the Janissaries will be seeking to speak to your commanding officer. I will offer no resistance."

24

He Was Always A Little 'Strange'

(Monday: Sultan, Pesh)

Jade lay on the mattress staring up at the ceiling and the single, fluorescent tube that had burned without a pause since their arrival. Beside her she could hear Margaret's steady breathing. Her sense of time might be a little off but given the meals they'd been served they'd probably been there for probably slightly more than forty-eight hours. So far, they hadn't seen anyone, and their meals had been passed through a flap at the bottom of the door. She didn't know whether to be relieved, or worried that no one seemed interested in talking to them. And with nothing else to do she found her thoughts constantly drawn back to Carlos, and what might have happened to him.

She heard the bolts on the flap on the bottom of the door being slid back and propped herself up on one elbow to watch the two trays being pushed through the opening.

She looked across at Margaret who gave her a wan smile, as the flap was dropped back into place and the bolts slid home.

"How are you feeling?" Jade asked. "You don't look too well."

"I don't feel well," Margaret admitted.

Jade leaned over to feel her forehead. "You're hot. What are your symptoms?"

"Tiredness, dizziness, cramping in my arm and legs. It could be flu . . ." she offered.

Jade pulled a face; it didn't sound like the flu. "Do you want me to tell our guardians?"

Margaret shook her head. "No, the less we tell them the better."

"I still think we should ask them to get your anti-depressants."

"And what, have me worrying about what they're giving me? I'll be fine."

"Promise?"

Margaret arched an eyebrow and waved a hand airily. "I am a Peric, a member of the Empire's ruling class. A kidnapping is as nothing to us."

"That's bollocks," Jade retorted. "I'm a Dame of the Empire, and I know precisely how wrong that particular statement is. Although I *would* like to know what they're going to do with us."

Margaret stared up at the ceiling. "Generally, terrorists only keep their hostages alive for two reasons," she said levelly. "One, they're trying to raise money by ransoming. Or two, they intend to execute us in some public manner for maximum publicity."

"If my vote counts I'd select option one."

"Ditto," Margaret said.

"It's certainly not five-star," Jade said, pushing one of the trays across to Margaret. It held a glass of water and two pieces of plain toast.

"Not even two," Margaret responded with a snort. "But at least they're still feeding us. Remind me to tell you what happened to my aunt during the war."

"Oh?" Jade said, taking a bite of her cold toast. "Your aunt, the First Leader's mother?"

"Aunt Isobel, yes. She was starved to death by Arnold."

Jade inhaled a mouthful of toast and sprayed crumbs everywhere. "And who was Arnold?" she asked when she had stopped coughing.

"My cousin. Donald's brother."

"Your aunt's son? You're saying Arnold killed his own mother?"

Margaret nodded. "He was always a little strange."

"Strange!" Jade couldn't believe what she was hearing.

"Although to be fair he didn't actually intend to kill her. He had locked her up in storeroom until she converted, but when Ivy launched her final offensive on the city most of those remaining deserted him and there wasn't anyone around who remembered she was there."

"Margaret, I'm not sure that that actually makes it any better —
accidentally forgetting to feed your mother!"

Margaret thought about it for a moment. "You're probably right. And
anyway, it was Arnold who ordered Donald tortured."

"The First Leader?"

"The same. Donald was in pretty bad shape when Rajko and I managed
to get him out."

"You're saying Arnold tortured his own brother?"

"Arnold didn't torture Donald himself. But he definitely ordered it. And
I know," Margaret said quickly, holding a hand up to forestall Jade's next
comment, "that doesn't actually make it any better."

Jade shook her head. "Arnold doesn't actually sound a very nice person."

"I don't know I'd say that," Margaret said defensively. "He was always
. . . different. I'll admit that. But it was only when he and Nedo got caught
up in the uprising on Dontfrey and Nedo was killed that he went a little
doolally."

"And who was Nedo?"

"My brother."

No wonder Margaret was as mixed up as she was with family like that,
Jade thought.

"They're not all loopy," Margaret protested, guessing what Jade was
thinking.

"I didn't say they were," Jade protested.

Margaret raised an eyebrow.

"Well, I didn't."

"I mean Donald turned out quite well, and Ivy's doing well for herself."

"Ivy? You mentioned her but . . ."

"My cousin, Donald's sister. She's busy at the moment trying to raise a
new crop of Clemhorns. She and Cador, her partner, had twins a couple
of years ago, and she just had another daughter this month." Margaret
pulled a face. "I was looking forward to taking a couple of weeks off to see
her. But enough about *my* family, what deep, dark secrets have you been
hiding?"

"Nothing like that; my family is as boring as they come. The worst thing
I can come up with was when my mother was five and she got detention
for pulling Lucy-Ann's ponytail during roll-call."

"Oh dear," Margaret said, trying to keep a straight face. "And what had
Lucy-Ann done to deserve that?"

"According to Mother, Lucy-Ann had been telling everyone that my mother had kissed Craig Prentiss during recess."

"And had she?"

"Mother never said," Jade said with a grin. "But it's possible. Five-year-olds are incorrigible."

"I can't remember being five,"Margaret admitted. "I think my first memory is from my seventh birthday party. Mother arranged to borrow an elephant from the circus to give rides, and then insisted that I let all my friends go first."

"That doesn't seem very fair," Jade said. "It was *your* birthday."

"That's what I thought," Margaret said, a tinge of bitterness coloring her voice. "Apparently I was so nasty about it I got sent to my room and missed most of the party."

Jade shook her head. "Did you get to ride it?" she asked.

"No, by the time I was allowed out the elephant had had to leave. I think I sulked for a week."

"I can't believe your mother arranged for an elephant for your seventh birthday," Jade said.

"I still can't believe she never let me ride it," Margaret replied. "But Mama was always very big on never taking advantage of our position."

"And arranging for an elephant wasn't taking advantage?" Jade said disbelievingly.

"I never thought of it like that," Margaret admitted. "I suspect Mama never did either." She took a sip of her water. "Tell me about your mother."

"My mother?" Jade was surprised. "What do you want to know?"

"I don't know. What happened to her after she stopped being five?"

"She trained as a nurse, but she's been a hospital administrator for years. We were always close, but after Dad died, we got even closer. If I think of her, it's how she smells. For some reason she always reminds me of the smell of fresh bread and rising dough." She paused, remembering the scent. "I know she never really got over losing my father. He was a professional musician for the New York Philharmonic and then after he died, she had to cope with a very mixed-up teenager."

"She did a good job," Margaret said.

Jade felt herself flush. "Thank you. I've told you she's descended from one of the Nayarit who accompanied Iapura through the portal. My great-great-grandmother in fact. Mother was the one who insisted I learn Nayarit."

"I remember that. It makes you one of a very, very select few."

"I certainly never felt as if I was."

Margaret leaned back, concentrating. "Nizhónígo ałhééhosiilzßßd,ö she said finally, and carefully.

Jade's face lit up. "Yá'át'ééh, Shí éí dinootł'izh-tse yinishyé, Haash yinilyé?"

Margaret's face had gone blank with the first word. "Woo, 'pleased to meet you' is the limit of my Nayarit."

"What I just said was: 'Hello, my name is Jade, what's your name?'"

Margaret frowned, replaying the words. "So what, Jade is . . . ?"

"'Dinootł'izh-tse' . . ." Jade shrugged. "Approximately. It's a dying language. I've never heard anyone else speak it, and my mother didn't know all the words, so 'Dinootł'izh-tse' actually translates as 'green-stone'."

"It's a pity it's dying," Margaret said.

"Why?" Jade asked, surprised.

"Because it's part of our heritage. Language shapes culture. So, to understand those who came through the portal you need to understand their language."

"I never really thought of it like that," Jade admitted.

"We should have you declared a living treasure," Margaret said with a smile.

"Oh great," Jade said with mock indignation. "First you get me declared nobility, and now you want to have me declared a living treasure."

Margaret suddenly winced and Jade eyed her with concern. "What?"

"Nothing, just my headache's getting worse."

"I think I should ask for some headache pills."

Margaret started to shake her head but stopped, and carefully laid herself back onto the mattress. "I really would prefer not to give them the opportunity to start feeding me drugs."

Jade thought of telling her that they could easily have added something to the water if they'd wanted, before deciding Margaret didn't need that worry.

There was the sound of a key being inserted in the lock and Jade looked round in surprise. "Margaret," she said warningly.

"Heard it," Margaret said, sitting up.

The door swung open, and Jade got to her feet. The person standing there was slight, with pale skin, red hair and a close-trimmed beard. He carried a weapon of a type Jade had never seen before. It looked a little like a flattened series of modules sitting around a standard pistol grip. It appeared functional, and obviously quite light despite its size as he held it braced into his shoulder.

"Dinootł'izh-tse?" he asked warily.

"Yes," Jade replied in Nyarit.

"Come with me," he said in the same language, waving her out of the room.

"Why?" Jade demanded, but he simply made a jerking motion toward the door with his gun.

25

COME IN, JULPE. I'VE BEEN EXPECTING YOU

(Wednesday: Nayarit Line)

"Julpe!"

Julpe looked round startled at the shift boss's voice, still not convinced of what he'd seen in the darkness beyond the light thrown by the grinders.

"What?" he asked Tupi. The large shift boss was scowling down at him threateningly.

"Keep your mind on your job. We're finishing here this afternoon, and I'd prefer it if we didn't leave bits of you behind when we leave."

Julpe nodded.

"Then get your arse into action. That pile of scrap that isn't going to move itself." Tupi gestured at the pile of cutoffs and coiled wire that the squad had been adding to all morning.

"Yes Tulpi," he said, and got back to transferring the scrap into the large dump that was waiting to be lifted to the recycling level. It seemed that was all he'd been doing for the last six months, ever since he'd become too big to crawl the ducts.

This far below the city's habitation levels the air was constantly damp and stank of wet concrete. At least the air was still breathable; in some of the areas they'd been working over the past year they'd had to use breathing masks.

The grinder suddenly cut off, and in the sudden silence one of the team shouted a warning from the other end of the hall as the beam they'd been working on collapsed. There was a tearing sound, and another beam ripped away from the concrete it was fixed to and bounced on the floor, throwing up more dust.

Tupi swore. "Get a move on," he told Julpe, "I want to be out of here before dinner." With that he headed off to check on what had happened.

Nawkaw appeared out of the gloom carrying two panniers filled with scrap suspended from a shoulder yoke. After dumping them on the ground he picked up one of the buckets and poured it into the dump.

"I think I saw a tunnel roach," Julpe said quietly, as he picked up Nawkay's second bucket.

"Down here?"

"It looked like it." Roaches generally stuck to the habitation levels. About the size of a small dinner plate no one had quite worked out what they ate, or where they lived, although Nawkaw swore they used the air ducts to move around in. Regardless, as servants of the gods, they were generally left to their own devices.

Nawkay gave a cautious look over his shoulder. "What was it doing?"

Julpe shrugged, unwilling to admit that it appeared to have been watching him. Even to him that seemed a little unbelievable, but the way its attention had remained fixed on him until Tupi appeared and it had disappeared seemed strange, to say the least.

There was a loud crash from overhead as the beam that was slowly being winched up the center of the stairwell to the recycling level eight floors above smashed into something. Both boys looked up nervously, but the source of the noise was hidden behind the haze and darkness that filled the shaft.

Nawkay shook his head unhappily. "I don't know if it's better, or worse that we can't see it," he grumped.

"Doesn't really matter where it lands, given the way they bounce when they hit the floor."

Nawkay nodded. A beam had broken loose from the rope a couple of days ago, and it had been blind luck that no one had been hurt. Julpe had measured the hole it had left in the concrete floor where it had landed, and it was big enough to take his whole hand up to his wrist.

"So, what do you think they're doing with all this?" Julpe asked, indicating the pile of scrap, and the beams ready to be winched.

"The Tletl?" Nawkay asked and spat.

Julpe nodded. The ruling caste was not exactly popular among the work gangs. Not that Julpe or Nawkay had ever seen one, but the Tletl did what the Marshall said, and in turn the city ran on the Tletl's orders, with the Macehualli, (the caste-less who made up most of the gangs) at the very bottom of the heap. And with the City Guards, or the Marshall's Militia, to enforce the Marshall's will he suspected it wasn't ever going to change.

Nawkay shrugged. "Who knows. It doesn't really matter, does it? So long as we get paid?"

"Five years ago, it was reclaim, recycle, reuse," Julpe protested. "Now all we do is just strip everything out. Where's it going?"

"I don't know," Nawkay said. "But if you don't start filling the dump, you'll still be doing it at midnight. And I won't be here helping."

Julpe looked at him, but Nawkay ignored him, and with a sigh Julpe bent to his task, once again turning his mind to the question of what the roach had been doing down here. Still, tomorrow was a freeday and if they were able to finish here today, he might be able to come back by himself to try and find out. And maybe he'd find something they'd missed that he could sell for himself.

"Julpe!"

Julpe rolled his eyes and turned back to see what his sister wanted. Not entirely unexpectedly, Nenetl was standing in front of the entrance to their room, hands on her hips, glaring at him.

"I want you back before they turn the power off," she said. "The lower caverns lost another child last week. I don't want you out after lights out."

He started to protest that he could look after himself but stopped when she tossed him a copper trade token.

"And see if you can get a couple of potatoes from Old Man Tocktli," she said. "Mother Coaxoch has given us half a rabbit."

"I'll see what I can do," he promised as he snatched the small token out of the air, his mouth already watering at the thought of the treat — actual, fresh meat.

"Good, see you do." Nenetl was only three years older than him, and despite just being sixteen she'd felt it was her job to mother him ever since their actual mother had died two years before.

"I'll see you later Mom," he said cheekily as he started down the dimly lit roughhewn passage that led from the cells to the main corridor. This far underground there was little power wasted by the Tletl on those who did all their work for them.

Julpe often wondered what it would have been like to have been born into one of the castes. They probably breathed the same stale air, and drank the same recycled water, but at least they weren't going to bed hungry each night.

Old Man Tocktli occupied his mat at the end of the corridor, just inside the intersection with the main corridor. His legs had been crushed in an accident five years ago, and he now earned his living trading knowledge and items between those on the bottom levels.

"Hi Tocktli," Julpe said, squatting down and placing the token in the old man's bowl. "Nenetl wants a couple of potatoes for tea tonight."

Tocktli pushed the copper around in his bowl with one, long, bony finger and pulled a face. "You'll need another half."

"What! For two potatoes?"

Tocktli shrugged. "Tithing for power and water went up again last week. The farmers get screwed by the Tletl, we get screwed by the farmers, and the Marshall's Militia screws all of us."

"And just how are we supposed to eat?" Julpe demanded.

Tocktli spat on the ground. "The Tletl don't care about us, and the sooner everyone understands that the better. The city is dying if it isn't already dead. We're just the maggots living in the decaying flesh of the city. Maybe it's simply time we acknowledged that and let the Tletl finish us off. But for the moment," he said as he tapped the copper with the tip of a boney finger, "you need another half."

Julpe stared at the bowl and shrugged. "One token for three potatoes and you join us for dinner. Mother Coaxoch has given us half a rabbit."

Tocktli raised an eyebrow at that news, then nodded. "Done," he said, and the token disappeared.

"You'll need to tell Nenetl what we agreed," Julpe said warningly. "I may not be back until late."

"You're checking out the last clearance?" He smiled at Julpe's jump of surprise. "Don't worry, I won't tell. But be careful, there may be others down there doing the same. And you've heard about the missing kid?"

Julpe nodded.

Tocktli gave him an evil grin and poked him with a bony finger. "You're probably safe, you're not even big enough for a half decent meal."

Julpe scowled at him and backed out of reach.

He took the main corridor for twenty yards before turning into a side passage. It being a freeday the corridor was still deserted at this time of morning, and no one was watching. There was a stairwell at the end of the passage, the door long since removed for firewood, and after winding up his torch he started the long climb down to the lower levels and the subway. At the bottom of the stairs, he turned his torch off and waited but there was no sign of anyone following him.

He turned the torch back on and headed down the passage that led at a gentle slope to the cross stations, one of the first areas that had been cleared out. From there he took the corridor that led past the water turbines. The thunder and vibration of the generators was obvious even through the yards of rock that separated them. The giant fans that recycled air from the upper agricultural levels through the rest of the city added to the din. It took another fifteen minutes before he arrived at the storage level they'd been working on for the last month.

At the foot of the stairs, he finally paused to catch his breath, turned his light off and sat down on the bottom step. There was a heavy silence that hadn't been there yesterday, and in the dark he wondered if Old Man Tocktli wasn't right, and they were maggots trying to survive in the city's dried and desiccated carcass. Leaning back, he stared up through the piercing blackness, imagining the weight of the city bearing down on him, and above it the dead sky smothering the city's corpse.

He had never seen the sky and had no interest in doing so. One hundred years of war had turned the surface outside the city into a wasteland of viral and radioactive poisons and acid rains. But he had once seen the city's farms in their hydroponic gravel channels. An endless series of green lines under their lights, and he couldn't help wondering what it might have been like on the surface before the wars.

Something rustled above his head, and he turned his torch back on to find a roach watching him from the ceiling. He frowned. It seemed larger than normal, perhaps the size of Tupi's hand, which he'd felt across the back of his head more often than he liked.

He blinked as the roach was joined by a second. His hand instinctively traced the shape of the cross on his chest: earth, air, fire, and water. Roaches were rumored to be the servants of the gods, and ones as big as these must indeed be their servants. Even as he watched, the two roaches turned away and took five synchronized steps away from him, then paused. When he simply stared, they flicked their posteriors at him and took another five steps. Cautiously, Julpe stood up and took a couple of steps after them. This time the roaches didn't pause and led him without stopping across the cavern. He was so intent on keeping up with them and not losing sight of them that he was unprepared for their sudden disappearance when they reached the far wall.

"Now what?" he demanded, but when they didn't reappear, he began to inspect the wall.

A piece of concrete had shed itself from the surface, leaving a thin, vertical crack, into which both roaches had apparently disappeared. He frowned as he inspected the crack and the concrete skim coat that looked as though it covered a brick wall. Why hadn't anyone on the team seen it? It was everyone's job to keep a look out for signs of hidden entrances or doors. Even as he watched, another thin piece of concrete sloughed off, shattering as it landed on the floor, and a roach waved at him from the crack.

There was a clatter of something landing on the concrete floor behind him and he whirled round to find four roaches clustered on the ceiling, a wrecking bar below them on the ground. He crossed himself. The roaches simply stood there, silently watching him. Cautiously he took a step toward them. The roaches scuttled back before settling down to watch.

He picked up the wrecking bar and hefted it, wondering where they had found it. It was better than anything he had ever seen before. Turning back, he attacked the thin concrete coat and had soon stripped enough of it away from the underlying brickwork to confirm that the concrete had covered what appeared to be a bricked-up doorway. Some of the mortar was fretting away, and it didn't take him long to loosen a brick enough to remove it. Shining his torch into the crack he cursed as he was almost blinded by the reflection of the light back into his eyes.

Pausing only to take a swallow from his water flask he set to with fresh heart to remove the rest of the bricks, piling them up beside the door as he worked. Finally, he had uncovered enough to realize he had found a treasure beyond reckoning: an untouched room from the time before the end of the war. The door itself was still locked, an unbroken expanse of polished steel. There was a panel set into the wall beside the door, and unable to help himself, and still not prepared to believe his luck and the rewards he would undoubtedly earn, he possessively stroked one finger across the smooth surface of the panel. There was an answering flicker of soft light from behind the face of the panel, and the silhouette of a hand appeared. Not really believing his bravery, he pressed his hand against it, only to jerk it away at the sudden sting he felt on his palm. Swearing softly, he shook his hand before checking it to find a small bubble of blood in the center of his palm. There was a grinding sound from the door, and he looked up, startled by a puff of hot, stale air on his face.

"Come in Julpe, I've been expecting you," came a female voice from the darkness.

26

So It's Someone Else

(Thursday: Sultan, Pesh)

"Carlos."

Carlos looked up from the meal he was pushing around the plate in the embassy's small refractory on Sultan — it was the Cardinal. "Any word?"

The Acting Ambassador shook his head. "Emre wants to see us though."

"About time. It's been seven bloody hours!" Carlos said, as he shoved his chair away from the table and stood up.

"Six hours and thirty-six minutes," the Cardinal corrected him, with just a glance at his watch.

He frowned as he took in Carlos's face. "That's one impressive bruise."

Carlos nodded, and winced. The whole left side of his face was turning a beautiful shade of green. "It's not knowing what's happened to her, to them."

"Maybe Emre has something."

"Where are we meeting him?"

"At the barracks."

"Did he say what he wanted?" Carlos asked, grabbing his jacket.

"No, but that's hardly surprising given the leaks we've been facing."

"Is Markus coming with us?"

"Just us. I sent Markus back through the portal a couple of hours ago to get some sleep. You should probably head back as well."

Carlos shook his head emphatically. "Not until we know something."

The Cardinal started to say something, then simply nodded.

"Any word on who planted the bomb?" Carlos asked, as the Cardinal held the door open for him.

"No, and that's strange . . ."

"Strange? How?"

"You know we're liaising with the locals about this . . ."

"Yes?"

"It seems the investigators found traces of boron."

"So?"

"That was my reaction. However, the locals were very excited about it. Apparently, boron has the *theoretical* ability to increase the heat of an explosion."

"In theory?"

He nodded. "No one on Sultan has been able to do it in practice yet."

"Oh great, so it's someone else. Another advanced line?" And wouldn't that be a nightmare! The C-T E had just got used to having to deal with one. And dealing with that one had almost destroyed the Empire. Having two, well . . .

The Cardinal shrugged. "I hope not, but it's something I need to speak to Emre about."

Emre had sent a staff car and motorcycle escort to pick them up, so they made the trip to the Barracks in less than fifteen minutes and were waved through the main gates with only a cursory check by the sentries on duty.

Emre met them in his office. "Cardinal, Carlos," he said, standing up from behind his desk and extending his hand.

"Emre," the Cardinal said. "Any word on the Ambassador and Jade?"

"I believe so. I've arranged for a briefing." Emre waved them toward his ready room.

"And any word on finding Karen's nuclear weapon?" Carlos asked, as they followed him out of his office.

"Some. We managed to find the ship it came in on, and there's clear evidence of radioactive contamination in the hold, but both the ship's Captain and First Mate have disappeared. However, the evidence we have was more than sufficient to put pressure on the Angevin Empire to start cleaning their house. I understand the Queen was not amused when informed how badly their security services had been compromised. The resulting assistance has been . . . useful."

He held the door to the ready room open, and as they entered, they interrupted a young Lieutenant busy writing on a large map of the city pinned up on a whiteboard.

"Kaymakam," the Lieutenant said coming to attention.

"At ease Lieutenant," Emre said. "Gentlemen, may I introduce Lieutenant Baris Erez. Lieutenant, this is the CT-E's Deputy Ambassador Cardinal Abbot, and Carlos Babineaux of the CT-E's Agence Nationale de la Sécurité."

"Cardinal, Agent Babineaux," the Lieutenant said, briefly coming to attention again.

"Lieutenant, perhaps you could ask the Miralay to join us?"

"Of course, Kaymakum."

"So, what is this all about, Emre?" the Cardinal asked.

"We believe we've located the warehouse where they're holding the Ambassador and Jade."

"Where?" Carlos demanded.

Emre placed his finger on a point well outside the city's outer ring road and only a short distance from the river. "Apparently the Angevin had been using it as a safe house."

Carlos considered the location for a moment. It was about fifteen miles south of the Barracks, and about five miles west of the warehouse he and Karen had been sent to scout.

There was a knock on the door. "Ah, Miralay," Emre said. "May I introduce you to Deputy Ambassador Cardinal Abbot, and Carlos Babineaux. Gentlemen, Miralay Ercan of the 5th Battalion."

The Miralay, a short, heavily muscled officer with a bald head and thick mustache shook the Cardinal's hand, then nodded to Carlos. "Mr. Babineaux and I are already acquainted," he said in heavily accented English.

As the Janissaries' 5th Battalion was responsible for intelligence and counter insurgency, the Miralay had led Carlos's debrief after his disaster at the port and Carlos gave him a wary nod.

"Are you ready to go?" Emre asked.

"The teams are just loading up."

"Gentlemen, I thought you might like to accompany the Miralay," Emre said. "The Caliph thought it important that you understand how seriously we consider the Ambassador and Miss Carvello's abduction."

"Thank you for the offer," the Cardinal said. "But I believe my presence might very well get in the way of the operation. And I'm not exactly sure how the Papal Father would take my involvement. I believe Mr. Babineaux' presence will be sufficient to represent the C-T E. But if I could have fifteen minutes of your time, Kaymakum, I believe you should be informed of the preliminary investigations into the bomb attack at the embassy."

"Of course," Emre said politely.

"Mr. Babineaux," the Miralay said, gesturing him toward the door.

"Carlos, please."

"Of course, Carlos."

There was an armored 6x6 already waiting for them, its fractal camouflage bringing back memories of the war when the movie news would have shots of such vehicles almost every week. Carlos hoisted himself into the back of the vehicle and nodded to the six soldiers already there. The soldiers were wearing tailored ballistic armor and helmets. Balaclavas covered their faces, and safety glasses hid their eyes. They carried a variety of weapons and Carlos felt seriously under-dressed. As he settled himself into his seat the Miralay passed him a Kevlar vest to slip over his head. Though bulky it was surprisingly light.

It was only a short trip to the landing field and Carlos barely had a chance to notice the unusual design of the five helicopters waiting for them as he climbed out of the vehicle, before the Miralay led him at the run for the closest, the rotors of which were stirring into motion. The stink of high-octane fuel was familiar, although different from the heavy diesel used by the Mainline's own airships. The engines were surprisingly quiet compared to the ones that the CT-E had started to develop. Taking the seat the Miralay pointed out to him, Carlos frantically searched for his belt as he realized he was going to fly in something for the very first time that didn't depend on either helium or hydrogen to hold it up.

The door slammed shut and the hum from the twin counter-rotating rotors overhead increased, as the Miralay passed him a headphone and microphone combination. Carlos was still struggling to do his lap belt up when he was pressed back into his seat, managing to drop the end of his belt as the helicopter broke away from the ground. The craft's single pusher propeller whined, and Carlos was pressed sideways against the Miralay. Finally managing to do his belt up he looked out of the window and gulped when he saw how fast they were going, and more importantly how low they were traveling as they powered along the river, at what looked like only feet from the surface of the water.

"How fast does this thing go?" Carlos asked, his voice sounding strangled over the headphones.

"Just over 250 miles per hour," the Miralay said. He leaned over Carlos and looked out the window. "We're keeping our speed down though. Probably only doing about 200 miles per hour."

"Of course," Carlos said dryly.

The helicopter banked suddenly, and Carlos grabbed at his seat.

"Stay in your seat until I tell you to disembark," the Miralay told him, "then stick with the Sergeant here."

The Sergeant gave him a nod, and Carlos responded nervously.

The helicopter banked right, and his belt cut into his stomach uncomfortably. A moment later the helicopter banked left and there was a thump from underneath him as the wheels extended. He was just bracing himself when he found himself thrown back into his seat, and the doors on both side of the craft slid back. Without orders the troops on board piled out of both doors and sprinted for the warehouse they'd landed in front of.

The Miralay tapped his shoulder. "Out!"

Carlos struggled out of his seat, his legs unsteady as he followed the Sergeant out of the helicopter. Around him the howl of five helicopter engines rose as they clawed their way back into the air. As the heli farthest from him left the ground, its wheels already withdrawing into its base, flames shot out of its body, followed a moment later by the heat and physical pulse of the explosion. Pieces of the helicopter scythed down around him as the helicopter reared up on its tail, its rotors slowing and disintegrating as Carlos threw himself to the ground.

Dear gods, what had he got himself into, he thought, as he curled himself into as tight a ball as possible.

He was still hugging himself when the rest of the helicopter hit the ground and a fresh explosion split the air. Their own helicopter spun on its on axis, and its twin miniguns sent tracer and AP into the front of the warehouse in a howling crescendo of destruction.

"Cease fire, cease fire!" he screamed into his microphone, panicked at the thought of Jade caught up in the middle of that holocaust.

The order was emphasized by the Miralay and the helicopter reluctantly ceased fire, and grumpily lifted away. Carlos was already on his feet and running for the warehouse.

Large holes had been torn in the metal skin that covered the front of the building while the closest corner looked as though it had been gnawed by a giant rat. He wondered if that had been where whoever had fired the missile had been standing.

He had almost reached the building when he was brought to the ground. He struggled round to find the Sergeant lying on him, his helmet askew.

"Wait," the Sergeant told him. "We need to make sure the building is safe."

Carlos nodded but made a mental promise to himself that if that meant Jade died, he would be seeking to put his views to the Sergeant in a considerably more physical manner.

The Miralay joined them, talking quietly into his microphone, one hand pressing the plug against his ear.

"What happened?" Carlos demanded, as the Miralay offered him a hand and hauled him to his feet.

The Miralay shrugged. A small group of soldiers was clustered around the doorway. There was a small spurt of flames from the lock, but Carlos's ears were still ringing, and he missed the soft fuzz from the explosion. He watched the first of the soldiers enter the warehouse, itching to be with them. There was a muttered: "Clear One, Clear Two, Clear Three," over the radio, before the final "Team Clear."

"Let's go," the Miralay said.

Inside the warehouse was a mess, as smoke and dust spiraled into the air from the damage caused by the helicopter's cannon.

Five figures lay sprawled across the floor, medics working feverishly over two of them. The medics' weapons were placed carefully out of reach. One of the casualties had been standing near the front wall, and his body had been torn apart by some of the 6,000 rounds that had shredded the front of the warehouse, and had sent concrete and steel splinters ricocheting across the enclosed space. The wooden structure built into the far wall, probably originally intended as an office, was pockmarked by the bullets and concrete that had split off from the floor. Its door hung half open from its hinges.

Carlos started for the office, imagining the worst. No one could have survived this.

"They're not here," the Miralay said, as a soldier emerged from the remains of the door and shook his head.

Carlos shook off the Miralay's hand on his shoulder and peered into the room. There were two mattresses laid out on the floor.

"They were here," he said.

"Yes."

"Miralay." The Sergeant was bending over one of the bodies.

"What?" the Miralay demanded, going over to see with Carlos trailing close behind.

"I thought it was a dog-tag, but . . ." the Sergeant held out the transparent disk he'd pulled off the body, suspended from a fine metal chain. "I've never seen anything like it. It's not Angevin."

The Miralay snorted. "I don't think even the Angevins would be stupid enough to wear something that would identify them as Angevin." He accepted the disk and hefted it experimentally. "It's heavy." He passed it to Carlos. "Recognize it?"

The disk was about two inches across, and maybe quarter of an inch deep. It was heavier than he expected, with two small notches cut into the rim on opposite sides of the disk. He pressed his thumb and forefinger into the notches and a picture appeared fractionally below the surface of the disk. Carlos frowned, looking at a snarling cat, fangs exposed. Perhaps a leopard, or jaguar.

"Sorry," he said, passing it back.

The Miralay pressed his finger to his ear plug. "Shit. We've lost another one."

"Just what did that dickhead in the helicopter think he was doing?" Carlos demanded.

"His job," the Miralay said.

Carlos wanted to argue that point, but the pilot probably had only been doing his job. That didn't mean he had to like it though.

"What now?" he asked.

"We keep looking," the Miralay said. "With luck we can get something out of that one."

"If he lives."

"If he lives," the Miralay agreed. "Perhaps this will give us some clue though." He hefted the disk experimentally, then passed it back to the Sergeant.

27

How Long Has She Been Like This?

(Thursday: Sultan Pesh)

"Breakfast," came the voice.

Margaret groaned at the sound of the tray being slid under the door. It had been three days since Jade had been taken and she had spent most of it lying on the mattress; sweating, dizzy, and trying not to throw up. Unfortunately, her best efforts had not been enough — at least they'd given her a bucket after the first day. Obviously, the stink had been too much even for her guards.

Turning over, she closed her eyes and waited to die.

"Miss Peric?"

She opened her eyes. Someone was leaning over her. "Wazup?" she slurred.

"Miss Peric, we have to go." It was a woman.

"Don't have to go anywhere," she said, closing her eyes again and letting her head fall back against the pillow. It was a cold voice; she didn't like it. She thought she knew its owner, but she wasn't up to trying to remember who it was.

"How long has she been like this?" the woman asked.

"Two, three days," a male voice replied uncertainly.

Margaret didn't like that voice either.

"And you didn't think to tell me? Gods she stinks. Why didn't you give her a shower?"

Who stinks? Margaret wondered.

"You told us she wasn't to leave the room."

"Imbeciles," the cold voice muttered. "Where's her handbag?"

"Outside."

"Go and get it."

Margaret kept her eyes closed and hoped they'd get the message and leave her alone.

Finally, she heard someone return and what might have been the sound of someone rummaging through her handbag. "Oh great," the cold voice said. "Paroxetine! Didn't you idiots think to check? She's on anti-depressants, or at least she was until you numbskulls sent her cold turkey. We don't have time to clean her up now. You're just going to have to ride in the back with her. Get her up."

She felt someone take her arm and pull her upright. She sagged; her legs unable to take her weight.

"Help him, Jules," the cold voice said.

The movement sent the world spinning again, unfortunately not enough for her to vomit, which was disappointing. She'd have loved to have spread the misery around.

They dragged her out to the van and slid her into the back on the floor.

"Pillow?" she asked hopefully, as she opened her eyes just sufficiently to see that her handbag had been placed in the back with her. Unfortunately, she wasn't well enough to make any use of it. In fact, a kitten could have beaten her in a fight — even with all four of its paws tied together behind its back.

"Get Miss Peric a pillow," the voice said.

Someone slid a pillow under her head, just before they slammed the door on her, and she felt the vehicle lurch into motion.

She didn't know how long she was in the van. She tried counting the seconds but kept losing track and having to start again. When they finally came to a stop, she heard the sound of a garage door closing behind them.

"Help her out," the voice said.

Standing, wavering, outside the van she found herself in some sort of lean-to attached to a house. She could feel uneven brick under her feet.

"Give her a shower first," the cold voice said, after they'd helped her up the three steps into the house. "I'll supervise that. You two see what you can dig up for her to wear."

The water was wonderful, and Margaret just stood under it, feeling it pulse onto her back. Finally, she turned to trying to get her hair clean. It would have been easier if her hair was as short as Jade's. Next time she was kidnapped she'd have to make sure she got hers cut.

She pulled the shower curtain open to find Karen sitting on a plastic chair inspecting her nails. Margaret quickly checked the rest of the bathroom, but they were alone. Karen threw her the towel she had on her lap, then pointed at the tracksuit neatly folded on top of the wash basket.

"You're looking better," Karen said.

Margaret grunted, starting to towel herself dry. She *was* feeling much better, but she didn't have to tell Karen that.

"What have you done with Jade?" she asked when she was dressed and was bent over fluffing her hair.

"I don't know," Karen admitted. "My . . . employers decided they needed to discuss some matters with her that could not be done here."

Although Margaret wasn't watching her Karen sounded genuinely surprised.

"And when do I get released?" she asked, straightening up to look at her.

"When whatever they want to do has been completed."

"And have they told you that what they want to do involves setting off an atomic bomb?"

Karen smiled. "You've worked that out? I would never have thought you would have had it in you."

Bitch! Margaret thought, smiling brightly at her. "You know you won't get away after all this?" she asked instead. "I can't see anyone on Sultan providing you with shelter once they find out what you've done. And the CT-E certainly won't."

"Oh, spare me the platitudes," Karen said, rising from the seat and opening the door. "I will admit this wasn't quite what I was planning six months ago, but if it pans out as I think it will I really don't think I need to worry about what Sultan, or the Empire think. Now, if your ladyship is ready I'll get Jules to show you to your room."

She was escorted down a rickety set of steps to the basement. Once again, the floor was lined with bricks. There was a bed with a small desk set up against the wall, and Margaret frowned, hoping they weren't going to shackle her to it.

"And you're through there," Karen said, gesturing around the stairs to what appeared an even smaller space, just large enough for the mattress laid directly onto the brick floor, and what might be a portable toilet squeezed into the far corner. A pillow and two folded blankets looked as though they'd just been dumped on the mattress.

Lucky me, Margaret thought.

"Here," Karen said, picking up a hardcover book from the table. After checking its title she handed it to Margaret. "You might be in there a while."

"What is it?"

"The Hadith, in English. You might learn something."

Margaret rolled her eyes.

"If you don't want it . . . ?" Karen asked, starting to put her hand out for it.

"No. I'll take it," Margaret said quickly.

As the door closed behind her and the lock snicked shut, she allowed herself to collapse onto the mattress. The energy the shower had given her was already evaporating.

Withdrawal symptoms she thought. No one had warned her she was going to feel like that. And now she had the depression to worry about returning. Well, she was damned if she was going to let that nonsense start up again. Markus and Jessie needed her, and there was no way she was going to let that bitch, Karen get away with going through her handbag. Going through her handbag! She gave a slightly hysterical laugh — Karen had kidnapped her and god knows what had happened to Jade, and she was worried about her going through her handbag. But damn it, that was wrong! Relaxing back into the pillow, she closed her eyes. She was getting stronger, and now she knew what had been knocking her around she was going to make sure that continued.

28

YOU'RE NOT SPEAKING TO ANOTHER OF YOUR CREATIONS NOW

(Saturday: Nayarit Line)

As the door ground its way open in front of him, sliding sideways into the rock, Julpe froze.

"Come in Julpe, I've been expecting you," came the female voice from the darkness. Even as she spoke the walls began to glow softly, showing a long corridor that disappeared into the distance.

"How do you know my name?" Julpe demanded, taking a step backward. Perhaps he should simply hand his discovery to Tupi and let the shift boss deal with it. Even the enormous wealth this find offered wasn't worth dealing with demons. And who else would be down here in the darkness, given all the gods had died bringing forth the priests? And now not even any of the priests, the Ejejatl caste, remained.

"My agents have been watching you," the voice said peevishly. "Now step inside so I can close the door."

"Who are your agents?" His hand smarted and unconsciously he licked the small bubble of blood that had formed in the center of his palm.

"Oh, in the name of Theresa and all that's holy!"

There was a scuttling sound from the ceiling, and he looked up to see that the area over his head was now a seething mass of roaches. Servants of the gods or not, instinctively he stepped into the relative safety offered by the corridor, and the door slid shut behind him.

"Thank you," the voice said pettishly. "Now move along, we haven't got all day."

"Who are you?" Julpe asked, starting to move cautiously along the corridor. "You're not a demon, are you?"

"No, Julpe, I'm not a demon. My name is Xipil, and I am, or was, a priestess and a follower of Theresa."

Julpe stopped. "But the Ejejatl are all dead!"

"How can all the Ejejatl be dead? If they were the demons would have broken free from the abyss and facing my irritation would be the least of your worries."

Well maybe he'd prefer that, Julpe thought, starting along the corridor again.

"Beside; I didn't exactly say I'm alive," she said crossly. "You need to listen to what I say."

"You mean you're a spirit?" There were stories of spirits who roamed the lower levels, unwilling to face the abyss without the prayers of the priests to keep them safe. Until now Julpe had given the stories little credence, but if true the number of dead must be into the thousands.

"No, I'm not a spirit! And no," she said, forestalling his next question, "I'm not going to tell you what I am until we can see each other properly."

Julpe rolled his eyes but continued along the corridor which sloped slightly downward as he progressed. He walked in a moving space of light, the dark pressing in behind him as he made his way along the passage.

Finally, he reached the end of the corridor and faced another closed door. Before he could press his hand against the panel the door hissed open.

"Come in, come in," Xipil said.

Julpe paused. He'd finally worked out who the voice reminded him of — Nana Tepin. She'd died when he'd been seven, but she'd ruled the lower levels with a will of iron. She had had a voice that could flay a man without having to set a hand on him. Had Nana Tepin been reborn into this spirit?

Cautiously he peered through the door. The room through the doorway was dimly lit, but enough light existed for him to see the small woman sitting behind the table on the far side of the room. She had a dark tan and a sun-wrinkled face. She wore a dark-blue gown gathered at the waist with a wide leather belt. Deep green eyes stared out at him from under gray hair, gathered in under a white wimple with blue edging. Julpe had never seen such richness of cloth. The colors were simple but the cloth . . . It would have fed him and Nenetl for a week.

"Come in boy and close your mouth before you swallow a fly."

Julpe realized he'd been staring with his mouth open and closed it with a snap, wondering as he did so what a fly was.

There was a soft woosh of the door closing behind him and he jumped, aware that he was now totally at the behest of what . . . ?

"You don't look like a demon," he said, the words escaping before he had a chance to think about them.

"I told you I wasn't," she said. She leaned forward and as she did so she — flickered . . .

Julpe found himself pressing his back up against the wall, eyes wide.

"Well, that wasn't supposed to happen," she said, looking at her hand. "But then what do you expect after 205 years?"

"You said you weren't a spirit," he said accusingly.

"And I'm not," she said, passing a hand in front of her eyes, apparently mesmerized by the movement.

"Then what are you?"

Her gaze sharpened on him, and then she, the table, and the chair she'd been sitting on, disappeared.

He edged into the corner of the room, eyes wildly scanning the room for the demon's return. And then there she was, her face looking out at him from a window that had just appeared in the middle of the far wall. Behind her he could see the room he was in, and in the far corner of that — himself.

"I am a whole brain emulation, an uploaded personality, and a priestess," she said, beaming at him out of the window.

"Huh?"

She flickered, then she reappeared in the room with him. "Perhaps you might call me a ghost in the machine."

That's when he fainted.

He came too, to find himself lying on the ground while a wiry tongue licked his face. He scrambled away, fetching up against the wall and found himself facing an animal of some type. It was covered in fur, about twice the size of one of the cats that still roamed the lower levels, although its head was bigger than he would have expected. It had a gray coat, with dark spots on its fur, tufts of fur on its ears, and a black tipped, stubby tail.

There was a cough from the far side of the room, and he looked across to find Xipil watching him from behind her desk again. "I have been told I have to apologize for my behavior," she said dryly.

She didn't sound very apologetic, Julpe thought. "And what is this, this, thing?" he asked wildly, indicating the animal that had sat down, wrapped its tail around its feet, and was now licking one of its front paws.

"Kenefer. You can touch her fur; she likes to have her ears scratched."

Hesitantly, surprising himself with his courage, he reached out and gently touched the monster, yanking his hand back at the softness of the fur, before reaching out again to scratch behind her ears. The animal started to issue a low purring sound.

"And what is a Kenefer?"

Kenefer looked up at him and said quite clearly, and distinctly. "Kenefer is not 'a Kenefer', Kenefer is a cat."

Julpe was never quite so proud of himself as in that moment. He didn't faint, his hand simply stilled for a moment, then continued to scratch behind her ears.

"You're rather large to be a cat, aren't you?" he asked calmly.

"That one"— the cat's flick of her tail indicated what she thought of the priestess—"has the mistaken belief that bigger is necessarily better. You just have to look at the roaches. In this case, however — "

"In this case her size is the result of the genetic material provided by her father," Xipil broke in.

"And you still haven't actually apologized," Kenefer told the priestess.

"I haven't?" Xipil sounded surprised.

"No," the cat said dryly.

"You see what I have to put up with. And from my own creations no less."

Kenefer glared at her.

Xipil returned the glare for a moment then shrugged and shifted her gaze. "Julpe, please accept my apologies. I have spent the last one thousand years ruling an Empire that stretched over six solar systems. To find myself constrained in the ways I now am is . . . difficult."

"One thousand years?" he asked, concentrating on the few words that he had actually understood.

Xipil shrugged. "Give or take a couple of years."

"What . . . what are you?" he demanded.

She sighed and considered her fingers before looking back up at him. "Before I was uplifted, I was both a priestess, and a scientist. My team was trying to develop a way to copy ourselves into silicon memory; to create a virtual world that would allow us to live forever."

"You forgot the 'secret' team," Kenefer pointed our dryly.

"Why secret?" Julpe asked.

"Because," Kenefer explained, "before she became the Undying Queen of the Six Systems it turns out that the particular school of thought to which our priestess belonged was not necessarily popular with mainstream priests who believed that some of the teachings of her Holiness Theresa of Kalpuyen verged on the heretical."

"The Undying *Empress* of the Six Systems," Xipil corrected her sharply.

"Forgive me, exalted one," the cat said dryly.

Julpe frowned thoughtfully. It hadn't even occurred to him to consider that there could be dissent within the priestly caste.

"And are there others of you here?" he asked, looking around uncertainly, wondering if more of these machine ghosts would suddenly appear.

"No," Xipil said, her face suddenly closed.

"Xipil, if you want his help, you need to explain," the cat said patiently. "You are not speaking to another of your creations now."

The priestess narrowed her eyes, then nodded slowly. "Very well, I will begin at the beginning. The Order to which I belong — belonged, had been working on developing a way to allow a human to be uploaded into a computer for many years before I joined the team. The theory itself is fairly simple. You scan someone's brain, layer by layer, then build a model of it in the computer. Practice proved considerably more difficult."

"Particularly when by 'scanning', you actually mean slicing someone's brain into really, really thin slices," Kenefer said, unconsciously licking her lips."

Xipil glared at the cat. "We were almost ready to accept our first volunteer when the Han attacked, and the government moved to close down any 'unauthorized' research. Of course, we couldn't allow that to occur, because we were so close, so it was decided to centralize our efforts here. This facility had been a secret military research laboratory before cutbacks forced it to close and it wasn't difficult to purchase it through one of the Order's shell-companies.

"As team leader I was never expected to be one of those uploaded, but circumstances dictated otherwise. Three of us were processed, but I was the only one who survived the upload. And even then, stabilization of my personality took longer than anticipated."

Kenefer snorted at that, possibly implying that she thought the priestess' personality still hadn't exactly stabilized.

Xipil continued, unfazed by the interruption. "By the time I 'awoke' the war with the Han had ended, but the subsequent Secularist uprising, and the resulting government crack-down had resulted in the forcible closure of my Order and the arrest of my fellows. As a result, when I finally roused, I found myself alone, and the facility running on automatic."

Julpe found to his surprise he experienced a pang of sympathy for the priestess waking up alone in a deserted facility.

"So what did you do?" he asked.

"I did what had always been intended and retreated into the world my Order had created for me. A virtual world."

"A place of dreams and fantasies," Kenefer said dismissively.

"Perhaps, but if it hadn't existed neither would you."

She caught Julpe's frown. "My virtual world might be imaginary," she admitted, "but it is neither a place of dreams nor fantasies. Rather it is a copy of the 'real' world. And more importantly for Kenefer, it runs on 'fast time'."

"Fast time?"

She nodded. "For every five years inside the computer, only a year passes outside, in your world. As a result, our science is now considerably in advance of what existed when I was uploaded and has allowed me to recreate tools such as Kenefer. Her kind was developed as saboteurs for the army during the Second Martian War of Independence."

"But why are you here?" Julpe demanded. "To come here, to this." He looked around disbelievingly.

"Because I had no choice," Xipil said. "My world was becoming . . . damaged, dying. And I could not allow my . . . people to die with it."

"You are aware that these people you are so concerned about aren't real?" Kenefer pointed out. "They are simply imaginary constructs created to give you a context."

"They're as real as I am," Xipil said shortly. "Regardless, it became clear that the source of the problem affecting the matrix came from an exterior source."

"The matrix?" Julpe said, confused.

"The matrix is the computer's memory," Xipil explained. "It was becoming damaged by random quantum effects within the event horizon of a nearby black hole."

Julpe looked blank.

"Someone has built a Gate near here," Kenefer said. "And it's leaking energy into the matrix, creating holes."

"A gate?"

"A way of moving between the stars," Xipil said, then held up a hand to forestall his next question. "I don't know how to better explain it for the moment," she said. "Suffice it to say — we need your help."

"Mine, why?" Julpe asked sourly, surprised.

"Because of who you are."

"I am no one. I am Macehualli, one of the caste-less."

"Even if that was the case, you would not be a no one. Theresa taught that everyone has a role in the endless fight to keep the demons at bay."

"Even the Macehualli?"

"Even the Macehualli," Xipil confirmed. "But you are Ejejatl; one of those from whom the priests, artists, teachers, and scientists are drawn."

Julpe blinked. "Ejejatl?"

"It appears so — brother," Xipil said.

"But how can you tell?" He remembered the pain and lack of food he and Nenetl had suffered as they grew. If he had known, their life could have been so different.

"I tested your blood."

Julpe remembered the sting when he had pressed his palm against the door panel. "So?"

Xipil sighed. "You are aware that a female has the same caste as their mother, a male that of the father."

"Of course."

"Approximately 690 years ago the Nayarit Confederacy began embedding genetic caste markers into DNA. Mitochondrial DNA for females, Y chromosome for males. Your blood marks you as Ejejatl as surely as if someone had written it on your forehead."

"But wouldn't they know? Shouldn't someone have told me? Wouldn't my mother have known?"

"Perhaps she did, or perhaps your father chose to keep his caste from her." Xipil shrugged.

"What do you want me to do? March into the city and command those to obey me?"

"Don't be ridiculous. You would be killed within the hour. The city's present rulers twist the words of the prophets for their own purpose. No, we must tread carefully, and I must have more information."

She sighed. "When I awoke, I found the links that my Order had built into the city's security systems no longer existed. My creations: the roaches and Kenefer, have tried, but they have been unable to penetrate into those areas controlled by the Ejejatl. That will be your job."

"Me?" he squealed, thinking she sounded as demented as Nana Tepin had been toward the end.

29

Vignette:
An Introduction to the Nayarit Line

Little is now known of this line, following the total destruction of its ecosphere in 1884 AE after eighty years of total war. The war, which involved both biological, chemical, and nuclear weapons, is now popularly referred to within the C-T E as the Nayarit cataclysm.

It was on Nayarit that the first trans-temporal portal was developed at Chiqu, a small training and research facility in the western foothills off the mountains that define the eastern boundary of the great central plains of the North American continent. The only survivors of the line were believed to be the fifty-three refugees who followed Iapura through the portal.

Cyclopedia of the Cross-Temporal Empire
Other Lines

30

WHERZ AM I?

(Sunday: Sultan)

The stink of vanilla flavored tobacco filled Jade's nostrils as she fought to open her eyes. But everything was too difficult. Her head lolled against someone's shoulder, too heavy to hold up. The motion of the vehicle they were in was making her nauseous — or perhaps it was the reek of the tobacco.

"Wherz am I?" she slurred, trying to pull herself erect.

"Apo, she's awake."

Jade frowned, trying to work what language he was speaking. She understood the words but couldn't place the language.

Her head slumped forward. As it did so, she jerked awake, and gazed blearily around the back of the car. "Who are you?" she demanded of the stranger sitting next to her.

"A friend."

She peered at him, woozily. "You're not my friend," she pronounced carefully. "Whotz your name?"

"Apo!" the stranger called worriedly.

"I need five minutes," the driver said. "Just keep her quiet till I reach the turnoff."

She knew she shouldn't be there, although she couldn't remember why. She lurched for the door, but her fingers slipped over the lock which refused to open.

She felt an arm over her shoulder and was pulled back. She struggled, but didn't have the strength to break free, and she felt the arm tighten around her shoulders.

"Stop it," he told her. "We're not going to hurt you."

"Then letz me go." She tried to jerk forward, but once again her strength failed and she collapsed back against him.

"Not long," the driver called over his shoulder as the car started to slow.

They turned off the road and she felt the car run onto gravel. As the vehicle pulled over there was a click and the doors unlocked. Jade threw herself at the handle and as the door swung open, she fell out, landing on her knees. Someone grabbed her arm, and she raked the back of his hand with her nails. He swore and yanked her arm back toward him. She threw herself backward and bit down on his hand — hard. A fist came out of nowhere and she collapsed.

She came to lying on the gravel, the stones pressing uncomfortably against her back and neck. There was a knee against her neck, and she pushed feebly at it as the sleeve of her coveralls was yanked up and a needle was thrust into her arm with no pretense at care. She felt the cold flow of liquid enter her armn and as it began to numb, she began to cry with sheer frustration. Then once again there was nothing.

31

THE DARK AND DREARY WALLS

(Monday: Sultan)

Just how the hell had he let himself get talked into this, Carlos thought, as he followed the prison trustee down the narrow passage between two high, concrete walls. Overhead the sky remained a sullen grey, screened off by rusting chain-wire fencing.

The one-piece green coveralls Carlos was wearing chafed his armpits. While the flip-flops he'd been issued with, and which he wore over his socks, threated to fall off with each step he took, restricting him to a quick shuffle. His arms ached from the weight of the plastic crate that was filled with the bedding he'd been given on his entry into the prison.

He still didn't know why they'd insisted on him coming in undercover, nor why he'd agreed to do it. His face still ached from the bruises he'd acquired during the fiasco at the port and the warehouse, and the Miralay's jokes to the effect that they added to the credentials for his role hadn't made him feel any more positive about this mission.

"So, you're a political then?" the trustee said, over his shoulder.

"What?"

"You're in Unit Four. That's politicals."

"I guess. Only got picked up today and they haven't told me the charges yet. I was with the Angevin Embassy, but they refused to recognize my diplomatic status."

"The Angevins still going? Thought we'd pummeled them pretty good in the war."

They were approaching a gatehouse and the trustee held up his ID card to show the officer staffing the gate behind a glass screen. "Prisoner Sarkis. I'm taking a new prisoner to Unit 4."

"Name," the officer said, bored.

Sarkis elbowed Carlos when he didn't say anything.

"Carlos Babineaux."

"Hold your card up to the reader."

Carlos looked around uncertainly, not sure what the reader looked like until Sarkis took pity on him, grabbed his ID card and placed it against the small black screen next to the door. There was a click and the door opened when Sarkis leaned on it.

Sarkis waved him through with a deep, ironic, bow. "Welcome to Maximum Security Prison 418. I take it this is your first time in?"

Carlos nodded as he found himself looking down a hill. At the foot of the hill, he saw a series of white-blocked two-story buildings that ran along the edge of a large, grassed playing field. Beyond them loomed the thirty-foot-high concrete wall that marked off the prison's inner perimeter. "I guess it shows," he said as the gate slammed shut behind them with an emphatic crash.

"Yep. Well, you'll probably be OK in Unit Four, but until you know your way around the prison steer clear of Five and Six."

"Why?" Carlos asked, hoping he wouldn't be in there long enough to need to worry about that.

"Five's run by the Mafia, and Six has a lot of the Nonos." He touched his forefinger to his thumb. He paused and pointed down the hill to the buildings in front of them. "That one's Six. Next to it is Five, then Four."

"So, is Barun Naim in Unit Four?" he asked, as they headed down the hill.

Sarkis looked at him suspiciously. "Why?"

"I need to talk to him."

"Well, that might be difficult, unless you've got someone who can vouch for you. He's in Wing One, and you're in what . . . Three?"

"Three," Carlos confirmed. "Unfortunately, I don't have anyone to vouch for me. I've only been in the country for a couple of weeks. But the operation I was involved in — Barun's name was mentioned a couple of times. And I've got some information I think he'd be interested in."

"One packet of cigarettes."

"What?"

"One packet of cigarettes and I'll see what I can do," Sarkis said.

"Two packets, if you can get me in to see him today."

"Two?"

"Two," Carlos confirmed.

Sarkis considered the offer, then nodded. "You're on."

They'd reached the entrance to Unit Four, and this time Carlos had his ID ready. There was a click from the door and the officer behind the window waved him through.

As he stepped through the gate, he found himself in a large open space from which two wings ran off at right angles to each other. Each wing consisted of two corridors stacked on top of each other. Cell doors lined each corridor, the doors presently propped open. On the ground floor soft sofas had been set up facing a large screen TV. There were a couple of guys sitting down at tables playing cards, while another group playing knuckle-bones sat on the ground round a green piece of cloth. A single officer occupied the glass walled control booth. Through the glass walls of the booth, he could just make out what looked like a mirror image of the space he was presently occupying on the far side of the wall.

No one seemed to be paying him any attention so he turned back to the control booth and knocked on the glass. The officer who was doing something with his phone looked up.

"Yes?"

"Wing Three?"

The officer simply pointed to the corridor on the left, before turning his attention back to his phone. To Carlos this . . . indifference . . . just seemed wrong. He considered his options and decided that wandering around looking for his cell would probably get him into trouble. He knocked again, and this time the officer looked up impatiently.

"What?" he barked.

"Cell 104," Carlos said. "Top or bottom?"

"Bottom," the officer said, and turned his gaze back to his phone.

Mentally tightening his belt Carlos headed off to look for his cell. The cell numbers were clearly marked on the doors, starting with 100, and counting up by ones on the left-hand side. He glanced in through the open door of the first cell. The room contained two double bunks. An open doorway seemed to connect with the next cell along. The room was festooned with drying towels, and there were lidded plastic crates stacked under the bunks and up one wall. Name tags were attached to the crates and one of the crates had its lid open and a prisoner was searching through the clothes it contained.

On reaching cell 104 he entered it to find the cell presently unoccupied. Given the made-up beds on the bottom of both bunks it had at least two occupants. Choosing one of the topbunks he dumped his crate on the floor and opened it to find it contained a single sheet, one blanket, and a pillowcase. As there was no spare pillow in sight, he didn't know what he was going to do with the pillowcase. Sighing, he made his bed then clambered up onto it. He had to sit with his head bowed so it didn't touch the ceiling. Now what?

There was a knock and he looked up to find a wiry looking prisoner standing in the doorway.

"You Carlos?"

"Yes?"

"Barun wants to see you."

That was certainly quick, Carlos thought, sliding back to the floor.

Without saying anything the prisoner led him back to the control booth, then outside, across the front of the booth, and back inside again. The officer in the booth barely looked up from his phone.

A green mat had been laid out in the center of the open area and two men stripped to their waists, their skin glistening with oil, were wrestling. A circle of prisoners surrounded the mat watching and making bets, the sound of their excited conversation merging into a loud and threatening background noise. His guide gestured him on.

In the far corner of the room a small group of men sat around a wooden table. Carlos did a double take when he realized that one of the 'men' was actually a woman. Her hair was pulled up under a cloth cap, and she was wearing jeans and a loose blue shirt with a scarf doubled round her neck, but there was no mistaking her sex. She had her arm draped around the one next to her, a small, swarthy prisoner with a large Turkish mustache and a heavy five o'clock shadow. He was wearing a fez; the first Carlos had seen on Sultan.

"Carlos?" the prisoner with the fez asked as Carlos came to a halt in front of the table.

"Yes. Are you Barun?"

"The same. I was told you had something to tell me."

Seeing the possessive way the woman sat, and Barun's reciprocal body language, and remembering the Miralay's briefing, Carlos decided to ditch the script that had been carefully worked out for him and stick to the truth.

"The information I have is not for general consumption." He looked around meaningfully.

Barun nodded, and two of those at the table stood up, creating a perimeter. With the noise from those cheering the two wrestlers that was probably going to be the best he'd get. He took one of the chairs just vacated and leaned forward.

"My name is Carlos Babineaux. I'm an undercover agent for the Agence Nationale de la Sécurité, presently placed within what appears to have been a splinter cell of the Angevin secret service."

Barun scratched the side of his nose. "The Agence Nationale . . . not sure I've heard of that.

"I'd be surprised if you have. I'm from the Cross-Temporal Empire." And that caused a reaction!

"The C-T E!" someone hissed.

Carlos nodded.

"We had heard the Empire was seeking to establish an embassy here," Barun said, looking at the woman.

"And had you heard that the Ambassador and her bodyguard were kidnapped nine days ago?"

"No. That piece of news hadn't reached me. Hasad?" He looked at a large, fat man sitting at the end of the table.

The fat man shook his head.

"What are you doing here?" Barun asked.

"As I said, I accidentally found myself working within a splinter cell of the Angevin secret service."

"How did you . . . no, it doesn't matter," Barun said. Carlos was impressed with the speed with which he seemed to be able to pick up on things.

"I was part of a group that had been tasked with arranging transport into Pesh of what turned out to be a nuclear bomb."

The woman's arm tightened around Barun.

"And what happened to that bomb?" Barun said, leaning forward.

"We don't know. Something alerted them to my true status. I was lucky to escape."

"And I suppose you don't know what they were proposing to do to the bomb either?"

Carlos gave a tight smile. "Unfortunately, I do. They're proposing to explode the bomb in Pesh. Possibly as some form of indirect attack on the C-T E, to disrupt our attempts to negotiate a peaceful entrance of Sultan into the Empire."

"And why do you tell me of this?"

"Because I have been requested by Emre Kaymakam of the Janissaries, at the request of both the Caliph and his Vizier, to ask for your help in locating the bomb."

"And they could not ask for the help themselves?"

Carlos gave a wry smile. "It was felt that given your past relationship with the authorities it would be unlikely that you would believe them."

"They were wise then. But assuming I believe you, what do you think I can do to help? Stuck in prison as I am."

Carlos simply stared at him. According to the Miralay, since Barun's arrest six years ago following a botched assassination attempt, his cell had grown from fewer than five active members to over a hundred. Carlos could still remember his startled response to that piece of news. "And he's done this from prison?"

"Well, he could hardly have done it from outside," the Miralay had replied evenly. "If that had been the case the Janissary's 5th Battalion would have been authorized to terminate him. From his perspective prison is the safest place for him to be. Besides, it's not as though it's any real hardship for him. He's even managed to father three children while he's been in there."

Carlos snapped back to the present as Barun nodded. "Perhaps, I should rather have said — why should I?"

"Because Miralay Ercan's analysts are convinced this is not following the normal pattern for a local terrorist operation, or even an Angevin operation. No one in their right minds would use a nuclear weapon. It's as if someone else is directing them."

"And what proof do you have of this . . . this act of heresy?"

"Miralay Ercan of the Janissary's 5th battalion will contact you shortly. In the meantime, you should contact the Acting Ambassador at the C-T E's embassy. He will confirm what I have said."

"So what, I am expected to expose my followers . . . possibly burn my entire network —"

"Barun, if you won't help you won't have any followers."

"Barun?" his woman, who had been increasingly fidgety, said. "If he's right . . . the children."

He nodded. "I know. You must take them to your parents. Phone me when you arrive." He kissed her hand gently, then waved for one of the two prisoners who had been acting as perimeter guards to escort her from the unit. He watched her until she had disappeared through the heavy prison door before he turned back to Carlos.

"I will speak to your acting Ambassador. And there are a couple of other people I will speak to. In the meantime, you will stay here."

Carlos nodded, hoping that Barun would be convinced by what he heard. He had the feeling that time was running out for Pesh.

It was close to five hours before he was escorted from the cell he'd been parked in, to find the Miralay seated at the table with Barun. Outside, the prison had descended into darkness but inside the wing the prisoners continued to mill around uneasily. Four Janissaries in full combat uniform stood against the wall.

"Well?" Carlos asked.

"I have agreed to help," Barun said. "There are conditions which the Miralay has agreed to. And the Caliph has also agreed to a general amnesty and a promise that none of my followers will be penalized for any offense committed before today."

He seemed surprised by this. Perhaps that was expected, given that he was not to have been freed for decades, and now suddenly he found he was to be released.

"It is perhaps over time that we work to bring our society back together," the Miralay said gruffly. "We came so close to destroying ourselves in the last war. We cannot allow these outsiders to use the cracks in our own society to destroy us in the next."

Barun started to open his mouth to argue, then stopped and shook his head. "It has been agreed."

32

ALONE

(Tuesday: Sultan, Pesh)

Margaret squinted at the room's single bulb that lit her small prison twenty-four hours a day. Without access to natural light, or a timepiece, Margaret had been forced to keep track of time by counting her meals. She was fairly sure she was being fed three times a day which meant, as best as she could calculate, she'd been locked up in the cellar for around ten days. They hadn't let her out, so she hadn't had another shower since she'd arrived. She presumed she smelled a bit 'high' — not that she could smell herself over the small portable toilet pushed up in one corner. At least that got cleaned out every couple of days, although she suspected that was as much for the comfort of the guards as for herself. Even the room's thick, solid wooden door wouldn't have contained the stench after a week.

The door had seemed over-kill for what might once have been a wine cellar, particularly given the substantial lock on the inside of the room. After all, who put a lock on the back of a door to a room that didn't actually go anywhere? It took her a while to work out the room might have been used as a play 'dungeon' at one stage. If so, being able to keep others out of the room while people were 'playing' would have had its advantages. It might even have been salacious if she didn't have to sleep there; as it was it just increased the 'ewhh' factor. She'd checked for any bolts or shackles left in the wall, which might have given her some useful weapons, but unfortunately, they'd all been removed.

All in all, it had been a singularly boring ten days. The most interesting part of her stay had been on the first morning after her confinement when the guard had delivered her breakfast: three pieces of toast, orange juice, and an apple.

She'd been sitting down with her back against the door, taking tiny bites of the toast and trying to make it last, when she heard the sound of voices and paused in her eating when she realized the second guard who just delivered the breakfast had stopped to chat.

"You heard?" the second had said.

"About what happened at the warehouse? Yeah."

What happened at the warehouse? she thought.

"So what, we lost Altu and Nuray."

"They also got Braelyn, Cwrig, and Ero."

"Ero! Shit. Fucking Janissaries."

"Yeah, they sure fucked us over."

"So, what happens now?"

"Who knows."

"And what about her ladyship . . . ?"

"Karen's trying to find out."

Oh great, Margaret thought, they no longer had a plan. If there'd been one thing she'd hated during the war it was dealing with the amateurs who'd made up a lot of the opposition. They simply didn't know what they were doing, which made them unpredictable. That unpredictability had ended up killing a lot of good soldiers.

Since then, she hadn't had the opportunity for any more eavesdropping, and given that the only radio the guards listened to seemed to play synthetic folk music she hadn't been able to pick up any further news. At least she hoped the music was synthetic; it would have been terrible to believe people could actually sound like that naturally.

At least her withdrawal symptoms had finally started to ease. She hadn't thrown up since arriving, and although she still had some dizziness, the sweats had also eased. Despite the lessening of her symptoms, she still found it difficult to sleep; although she wasn't sure if that was because of the withdrawal, the light that was left on twenty-four hours a day, or because with nothing to do she wasn't getting tired enough to sleep. The book, the *Hadith*, Karen had given her on her arrival had helped a little to pass the time. It wasn't exactly riveting reading, being a record of the words and deeds of Muhammad, his family, and his companions, but after reading through it she had decided to set herself the task of memorizing a page every day. Now, with six pages memorized she had only another ninety-four to go.

Unfortunately, even that task hadn't helped with her sleeplessness, or the concern that her depression might return. Finally, she decided enough was enough and created an exercise regime. Without weights, and with the ceiling being just above her head she'd been a little restricted in what she could do; but between pushups, lunges, and walkouts she'd managed to create a regime that had her working up a solid sweat after twenty minutes. More importantly, sleep became easier.

She was in the middle of her last set of morning sit-ups when she heard the sound of the key turning in the lock. The door opened just as Margaret stood up, wiping the sweat off her face with an old towel she'd persuaded one of the guards to give her. To her surprise it was Karen. One of the guards was standing behind her, covering her with his revolver.

"Long time no see," Margaret said, as Karen entered the room.

Karen pulled a face. "This place stinks," she said.

"And hello to you as well. To what do I owe the pleasure of your company?"

"We're leaving."

"Why?"

"Because this place, and the rest of the city, is slated for destruction in a couple of hours."

Margaret froze — they'd got the bomb into the city. "Can I ask why you're taking me with you?"

"Because once the bomb goes off, we might need some insurance. Let's go," Karen said, gesturing for her to step out of the room. "We don't have much time. If you want to stay, though, I'm quite happy to leave you."

There was a shouted query from upstairs and the guard took a step backward, looking away to shout something up the stairs. Margaret seized her chance. Stepping forward, she drove the heel of her palm up against Karen's chin. Karen jerked back instinctively but Margaret's hand connected, and her head snapped back. There was a loud crack as the back of her skull connected with the door frame. Margaret would have preferred to have left it at that but there was still the guard outside and no time to try and disarm her. As Karen collapsed, Margaret slammed her forehead into Karen's face. There was a crunch of broken cartilage, and blood spurted from Karen's nose. Bitch, Margaret thought.

Without stopping, Margaret lunged for the other guard, but he was already turning, and she was too far away. Instinctively she grabbed the door and slammed it shut to act as a shield. She heard the shot and flinched at the sound of the bullet as it embedded itself in the thick wood.

Without letting go of the handle she forced the bolt on the back of the door into place, locking themselves in the room. OK, maybe not the best idea she'd had, but at least she was alive and now had a hostage. Or perhaps not, she thought, as she turned back to check on Karen, who seemed to be in danger of drowning in her own blood. She must have bitten through her tongue and the gods knew what the effect of the knock on the back of her head was going to be. With a sigh, Margaret rolled her into the recovery position.

"Karen?" the guard called from the other side of the door as Margaret quickly ran her hands over Karen, hoping to find her cell-phone. Unfortunately, it was a fruitless hope. Despite Karen's position she seemed to be losing the battle to keep breathing.

"Karen?" the guard called again.

There was muffled conversation outside, then she heard the sound of the guard turning the key in the outside lock.

"Doesn't sound as if they consider you important enough to try and save," Margaret told Karen conversationally. She was met by silence, and when Margaret checked her pulse, it was obvious that Karen no longer needed rescuing.

After propping Karen up into a sitting position in the far corner of the room Margaret started a more thorough search of the body. Finally, squatting back on her heels, she considered what she'd found. There was one baton, extendable; a small ankle knife; belt buckle; and boots. The baton and boots didn't seem immediately helpful, but the knife and belt buckle — oh yes!

The enameled plate they'd served her breakfast on hadn't been retrieved yet, which at the time she had thought was a bit slack. Now she realized it was because they had already been intending to move her. It was a very nice enameled disk, with brightly colored flecks worked into its surface. That finish would undoubtedly be unrecognizable when she'd finished with it.

She'd identified the major weakness of the basement as its brick-paved floor within a couple of minutes of being placed there. However, to make use of that knowledge she needed uninterrupted time to find out what actually lay beneath the bricks, and something to lift the bricks with. Now she had Karen's belt, she could use the prong of the buckle and the knife to dig one of the bricks out. If the bricks had been laid directly on soil, then she had a chance to dig her way under the door. On the other hand, the bricks might have been laid on an earlier floor. If they had, and that floor had been constructed of flagstones then that would only delay her. If it was stone blocks, however, she might not be going anywhere.

The first thing was to cut into plaster near the door, removing enough to create a hole in the wall large enough to get her fingers in to be able to work that first brick lose. She set to work.

33

THEY'VE GOT A LEAD

(Tuesday: Sultan, Pesh)

Carlos swore as he slammed the phone back into its cradle.

"What?" Markus asked, as he looked up from boxing files in preparation to evacuate with the rest of the staff.

Carlos shook his head, trying to control his anger. "That was the local police. Same old platitudes. They've got everyone on the job. It's just a matter of time. But eleven days, Markus, and still no sign of them!"

"Everyone's trying their best."

"Their best isn't enough. Damn it, Markus, how can you remain so *calm?*"

Markus paused and looked at his hands. "Because I don't have any choice. Jessie's already waking up five times a night. If I lost my temper . . ."

Carlos looked at him, reminded that he wasn't the only one who was suffering. But dammit, neither of them was probably suffering as much as Jade and Margaret were.

He looked around the empty office, most staff having already been evacuated back to the Mainline over the past couple of days.

There was a knock and the Cardinal looked in. "Emre wants to see you, Carlos."

"Have they found them?" Carlos asked, as he got to his feet.

201

"No, but they've got a lead on the bomb."

"Where?" He was already reaching for the torso armor and helmet he had hanging from the coat rack next to his desk.

"Here, they're picking you up from the roof."

"Now?" he asked as he dropped the vest over his head and tightened the strap, checking his pistol at the same time.

"Five minutes ago. On no you don't, *Agricultural Specialist* Ackov," the Cardinal told Markus, as Carlos headed for the stairs. "I've been ordered to evacuate all remaining staff through the portal immediately!"

The helicopter was just landing as Carlos opened the door and stepped out onto the embassy's roof. The ImpSec officer on duty there had a hand over his earplug and was obviously trying to listen to the radio over the noise of the helicopter. He nodded, gave a thumbs up to the pilot, and waved Carlos forward.

Crouching, Carlos raced for the helicopter as the side door slid open and arms reached out to pull him in. Even before he had finished securing himself in his seat, the helicopter had left the ground and was accelerating away over the city. Someone handed him a headset, and Carlos recognized the Sergeant who'd been tasked with looking after him last time.

"Where is it?" Carlos asked, as he settled it on over his ear.

"North, not that far from the safe house," the Sergeant told him.

"How good's the intelligence?"

The Sergeant shrugged. "The Miralay said it's from Barun."

Carlos had a flashback to the prison cell door slamming shut behind him and suppressed a shudder. Gods, he'd hated that place.

It was only ten minutes, but Carlos spent the entire trip willing the craft to even greater speed. As they swept in toward their target, a three-story building sandwiched between two rows of terraced housing, he could see two helicopters hovering above the roof as soldiers rappelled down to it on ropes. Below them, another helicopter disgorged its troops onto the street.

For a moment, the sight of the terraces reminded Carlos of the safe house he had stayed in at Boston less than two months ago. Had it been only two months? Things had been so much simpler back then when all he had to do was penetrate the Anarchist movement. Now he was representing the Empire, and trying to track down a nuclear bomb, while working to recover a kidnapped Ambassador and a recently ennobled girlfriend. When had things got so difficult?

The Sergeant was talking to the pilot, and their craft abruptly swung round, plunging down toward a tiny park at the end of the street. As it did so the hatch slid open, and the helicopter tilted dangerously to the left. Carlos gasped, petrified as he found himself hanging from his harness, staring down at the ground rushing up to meet them. The helicopter landed heavily, slamming Carlos's helmet back into his seat.

"Out," the Sergeant ordered as Carlos fumbled with the release on his belt. Around him the other soldiers were fixing their gas masks into place. Finally, Carlos's fingers found the release and his belt sprang back into the seat. Crouching low he slid out of the hatch, his legs almost giving way under him as the rest of the squad piled out of both sides of the craft and took off at the run for the house.

The wine of the engine screamed in his ear as the helicopter launched itself back into the air, the wind from its rotors almost knocking him back down. He crouched lower, wondering what the hell he was doing there. There was the sound of breaking glass and a muffled series of explosions as the Janissaries launched flash-bangs through all the ground floor windows, followed a moment later by a larger explosion from the front door as someone set off an explosive breaching device.

The Sergeant, who had been holding back with Carlos must have heard something on his radio, because he suddenly swore.

"What?" Carlos demanded.

"They've gone — hold it," he said, suddenly stiffening.

Carlos clenched his fists. Not again!

"Wilco," the Sergeant said to the radio. "OK, put this on," he told Carlos, handing him a gas mask.

"Why?"

But the Sergeant ignored him and simply helped Carlos to do the straps up.

"Ready?" the Sergeant asked.

Carlos nodded. The mask was heavy and smelled of stale sweat.

The Miralay was waiting for them at the entrance to the building. "Special Agent," he said.

"Miralay."

"We need you to see this," the Miralay said, ushering him inside.

Smoke filled the corridor, and Carlos' sonorous breathing echoed in his ears, the mechanical valve on the mask clicking in time to his breathing.

He strained to peer through the smoke, stumbling blindly as he followed the Miralay toward the back of the house.

The Miralay led him to the kitchen where two soldiers nervously watched a third dressed in white coveralls run a Geiger counter over a body sprawled on the floor. The loud chattering of the device made it quite clear the body had been in contact with the bomb and Carlos felt his scrotum trying to crawl up into his body. The body's position, a neat hole in the back of his head, and the absence of most of his face indicated he'd been kneeling when someone shot him through the back of his head.

"Recognize him?" the Miralay asked.

Carlos squatted down, trying to keep his shoes out of the worst of the blood. After a quick examination of the body, he shook his head. "No. Sorry." Standing back up he quickly moved back from the body, and the radiation.

The forensic scientist, who had continued to pat the body down, gave a pleased exclamation as he pulled a cell-phone out of the body's coat pocket.

"Miralay, his phone. It's on."

The Miralay took the phone, hit a couple of keys, then smiled. "We've got his number."

"Is that important?" Carlos asked.

"It means we can track where he's been."

"Oh?"

But the Miralay had already turned away and was talking quickly on the radio, passing the phone's details to the operator on the other end.

"Right," he said, when he'd finished. "The Kaymakam wants us back at the barracks with the phone. Carlos, you'd better come with me this time."

Scrambling on board the helicopter Carlos was still struggling with his harness when the whine of the engine shifted up an octave and the helicopter launched itself into the air, pressing Carlos back into his seat. The engine continued to whine as the pilot red-lined the motors, and Carlos's teeth ached painfully from the vibrations. As they approached the barracks Carlos gripped the edge of his seat with both hands, terrified by the speed of their approach. The helicopter actually bounced twice before settling back to the pavement, and as the Miralay slid the door open an officer was already running forward to take them inside.

He and the Miralay were escorted to a part of the barracks Carlos hadn't been in before. Down three flights of stairs to a bunker, then into a large control room. Three rows of raised desks were in a half circle round a pit that backed onto a large screen that lined the entire wall. At the moment the screen was showing a map of Pesh. Emre was talking to someone and looked round as they were ushered in.

"Carlos," Emre said with a worried smile.

"You haven't got anything from the phone yet?" Carlos asked, gesturing at the screen.

Emre glanced behind him, then leaned forward to press a button on the keyboard on the desk next to him. "Sorry," he said, as a red path appeared on the screen, overlaid on the street plan. The trail entered the city from the south, following the main arterial road through the city.

"He apparently arrived in Pesh yesterday morning. Now, this is where we found the phone." Emre touched the keyboard again and a circle pulsed on the screen. "But this is the important one." A second circle pulsed on the screen. It was on top of the Sultan's palace, dead center in the city. "He stopped here for perhaps thirty minutes."

"How did he get through security?" Carlos demanded.

"I don't know, and you can rest assured we'll try to find out. For the moment though, we've got bigger problems." He raised his voice. "Have we got vision from the helicopters yet?"

A window opened on the top left corner of the screen. It was from the camera on one of the helicopters racing for the city. The helicopter swerved around a building, then accelerated upward over the trees that blocked the end of the road. For an instant the camera showed the Palace directly ahead; the large, white, Christian based revival edifice with its domes, columnar arches, and mosaics with the river spread out behind it. Then the center of the feed went white, and the helicopter pitched, the picture plunging as the helicopter slammed into the ground and the picture died.

Someone, acting quicker than Carlos would have thought possible, punched the alarms and the eerie wail of the sirens could be heard in the distance even before the giant airtight doors slammed shut and the sudden increase in air pressure made Carlos's ears pop.

"All to bunkers. All to bunkers. This is not a drill," an automated voice announced unemotionally.

Another window opened on the screen, from the second helicopter that had been shadowing the first. It showed a dark cloud mushrooming up into the sky, just seconds before a solid wall of wind hit the craft, and sent it cartwheeling through the air. The picture froze, and then the earthquake hit the bunker.

As the bunker settled back in the stunned silence of its passing, Carlos stared horrified at the screen.

34

THOSE STUPID BASTARDS DID IT

(Tuesday: Sultan, Pesh)

Margaret stretched exhaustedly. At least she was making progress, she thought. It was slow, but so far nothing had happened which had meant she'd had to reconsider her plan to get out of the cellar. The important thing was that she'd been able to confirm that the bricks *had* been laid directly onto the earth. In addition, the plaster on the wall had been every bit as soft as she'd hoped, and she'd quickly been able to dig a trench into the wall that gave her enough room to wriggle that first brick out. Unfortunately, the bricks had been packed tighter than she'd hoped, and she'd had to be very careful when she'd forced the knife between the bricks not to break it. A mallet and a flat head screwdriver would have been better, and she snorted at that thought — might as well wish for a pneumatic hammer. Regardless, she'd now been able to remove about a square yard of the bricks and was ready to actually start digging her way out under the door.

As she reached for the enamel plate she was planning to use as her shovel, the ground lurched under her, and she curled herself on the floor as dust rained down on her from the ceiling. And then the light went off.

She swore angrily. Those stupid bastards had actually done it!

She lay there a moment, waiting, then the wind-front hit the house. It slammed into the building, shattering its windows as it tried to tear it free of its foundations. All she could do was curl herself even tighter on the floor and pray as a low-pitched roar shook the building. Eventually the roar died away to be replaced by the ominous creaking of the house as it settled back into place around her. Finally, silence descended over the room and she cautiously sat up. The darkness pressed down on her and taking a deep breath she let it out slowly. She was in control, she told herself sternly. Reaching for the plate she found her hand clutching on nothing. She closed her eyes and as she let her breath out, she tried to relax. OK, that wasn't working.

Spreading her fingers, she carefully swept the floor around her. Finally, her hand knocked against the metal of the plate, and she clutched at it thankfully. Given how long it had taken her to find itn, perhaps it might be an idea that before she started to dig up a large pile of sand, she should make sure she wasn't going to bury anything important. It took a while but eventually she'd located the baton, the knife, belt, and boots and placed them to one side of the door where they would be safe, and she'd be able to find them again. Then, retrieving the plate, she started on the hole.

After the time it had taken her to remove the bricks, digging the hole proved remarkably easy. Even having to dig it deep enough to lie in to reach under the door and remove the bricks on the other side didn't unduly delay her. She was gaily turfing the bricks into the far corner when she heard the unmistakable sound of one hitting soft flesh.

"Sorry Karen," she giggled.

At last, the hole felt large enough, and after placing the items she'd taken from Karen onto the plate she passed it under the door, lifting it out to balance precariously on the bricks next to the hole. She paused for a moment, wondering if she shouldn't try and dig more out, but really, she'd reached the limit of how far she could reach under the door, and it was only getting more difficult. Every time she removed some sand it seemed that twice as much fell back into the hole.

Sitting down with her back to the door she took a deep breath, then carefully lowered herself awkwardly backwards into the hole.

Sand forced its way under her collar and down the back of her neck as she wormed her way under the door. She stopped as her forehead scraped against the bottom of the wood. The space definitely felt narrower, and shallower than when she'd been digging it out. Closing her eyes to stem her panic she turned her head and continued to inch her way into the hole. The bottom of the door scraped across the side of her face, but finally her head was free.

For a moment she lay there, just gathering her strength. Before, with a sigh, she started to wriggle her way onwards.

Sand crusted her left eye, and she couldn't even brush it away as her arms were trapped by her sides. She increased her efforts, and sand cascaded around her as the bottom of the door scraped painfully across her chest. Her feet, still unable to fit into the hole with her, scrabbled uselessly against the bricked floor of the cell. She couldn't even use her hands against the side of the tunnel now to push with, because every time she tried sand poured down into the hole on top of her. She swore, knowing she should have taken the time to deepen the hole. Unfortunately, it was too late now, she was committed, so she continued to try and work her way further under the door.

Finally, she'd got herself far enough along to be able to work her feet into the hole behind her. Bracing, she shoved with her feet, and immediately found herself covered in a fresh layer of sand and grit as the top of her head slammed against the end of the tunnel. She grunted in pain. Trying to lift her head she found she'd managed to jam herself in so tightly she couldn't move.

She stifled a sob, as the hole embraced her as tightly as a coffin might its occupant. She couldn't even breathe properly because of the weight across her chest from the bottom of the door. She tried to throw herself from side to side, to bend, to wriggle free, but all she succeeded in doing was to bring more sand down on top of her. At last, her strength exhausted, she slipped into a torpor.

She roused at the sound of movement in the dark beyond her feet.

"Who's there?" she whispered, spitting out sand.

"Well, well, well," a voice said from the darkness.

"Karen?"

"The same. Looks as though I'm going to have company when Charon ferries me to Hades."

"Fuck you!"

"Oh, I don't think so."

Margaret flinched as she felt a hand touch her ankle, and as it started to work its way up her leg she kicked out. She continued to kick frantically, twisting her legs up and to the side, and suddenly she found she could move again. Cursing, twisting, and struggling she fought her way free of the sand as bricks slid into the hole around her.

As she pulled herself out, great hacking coughs racked her frame as her body struggled to clear her lungs of the sand she'd inhaled.

Eventually, exhausted and shaking, she forced herself to carefully feel around for the plate and its contents. For once luck seemed to be with her and she found them exactly where she had hoped. Retrieving the knife, she leaned cautiously back into the hole.

"Karen," she called softly. She listened, but there was no response from whatever she had heard, or felt she quickly reminded herself, shivering at the memory of that hand feeling its way up her leg.

Still on her hands and knees, and using the knife to feel her way, she crawled her way toward where she remembered the stairs to be. She almost lost her grip on the knife as it hit the edge of the bottom step. She was much weaker than she had thought. Wiping her hand on the leg of her overalls she clutched the knife as tightly as she could and started up.

She counted her way up the stairs, reaching fourteen before her hand felt the solid surface of the door blocking her way. Sitting down she considered the door. She thought she could just make out the hint of light leaking in around one edge. But how was she going to pick the lock, or alternatively break through the door? Nothing she had seemed suitable, although there might have been something downstairs. Perhaps the bed. She remembered seeing it when she was put into the cell.

She stood up, carefully reaching for the banister, then paused as an idea struck her. Turning back, she tried the handle. It turned effortlessly. Hardly daring to believe her luck, she shoved. The door squealed as it swung open and she had a moment to consider the risk of doing that, without knowing how close she'd been to ground-zero, before light flooded her vision and she had to blink to clear the tears.

Glass from the window inserts in the door littered the floor, glinting in the light. Looking up the stairs as they continued to the next floor, she could see the shattered windows on the landing. Surprisingly there didn't seem much in the way of visible damage, which might mean they'd been far enough away from ground-zero not to have to worry about the radiation — or at least not immediately. The terrorists had kindly left the key in the front door for her, or else they'd left via the garage and hadn't bothered with the key. Holding her breath she opened the front door, and stared stunned at the scene of devastation that greeted her.

She could see Pesh's skyline in the distance, or what remained of it. The skyscrapers that had survived the aerial bombardment of the Etehad Sho'mali's Kinetic Orbital Weapons were now shattered stumps — the glorious dome of the Caliph's Palace completely gone. Smoke stained the entire horizon while the wail of sirens could be heard in the distance.

On the street the windows of the buildings opposite, empty and desolate, stared back at her. Two small bodies lay lifeless on the street, while a short distance away a father cradled a small child to his chest, rocking backwards and forwards over the body of its mother. Shattered clusters of stunned people stood uncertainly or worked frantically on those who had been injured by the blast. Glass covered the ground like broken snow. She could smell smoke —

> — and then between one breath and the next she found herself watching the sun climb slowly into the sky above the Charterists' hill fort, as smoke from the summit eddied around her in the heavy air. Behind her the Battle Group was shaking itself out in preparation for its final attack — but it was an attack she already suspected would be unnecessary after the massive explosion that had woken her shortly after midnight.
>
> She watched the Battle Group climb the hill, then when confirmation arrived about what had happened, she followed.
>
> At the top of the hill, standing on the bulwarks of the fort she found herself staring down into the massive crater that filled its center, and the burned and dismembered bodies that littered the ground around it. Smoke drifted up from the pit, carrying with it the stink of gunpowder and burned flesh that clawed at the back of her throat, and she gags, abruptly lost in the memory.
>
> A soldier, face covered by a rag against the smell stumbled, their foot catching on the outreached arm of a small child. Margaret swallows, then bends, vomiting, and vomiting again until there is nothing left. Uncapping her water bottle she swirls the water round her mouth, then spits it out. For a moment she stands there, then dropping the bottle turns her back on the carnage and walks away down the hill.
>
> Her uniform chafes at her skin, carrying with it the reminder

of the blood she has spilled over the last couple of years, the innocents she had killed, and at the bottom of the hill she undoes the buttons on her jacket, letting it slip from her shoulders, to fall forgotten to the ground. Her mind numb, she bends to unlace her boots. Toeing them off she starts walking again, trying to undo the buttons on her shirt until frustrated by the time it's taking she simply pulls the shirt off over her head.

"Leader." It is Sarah, her aide, concern in her voice.

Margaret ignores her, only pausing for a moment to undo her trousers and slide them off. She doesn't know where she's going, but she's finished with this damn war. She's lost too much, seen too much, done everything that has been asked of her. She starts walking again, pulling her camisole off over her head as she does so and dropping it on the ground.

There is something happening behind her but whatever it is can't penetrate her inertia. She releases the ties on her drawers, and with one hand on a tree to balance her kicks them off. And then there's nothing left, and like a puppet with its strings cut she collapses on the ground, pulling herself into a ball. All she wants is for everything to end, for the pain to stop, but it won't. It goes on and on and she feels a blanket tucked over her and Sarah demanding that someone get the medic. And Margaret closes her eyes and wishes it all away.

Margaret blinked. So that was what happened, she thought, as the memory slotted itself into place. Doctor Rubenstein had tried to bring the memory back without success, and all it had required was this? Cold certainty coalesced in her chest. She was not the same Margaret who had fought through the war, had lost her brother and friends, people who had depended on her. She was not the same one who had broken. She was a Peric, and this was not going to happen again. She had lost so much but enough was enough and she was not going to crawl away and hide as she did last time. She was going to face this down. But more importantly, she was going to do what she had been unable to do last time. She was going to bring succor to the wounded – and then she was going to track down who had done this and make them pay.

She scrubbed at her face, feeling the dirt running down the inside of her coveralls. Gods she could do with a shower, although that could take a while, she told herself, looking around at the devastation surrounding her. That reminded her. Turning, she retraced her steps and picked up the handpiece from the phone on the small hall stand.

She raised an eyebrow when she got a dial tone, but immediately keyed in the embassy's number. She was rewarded with the burr of a dead line, and swore softly. If that meant the embassy had been destroyed, then she was damn well going to do more than just make whoever had done this pay. On a chance she tried Carlos's number. She was more than a little surprised when she got the sound of ringing.

"Hello?"

She felt like doing handsprings as she recognized Carlos's French accent.

"Carlos, it's Margaret."

"Margaret! It's the Ambassador!" he called to someone in the background. "Margaret, is Jade with you? Where are you? Are you all right?" His worry was clear in his voice.

Margaret shook her head, aware as she did so that he couldn't see her. "No, she's not here. We were separated days ago. I'm OK. I'm in Pesh, somewhere south of the Palace. I can see it in the distance, or what remains of it. Did the Embassy survive? I can't get through to them."

"No. We evacuated all personnel back to the Mainline before the bomb went off though. I know Markus got through safely, but the Cardinal stayed behind, and I haven't heard anything from him since —" He broke off.

There seemed to be some discussion occurring in the background.

"Can you give me a more precise location of where you are?" Carlos asked finally.

"I'm not sure. Perhaps two or three miles from the Palace. I could ask someone," she suggested, as she caught sight of two survivors walking listlessly along the road through the open door.

"No, it's all right. Emre says we have your number and can pull an address. We should have a helicopter there in less than half an hour. Are you going to be all right until then?"

Knowing the multiple situations they must be trying to cope with, half an hour would be fine. "I'm good," she said. "And Carlos . . ."

"Yes?"

"I'm sure Jade's all right."

"I hope so, and thank you."

35

Vignette:
Nayarit's Pre-History

The Nayarit Line is generally considered a low probability line that split from the Mainline around 8000 BC with two separate, but associated Points of Divergence (POD).

The first POD occurred in 8000 BCE when the indigenous inhabitants of the Northern American continent successfully domesticated the native horse. It is now believed that the horse was initially domesticated by the Ute (near Mainline equivalent Colorado). Domestication was initially for food, but subsequently as a beast of burden. This was almost 4,000 years before domestication of the horse in Europe and it gave North America a significant technological/cultural lead over the rest of the world (as well as preventing the horse's extinction in America).

The second POD involved the domestication of wild rice around the Great Lakes in 7,000 BC (having been harvested from a much earlier period). When introduced to the Mississippi valley, cultivated rice allowed the Mound Builder culture to develop from a hunter-gatherer society to one based on farming and the establishment of the first cities.

Cyclopedia of the Cross-Temporal Empire
Other Lines

36

Margaret's Back

(Thursday: Mainline, Budapest)

Markus was waiting on the other side of the portal, Jessie by his side, as Margaret stepped through it. She looked tired, but there was nothing of the utter exhaustion he had sometimes seen in her eyes before she had disappeared, and which had made him so worried.

Seeing the two of them, her face, so serious and fixed with purpose lit up, and he had to catch his breath.

"Miss Peric!" Jessie called and dashed forward to wrap her arms round her waist. Without breaking her stride Margaret bent down and swung her up onto her hip.

"Hello Jessie," she said kissing the top of Jessie's head. For a moment Markus wished he could have been his daughter, but then Margaret had reached him and kissed him soundly on the mouth.

"I missed you," he managed to say as she swung her other arm around him.

"Good. Come on."

"Where are we going?"

"The conference room. I need to speak to my cousin."

"Of course. How bad is it?" he asked, allowing her to lead them, staff trailing them as she strode for the cloisters.

"About as bad as could be," she said, her face suddenly still. "Nearly three-quarters of a million dead or wounded. The center of the city is completely gone, and most of the northern suburbs were flattened. They were still trying to recover from the last war and now this."

"Any word on the Cardinal?" he asked.

"They identified his body this morning."

He paused. "And the Caliph?"

"Dead. His entire family."

"So who's in charge?" he asked, dumbfounded.

"At the moment — Emre. The Janissaries control the city, and for now the rest of the military seem willing to go along with him. The Vizier is acting as his liaison with the civil service."

"And that's working?"

"Until they can negotiate an agreement with the Caliph's brother for his return. He wasn't exactly popular with his elder brother and has been in semi-official exile in Serbia for the last ten years."

"What did he do to deserve that?" He gave a mock shudder.

She gave him a fond smile, knowing he'd been born in Serbia. "I understand he was a little too outspoken in favor of a more liberal re-interpretation of Islamic practice. Specifically, as to how it relates to Islamic feminism."

He looked a little uncertain as to how he should respond to that. "And how does he feel about the Empire?"

She rocked her head. "That's one of the things Emre and the Vizier are negotiating."

At the doorway to the conference room, she paused uncertainly.

"What?" Markus asked.

"I'd like you in on my phone call, but I'm not sure about Jessie . . ." She looked down at the small girl who looked up at her and gave her a bright smile. "I'm going to have to call in some favors."

"Here," he said offering to take her. "Helena's around somewhere. She can look after her for us."

"Helena?" Margaret was surprised at the reluctance she felt to release Jessie.

"Your psychiatrist."

Margaret raised an eyebrow. Markus was on first names with her psychiatrist? "She's still here?"

"She's still got another week to go before she has to head home, and she wants to see you."

"Of course. What's she been doing with her star patient absent?"

"She's been working with Jessie."

"Oh?" she asked worriedly.

Markus grimaced. "Apparently Jessie's been hiding how she felt about her own kidnapping, then when you disappeared . . ."

" Doctor Rubenstein says I have post-traumatic stress disorder," Jessie said brightly. "But I'm getting better," she added quickly.

Margaret planted a kiss on the top of Jessie's head, and reluctantly handed her over to her father.

She sat at the head of the table, gently rocking on the chair until Markus returned.

"Close the door," she told him, moving the conference phone so he would be able to join in without having to lean over the table.

Donald had obviously been waiting for her call as she was put straight through to him.

"Margaret," he said. "I am so glad to hear you're all right."

"So am I," she told him sincerely.

"For your information I've got Arni and Heidi here with me. Christobel has just had to step out for a moment."

She nodded. That meant the Military, Imperial Security, and media liaison were all represented. "Markus is sitting in on my side."

"Sir," Markus said.

"Markus," Donald acknowledged him. "Right Margaret, first things first. Do you have any news on Jade?"

Trust Donald to focus in on the human problem, Margaret thought. "Not at the moment. I know Carlos is convinced that she was moved out of the city well before the bomb went off, but I don't know how much of that is based on blind hope. I'm due to meet with Emre tomorrow and he intimated he had some news for me. I'll make sure tol keep you copied into anything I find out."

"Thanks. Right, Colonel Ferai's been keeping us informed about the general situation on Sultan. What do you need?"

Margaret shook her head in disbelief. "Donald, I've been psyching myself up for an argument for the last hour, and you've just shot the ground out from underneath me."

He laughed. "I didn't say you were going to get everything you wanted, but you never know."

"Fair enough." She paused to collect her thoughts. "Firstly, the C-T E *must* stand with Sultan. Whoever did this has access to portals, so what happened on Sultan can, and probably *will* happen to the Mainline if we don't stop them. More immediately though, we have to provide as much assistance as we can. Pesh has three-quarters of a million dead or wounded, and at least four times that number presently homeless."

"Done, and done," Donald said. "I understand from Colonel Ferai that access to the city has been badly disrupted. We're looking at establishing at least one large portal from the Mainline within a week and can start shipping through supplies by the truckload. We're already starting to build up stockpiles. Speak to Emre and find out where he wants us to put the portal.

"I've also authorized the release of two Battlegroups," he continued. "The first should be there by the day after tomorrow. They'll be under Emre's direct control. You might want to let him know that I would like them back before the end of the year, though."

"Thank you," Margaret said.

"Then if that's all, Madam Ambassador, I won't keep you any longer. Let me know what Emre tells you tomorrow. And Markus, make sure she gets *some* sleep tonight. I don't want her collapsing again."

"Yes, sir."

"Goodbye Donald," Margaret said sharply.

There was a laugh, and the line went dead.

Margaret let out a sigh. "That went better than I expected."

"Why?" Markus said, surprised. "You were right."

"Being right does not always get you the resources you need to tackle a problem properly."

"What now?" he asked.

"I have to phone Jade's mother."

"Can it wait until tomorrow?"

She shook her head. "If I don't do it now, I'll spend all night worrying about what I'm going to say. And you heard what my cousin told you about making sure I get to sleep. Better get it out of the way."

He rested a hand on hers for moment, until regretfully she pushed the call button. Getting Jade's mother to the phone took considerably longer than it had taken to get put through to the First Leader, which gave some indication of how seriously Donald had viewed the situation, she thought with a sigh.

"Miss Peric," came the quiet voice when the hospital had finally managed to track her down. "This is Ruth Carvello. I was told you'd managed to escape. Can you tell me how Jade was when you saw her last?"

"She was in good shape, Mrs. Carvello," Margaret said, thinking Jade had actually been in better shape than she'd been, given Margaret was still coming off her anti-depressants. "I'm sorry I can't tell you more, but we were separated about fifteen days ago. I just phoned you to let you know that we are doing everything in our power to find her."

"That's just what the First Leader told me." There was an amount of disbelief in her voice that the First Leader had spoken to her personally.

"It's highly unlikely that Jade was in the city when the terrorists set off the bomb, a view Carlos also supports," Margaret said reassuringly. "It's only a matter of time before we pick up her trail again."

"Carlos is her . . . Canadian friend?"

"Yes, I had presumed Jade had told you of him."

"She mentioned him in passing."

"Only in passing?"

"Yes. It raised my suspicions immediately. Jade is normally much more forthcoming about her beaus. I had my suspicions it was more serious than she was letting on."

"Can I tell her that when I see her next?"

"Please do," Mrs. Carvello said with a laugh. "It will serve her right."

There was a pause.

"Is there anything I can do for you?" Margaret asked. "I have to go back to Sultan tomorrow. We're coordinating a relief effort, but I'll make sure you're kept informed if we find out anything about Jade."

"Those poor people," Mrs. Carvello said, a catch in her voice. There was a ragged breath. "Boston Hospital is identifying medical equipment we can donate, and I'm pulling a team together to go with it. If you could let me know who I should coordinate with . . ."

"Of course," Margaret promised.

"Thank you. And thank you for phoning."

There was a click, and Margaret slowly replaced the handset. For a time, she simply stared at the table, her eyes pricking, teetering on the edge of a cliff, arms wheeling. And then Markus's arms embraced her and for a moment she was free to grieve.

37

NENETL!

(Thursday: Nayarit)

It was late when Julpe arrived back at the room he shared with his sister. The curtain was closed, and the room was in darkness.

"Nenetl?" he called uncertainly, as he lifted the corner of the curtain.

"Don't come in!" Nenetl's voice was sharp.

Julpe pushed the curtain aside but as he took an uncertain step into the room his foot connected with something on the floor. He stumbled badly, landing on his knees. He flinched as one hand touched someone's face, and he threw himself backward, scooting on his bottom until he ended up colliding with the wall. "Nenetl!" he protested.

"I told you not to come in," she said, tears shading her voice.

He stood up carefully and felt along the wall for the shelf where they kept the candles. He lit one with shaking hands and placed it carefully on the shelf before turning to look.

His sister was jammed into the corner, knees pulled up against her chest while Tupi lay across the shattered remains of the table, a pool of blood spreading across the floor from one ear. The frypan lay on the ground next to him. He looked dead, and Julpe cautiously crouched down and slowly extended a hand to feel his throat. There was no hint of any life. There was a soft rustling from the ceiling, and he looked up to see one of Xipil's roaches watching him.

He waved it away, but it ignored him. He grimaced. He didn't like being under constant observation. Carefully he made his way around the body, half expecting Tupi to sit up and grab his leg.

"Nenetl." He squatted down in front of his sister. "What happened?"

She looked up at him. "I hit him."

"Why?"

"Because he wouldn't stop touching me. And then when he ripped my shirt ... I didn't intend to kill him!"

Her voice rose, and Julpe looked around worriedly.

"It really doesn't matter why," he said sourly. "He's dead. And we don't have the credits for a penalty, even if they were prepared to consider one."

He cast a look at the ceiling. Perhaps there was a way of raising the money.

"I am not going to the farms!" She lunged for the knife that was among the shattered remains of the table.

"No," he protested and there was a mad scramble for the blade.

"I'm not going!" Nenetl said hysterically as he managed to pull it away from her.

"I know," he said, trying to calm her. He looked up at the roach, not really surprised to find that there were now two of them.

"I need to speak to Xipil," he said. One of the roaches waved its antenna at him, which he presumed meant it had understood him.

"Who are you speaking to?" Nenetl demanded.

"A friend," he said, hoping he wasn't wrong. He settled himself down beside his sister, putting an arm round her shoulder and pulling her against him. She resisted for a moment, then finally allowed the comfort, tucking her head in against his shoulder.

Less than fifteen minutes later the curtain stirred and Kenefer slid inside. The cat settled, wrapped her tail around her paws then looked him up and down.

"And just what did you want to speak to the priestess about?" she asked.

He felt Nenetl start beside him, and he put a hand on her arm to still her.

"How?" she demanded.

"I'll explain later," he said hurriedly. "But Kenefer is a messenger of the gods." He glared at the cat, daring it to correct him, but the cat simply stared back at him.

"I . . . we have a problem," he said gesturing at the body.

"So Xipil surmised," Kenefer said primly.

"I thought that, perhaps, as I wouldn't be of any use to you as a convict, that you might, you know, in exchange for my services, make this problem ... disappear."

Kenefer stared at him, and he felt himself start to squirm. In hindsight this might not be such a good idea. He thought about the stories their mother had told them about what happened when humans tried to bargain with a god, and how it always ended badly. And while he knew Xipil wasn't a god, her powers were close enough to those of a god to make no difference.

Finally, Kenefer gave a very human sounding sigh. "Xipil felt that you might try this, and she tasked me to tell you that her assistance cannot be bought. That any assistance she provides will be because *she* wishes it."

"I knew that," Julpe said quickly.

Kenefer gave another sigh. "Under normal circumstances I might have counseled Xipil against the path she has decided but this time my preferences align with hers." She rose and walked across to stand before Nenetl before leaning forward to press her forehead against Nenetl's. "Little Sister, this man deserved to be punished for what he attempted. Perhaps not killed, but then that was not your intent so he too must be held responsible for that."

Julpe stared at Kenefer, trying to work out what it meant.

Kenefer gave a third sigh and looked back at him. "Yes, Julpe, we will help, and there will be no debt put on you for this."

"Really?" What sort of a bargain was that?

"Really," she said. "Xipil has spoken." Giving a yawn that displayed her fangs, she lay down and proceeded to wash her face using her front paw.

Nenetl looked at him. "It's a cat."

"Yes."

"But it talks."

"Yes."

"How?"

Julpe sighed and Kenefer looked back at him. "It's a long story," he said.

"We don't have anything else to do."

Nenetl was definitely sounding more like her normal, bossy self and Julpe wished she could have taken a little longer to recover. He really didn't want to have to explain about Kenefer and Xipil, primarily because he didn't know how to. He glanced at Kenefer for guidance, but she was ignoring him while she continued the washing. He had the feeling she was enjoying his discomfort. Steeling himself, he proceeded to tell his sister what had happened to him over the past couple of days.

"So, let me get this straight," she said when he had finished. "You've been offered a job by a genuine priestess of the Ejejatl caste and you turned her down?"

"I haven't turned it down," he said defensively. "I said I'd think about it."

"Think about it. *Think about it!*" She cuffed him over the top of his head.

No, he thought regretfully. Nenetl was definitely over her shock.

"You may tell the priestess that my dim of a brother accepts her offer," she told Kenefer, who simply smirked at him.

Julpe rolled his eyes. "What happens now?" he asked.

"We wait," Kenefer announced.

"Could we have dinner?" Julpe asked, looking at his sister hopefully, as his stomach rumbled.

"No," Nenetl told him, with a glare.

Julpe slouched back against the wall.

After finishing her toilet Kenefer took up a position next to the door where she went to sleep. Julpe was just wondering how quickly she would respond if he pulled her tail when the top of the curtain wavered, and with a rustling another of Xipil's roaches appeared. It seemed bigger than the ones he had seen before. He heard Nenetl's sharp intake of breath.

"You might want to close your eyes," Kenefer, who had woken up with the appearance of the roach, suggested.

"Why?" Julpe asked, but Kenefer had already followed her own suggestion and had closed her eyes again, apparently going back to sleep.

There was a soft scratching from the top of the curtain and Julpe watched as another roach appeared, flattening itself to push its way between the ceiling and the top of the curtain. His gaze followed the two as they descended to the floor, then scuttled across to Tupi's body. A soft scritching sound began as though that of a file scratched across skin.

"Nenetl?" he asked softly as another roach forced its way through the grilles that blocked the air-vent, but his sister had her eyes tightly clamped together.

Julpe turned back to the body to find that another five roaches had crept in. He closed his eyes when he saw the muscle that had already been exposed on Tupi's cheek as the roaches attacked the body. The stink of blood and feces filled his nostrils even as the sound of scratching and mastication continued, growing louder, until unable to contain his curiosity he opened his eyes to find a heaving, writhing pile of roaches covering the body. He stared fascinated until he felt Nenetl poke him.

"Close your eyes," his sister told him.

Julpe scowled — how was he supposed to learn anything if he wasn't allowed to watch?

Finally, the sound of eating died away and he opened his eyes just in time to see the last roach climb laboriously up the wall and force its way through the gap it had easily managed before its meal. There was no sign that Tupi had ever been there. He noticed with macabre horror that they had even polished the floor after them.

As it disappeared, Kenefer cracked her eye open and sat up. "We will see you tomorrow," she said and slipped out through the curtain.

Julpe looked at his sister hopefully. "Dinner?"

"No," she started to say, then paused. "How much will this priestess pay you?" she asked.

"I have no idea. *I* would have bargained for something, but someone told them *I* was going to work for them without sorting that little matter out." He was quite bitter about that.

Nenetl stood up, reached into the money jar and pulled out their last two tokens. "Go and ask Mother Coaxoch if she has anything left to sell us."

Julpe's eyes lit up, and before she could change her mind, he was off.

38

Vignette:
Nayarit's Caste System

A significant, and primary driver of history following domestication of the horse on the Nayarit line was the caste system developed by the Hutanga nomads of America's Great Plains. The meme spread rapidly across the continent following the diaspora of the Great Plains in 6,000 BC as a result of the beginning of the 3,000 year drought. The diaspora sent the nomads crashing into the newly developing civilizations along the Mississippi and on the west coast. Subsequent active proselytization of its religion by the priesthood caste allowed other ruling groups to be suborned into this new meme. It has been postulated by Emila Rodrigues of the University of Constantinople (Mainline) that the Hutanga caste system actually had the effect of slowing the development of technology on the Nayarit Line.

In theory, and usually practice, females acquire the caste of their mother, while boys that of their father. In 1402 (CE) genetic caste markers were embedded into the DNA of Nayarit Commonwealth citizens: mitochondrial DNA for females, Y chromosome for males.

There are four major caste groupings (not including those caste-less individuals who initially would have been cultural outsiders), with the traditional role of the Tletl, Atl, and Tlalli to support the Ejejatl in their constant struggle to ensure the demons do not escape the abyss. The castes consist of the following vocations:

Ejejatl (air) - priests, artists, teachers, and scientists
Tletl (fire) - ruling and military elite
Atl (water) - agricultural and traders
Tlalli (earth) - assistants and technicians
Macehualli (caste-less) [maːseːˈwalːi]

CYCLOPEDIA OF THE CROSS-TEMPORAL EMPIRE
OTHER LINES

\# \# \#

39

I Will Make My Arrows Drunk With Blood

(Wednesday: Sultan, Pesh)

Emre glanced at the framed photograph of Darda on the corner of his desk. Her eyes stared back at him. Unable to face her accusing gaze anymore he turned the frame face down on the table. Abruptly his eyes pricked, and he removed his pince-nez to massage the bridge of his nose. He replaced his glasses and his eyes flicked to the time in the top corner of his screen. Forty-eight hours since everything had changed — since he'd lost Darda. With a sigh he reached for the container of modafinil in the drawer and dry-swallowed the last tablet in the box. He crumpled the empty packet and dropped it back into the drawer, wondering how much longer he could keep going without sleep, even assuming he could find some more of the modafinil.

There was a knock on the door, and he looked up to see his Lieutenant hovering uncertainly.

"Yes?" Emre said.

"The CT-E Ambassador has returned, Kaymakam. Carlos Babineaux is with her."

"Show them in then, Lieutenant."

"Margaret, Carlos," he said, rising to greet them. "I was sorry to hear about the Cardinal."

Margaret's face clouded. "Yes. We'll miss him. Is there any news on Darda?"

He shook his head. "We still have teams in the area, but they haven't found anyone alive in the last twenty-four hours so I'm not holding out any hope. But not even being able to bury a body . . ." He gestured helplessly.

She touched his hand in sympathy.

Unable to get any words out, in the end he simply nodded and waved them into their seats, before taking his own.

"I'm glad to see you again," he said. "I hope you bring good news; we're racing against time to save those who are still trapped in the debris." Hands gestured the helplessness of his situation.

"I do have some good news," she said. "The First Leader has authorized the release of two Battlegroups. That's about 2,000 troops. The first will start arriving tomorrow morning. They will self-supply and will operate under the direction of your emergency coordinating committee. I also understand we should have a larger portal in place within a week and can start shipping through supplies by truck. We're already stockpiling supplies in preparation. We need to know where you want it to come through, though."

"Thank you." He felt some of the pressure lifting. Little as the help was it was more than he had dared hope for. And with the promises of support he was getting from both former allies and enemies he had some hopes that when they had finished with this crisis his world might actually survive. He glanced at the photograph lying face down on the desk. That is if they survived *this* crisis. With a certainty he hadn't had before he reached into his top drawer and pulled out the file his aide had prepared for him, laying it on the table before him. He then pulled out the small vial of potato virus, placed it on top of the file and pushed them both across to Margaret. She eyed them doubtfully.

"It doesn't seem worthwhile holding onto it any longer," he told her. "I doubt we'll be able to finish the tests we wanted to as the lab doing the tests was destroyed in the attack. I can confirm that the blight was artificially created. Further, the lab indicated that certain 'markers' they found in non-coding DNA meant they were 97 percent confident it was not created on Sultan."

Margaret raised an eyebrow. "That appears . . . confident."

He nodded. "That's what I thought, so I queried it. Apparently, the level of confidence is because they were able to match the 'markers' with some already on file."

Carlos leaned forward interestedly. "When you say 'markers', what do you mean?"

"I was told it looks like some sort of identifying code for the person, or persons, who inserted the code, or in the case of the virus, created it."

"So, it's sort of like 'Kilroy was here'?"

Emre looked at him, confused.

Margaret directed a frown at Carlos before turning back to Emre. "But if they know about the marker, surely that means it originated on Sultan?"

"If the source of the matched markers came from Sultan, yes. But in this case, it matched with an individual they already had on file who wasn't from Sultan."

"Who?"

"Donald Clemhorn."

"Donald? My cousin? The First Leader?"

"Indeed."

Margaret's eyes narrowed warningly. "And they had his DNA on file — why?"

"From his kidney transplant. They needed samples of his DNA to ensure maximum compatibility for the kidneys."

"But why did Donald have this . . . code?"

"I don't know," he admitted. "But it gets even more interesting. The tests of the staff of those at Embassy also threw up one other individual with the same markers."

"Who?"

"You don't want to guess?"

"Emre," she said threateningly.

"Jade."

"Jade!" Carlos exclaimed.

Emre nodded.

"And no one else?" Margaret asked.

"No one else. Up until yesterday we were continuing to run checks against as many Mainline samples as we could."

He could see Margaret start to ask where they had been getting the samples from, before deciding that she didn't want to know.

"How many did you test?"

"We were aiming for a thousand , but the lab had managed to test only five hundred and eighty-nine before ..." His shrug indicated the disaster.

"And no other matches?" she asked.

"No."

"So what is the link?"

"I was hoping you could tell me."

Margaret leaned back in her chair. "I'm not sure that either of us is actually operating at our best at the moment," she admitted, then shook her head. "No, I'm sorry, Emre. I can't think of any reason why Donald and Jade are the only ones with those specific markers."

"They're not related?"

She shook her head thoughtfully. "Not that I . . . oh!" Her eyes had gone very wide.

"What?"

"It couldn't be. Oh gods . . ."

"What?" he demanded.

"The Hraffor."

"What?" Emre said, not understanding.

"Donald and Jade are both descended from the Hraffor who followed Iapura through the portal from Nayarit when he conquered the Mainline a hundred years ago. In Jade's case it was her great-great-grandmother. Donald claims descent through his father."

"But you don't have the marker, and if Donald — "

"Donald and I are related through our fathers, but none of my female ancestors claim any Nayarit descent."

"And why is that important?" Emre asked.

"If I remember correctly from my Academy days, what you're probably picking up is some sort of caste identifier. And on Nayarit women recieved the caste of their mother, while boys that of their father."

Emre narrowed his eyes. "And if none of your female ancestors came from Nayarit..."

"I don't have a marker. But I suspect if you tested my brother Rajko's DNA you'd find the marker."

"But Jade said the Nayarit Line was destroyed," Carlos said.

"That's what we believed. Obviously, we wrong. Oh —" She struck her forehead with her hand.

"What?"

The people who took Jade shortly after we were captured. At least one of them spoke Nayarit. I didn't think about it at the time. But now . . ."

"She's on Nayarit," Carlos said definitely.

Margaret looked at him. "We don't know that for sure," she warned.

"No," he admitted. "But it makes sense." He looked at Emre. "Do you still have that disk we found on that terrorist at the first warehouse we raided?"

Emre shook his head. "It was still getting examined. Now . . ." He shrugged.

"What disk?" Margaret demanded.

"It looked like some sort of high-tech dog-tag," Carlos explained. "A disk of transparent metal about two inches across. If you pressed it with your fingers a picture of a snarling cat appeared within the disk."

"Nayarit?"

"I didn't recognize it at the time, but I'd lay my life on it now."

"Let me guess, the cat was a jaguar."

Carlos nodded.

Emre's head had been swiveling between the two of them.

"The jaguar was a common symbol among the Nayarit military caste," Margaret explained. She stood up. "I need to speak to the First Leader again."

"Of course," Emre said, standing up as well, as Carlos jumped to his feet.

"And Emre," she said with a smile, "this time let's keep each other informed of our suspicions."

He grimaced and picked up the file to pass it to her. "I think that might be a good idea. With your permission I'll arrange for my Lieutenant to return with you. I believe he might work well with your Mr. Ackov."

"Give the poor boy time to pack, Emre. I'll leave a message at the portal to expect him. That will also give someone time to find where he can bunk."

"Thank you."

"No, thank you!" she said. "Without this," and she gestured with the file, "we wouldn't know who was behind all this. Now we know and they are going to pay."

"In truth," Emre said fervently.

He watched them leave, then with a sigh he reached for the next folder in his tray. His eyes were caught by the photograph frame still lying face down on his desk. He paused, then slowly reached out and lifted the photograph back up. He ran a finger softly over her face, stroking the memory. "For you, Darda, 'I will make my arrows drunk with blood, while my sword devours the flesh of the slain'. There will be no escape for them."

40

THIS IS NAYARIT

(Monday: Nayarit)

Jade struggled to open her eyes, fighting against the smothering lassitude that gripped her. She seemed to remember someone pressing a needle into her arm, promising her it would help, but if it hadn't been a dream — they'd lied. She ached everywhere.

She forced her eyes open, squinting against the glare of the overhead florescent light. Just where the hell was she? Her left eye had something stuck on it and when she tried to rub it, she discovered that both her hands were restrained.

What had happened to her? All she had was memories of ill-formed dreams. Of flashing lights and swirling patterns; of angry faces and the cold flood of liquid into her arm. She began to raise her head and the world spun crazily around her. She vomited and bile stung her throat, filling her mouth. Some got into her lungs, and she started to cough, unable to breathe.

Hysterical now, tied down and unable to breathe, she struggled frantically. Then her arms were released, and someone heaved her onto her side. She coughed and vomited again. The bile dribbled from her mouth and soaked the collar of her top. Finally, her throat raw, the urge to cough slowly eased and she was able to take notice of the fact that she appeared to be on a hospital trolley.

How long had she been sedated? Her memory was a disorganized series of out-of-focus-images. But she knew she'd been moved, and some of what she remembered implied the move had involved long trips by truck. She was fairly sure she'd been held in a small cell for a time. She seemed to remember someone feeding her, of trying to fight someone, but it was a blur of nightmares. She flexed her fingers and flinched as she realized from the length of her nails that she'd lost at least a month.

Her arm hurt. There was a drip plugged into it, connected to a bag that hung limply from a metal wheeled stand. The bag looked almost empty, and she needed to pee.

"How are you?" someone asked.

She looked up. It took her a moment to recognize the speaker as one of the men who had taken her from the room she'd shared with Margaret. And a moment longer to realize he'd spoken in Nayarit.

"I need to use the toilet."

"Speak Nayarit," he said.

She had to think about it for a moment, then repeated the question.

He looked uncertain, then nodded. "Come with me," he said, and stepped back to allow her to swing her legs over the edge of the trolley. The world spun wildly, and she grabbed at the trolley's rails, grimly hanging on until everything stopped moving. When her balance had stabilized, she carefully stood up, using the stand holding the drip next to the bed for balance. It was only then that she discovered she was wearing some sort of dark-blue overalls, although she couldn't remember putting them on. It was another minute before she felt able to take her first step, and even then, her weakness ensured she kept a firm grip on the stand. On her second step, however, her right leg started to shake, and she had stop for a moment until she felt able to take another, careful step.

She progressed slowly, propelling the stand holding the drip before her, until she reached the doorway. The corridor seemed newer than the room she'd been held in, all sharp corners and vertical walls, rather than the gentle slump of the walls in the room behind her. She wondered if it had been built on. The toilets were at the end of the corridor. The door to the female toilets was wedged open, and given the boxes and buckets stacked up against the far wall it was obvious it was being used as a storeroom.

When her escort tried to follow her through the door, she shook her head. "No. You stay outside."

He frowned. Then he jerked his head at the door. "Leave it open."

She was fidgeting, almost crossing her legs now so she was in no position to argue.

The cubicle was out of direct sight of the guard and quickly wriggling the overalls down, she squeezed past the stepladder, and the bucket and pail leaning against the wall inside the cubicle and sat down to relieve herself. As she stretched her right leg out, she found her gaze following the ladder up to the ceiling which consisted of narrow plaster panels set into thin metal straps in a rectangular pattern.

"Oh *please*," she muttered.

Finished, she yanked the catheter out of her arm, shrugged herself back into her overalls, then flushed the toilet. Under cover of the noise of the toilet, she swung the cubicle door closed and flicked the lock to occupied. After opening the stepladder she jammed one end under the door, grabbed the mop as a possible weapon, and started to climb.

Five rungs later her right leg had begun to shake again, and it was clear adrenaline was only going to take her so far, but she was now high enough to push the panel out of the way and shove the mop through the gap. For a moment she paused, then, grasping both sides of the hole, she hoisted herself up, into the narrow space beyond.

There was barely enough room to fit below the roof, and she could now see that the ceiling on which she crouched consisted of thin metal beams suspended by rods fastened to the overhead beams. Behind her, a brick wall blocked off access to the older part of the building, including the room she'd woken up in. A sudden shout from below warned her that her escape had been detected.

Cautiously she started to make her way across the ceiling, carrying the mop, and holding onto the overhead beams with her free hand. The struts groaned and swayed alarmingly under her as she did so. She'd reached the far side of the cavity when she heard a noise behind her and looked back to see that the guard had managed to join her in the ceiling space and was now moving tentatively across the space toward her. She giggled at the thought of what would happen if he caught up with her. There was no way the ceiling would support them both. In fact it was questionable if it was going to support *her* for much longer, which gave her an idea. Taking a deep breath, she smashed her foot down on the tile just in front of her. The plaster tile shattered and, dropping the mop through the hole, she grasped the sides of the panel's frame and lowered herself into the space beyond.

It was only when she was hanging from her arms from the bars that she realized she couldn't see anything. There was a dim, blue light coming from somewhere out of sight behind her but the rest of the room below her was in darkness. She couldn't even see the floor below her. A tremor racked her body and as one of her hands gave way, she closed her eyes and opened her fingers. She had time to realize the floor was a lot farther away than she'd thought, before she landed and her ankle gave way under her. She collapsed, and momentarily disorientated, simply lay there until her pursuer shone a torch down on her through the hole in the ceiling. At least he didn't look as though he was preparing to follow her. The drop must be at least twenty feet, but his shouts would already be bringing others.

She started to straighten, then stopped, shocked. Directly in front of her, only ten yards away, was the swirling chaos of a portal! So that was how they'd got her here, wherever 'here' was. It was only a small portal, about the size of a door, but if she could get to it, she could at least get back to her own line. She could hear someone banging on a locked door behind her, trying to break in, and she knew she didn't have long. Picking up the mop, she gritted her teeth and hobbled as quickly as she could toward the portal, throwing herself forward into the portal's shimmering curtain of light.

She fell out of the portal on the other side onto her hands and knees. Using the mop as a crutch she struggled to her feet. She felt a sharp stab of pain from her ankle and gasped. Her breath misted into the frigid air, and her hair crackled and rose as the air hummed with suppressed power.

She was alone, at least for the moment, in a long, thin, stone-lined room. Tables lined both sides of the space, their surfaces crowded with screens and oscilloscopes. The walls were of age-darkened stone, lit by three small lights that hung from old metal torch holders, the lights' cables strung along the wall between the brackets like something from a 30s B-grade horror movie. There were some empty alcoves cut into the walls about head height. Perhaps they had once housed statutory. The whole room appeared ad hoc and jerry built; nothing seemed to match, which left her wondering where she was. It seemed impossible that someone from Sultan would have cobbled together something like this. Surely even the anarchists would have managed a better job! Under her bare feet the stones were already leaching the heat from her body. She shivered, and paused to wait for her right leg to stop shaking.

When the tremors eased, she cast her eyes hopefully over the portal's power cables, but they were too thick to cut. The cables snaked their way under the tables on her right to disappear through an open doorway, and into what appeared to be a dimly lit corridor beyond. She needed to start moving. It wouldn't be long before someone came through the portal. Just where the hell was Carlos? She didn't want to start depending on him, but surely if he was going to turn up with a squad of ImpSec goons now would be the time to do it. She had started to hobble toward the open doorway when something made her pause and look back.

Whatever she had done to her ankle meant that she couldn't outrun those who would come through the portal at any moment. But what if there was something *behind* the portal? Reversing direction, she peered around the portal's massive metal frame. Yes! There was a door set into the wall, with a table pushed up against it. She hobbled over to it and tried the door handle. It moved, but she had to work the table away from the wall before she could pull the door open enough to squeeze through it and into the corridor outside.

Easing the door closed behind her she found herself in a broad, roofed area with enormous carved pillars that marched off in serried ranks into the distance. Overhead a series of smoke stained stone vaults linked the pillars into a sequence of continuous arches. Between the arches the walls were pierced by the shattered remains of small, circular, openings. The light that leaked in around the broken glass of the openings seemed shuttered and dim, as though from a New York winter day rather than early autumn. And the cold! It clawed at her nose, her breath steaming with every wheeze as she sucked the cold air into her lungs. The soles of her feet and toes were already numb from the biting cold.

Something about the carved columns struck a chord, and she squinted, trying to get a better look. She traced a curve up one column to where it swept out to support the roof. Recognizing a wing, memory started to nag at her as she finally made out the leering face of the stone demon staring down at her. And then another demon caught her eye, and a frisson of fear ran down her spine as she felt the hair on the back of her neck begin to rise in ancestral memory. It couldn't be — but with that thought came the cold fear of certainty. The crypt at Naisre on the Mainline. She'd seen photographs in a book on those who had come through the first portal, leaving their dying world behind them. This was Nayarit!

The frozen statues seemed to delight in her shock. One of them even appeared to wink at her. She bent over, trying to control the spasms that gripped her. It was only stone! If she was on Nayarit, that meant she had escaped into even greater danger. But how could it be? The first portal had been established on America's east-coast. She didn't think she had been knocked out for that long!

As the tremors slowly eased, she straightened carefully. She couldn't stay here to freeze to death, and she couldn't go back. And yet this was a dead line. Everyone knew that. Unfortunately, no one appeared to have told those who had built the portal. Pulling the thin cotton of the overalls tighter around her she started to hobble toward what passed as the sun on this line. Her ankle didn't seem to be hurting as much but she certainly wasn't prepared to put any real weight on it. At least she could see what this building looked like from outside.

The sun was approaching the horizon by the time she reached the outer edge of the building. In the gathering darkness her neck continued to prickle from the gaze of the demons carved into the columns high over her head. Just what type of religion would frighten their flock? And yet that was precisely what was intended. A reminder, as her mother had explained it, of what would happen if the priests failed in their prayers and the demons escaped the abyss. Mythical or not, the statues gave her the creeps.

Outside the air was sodden with a heavy mist. From what she could see though, the ground surrounding the temple was bare, broken shale, with only the occasional, stunted, lichen-covered shrub to break the monotony. She couldn't feel her feet now, the cold had leached up her legs, and she was shivering so hard her teeth were chattering. Something she had thought, up to now, was only a figure of speech. She considered returning to the portal, but if she did that, she doubted she'd ever have another chance to escape. With visibility now down to ten feet she decided to strike out, away from the building.

The ground was rough, littered with loose stones, and continued to rise steeply as she struggled up the slope, picking her way through the worst of the shale, trying to avoid cutting her feet. The handle of the mop slipped on the mist covered rock. She reversed the mop, but it didn't help much. She couldn't feel anything now; her feet were completely numb, with the cold continuing to creep up her calves. It wasn't long before she was moving in shrouded, eerie darkness. She didn't know if that was the mist, or the fact that the world was actually dead. Whatever the answer she needed to find some sort of protection, or the question would become moot.

Darkness had descended by the time the ground began to level out, and she faced the problem that if she continued to push on, she ran the risk of becoming completely lost, yet remaining where she was, would be just as dangerous. Her teeth were continuously chattering now, and she was physically shaking from the cold, the moisture in the air continuing to wick out any warmth she had in her body. If she couldn't find shelter, she wouldn't survive the night.

She felt her way forward, one step at a time. She didn't know how long she'd been doing that, but her steps were becoming shorter, and the breaks between each movement longer. Finally, she saw what seemed to be a darker shadow to one side, and with what remained of her energy she struggled over to it. It turned out to a concrete wall. She didn't know how high it was, but it wasn't the temple with its demon guards. As though that were a signal, something called from the darkness, a howling, whistling cry that momentarily froze her. Gritting her teeth, she worked her way along the wall until she came to what might be a doorway. A panel was set into the wall next to it, with a numeric keypad. But the panel remained dead when she pressed it. As her last hope deserted her, she sank to the ground, her back sliding down the metal of the door, and closed her eyes.

41

When You're Older

(Monday: Nayarit)

"Are you sure this is a good idea?" Julpe asked, trying to hold himself steady as Kenefer balanced on his shoulders and peered into the control box next to the airlock. A roach, serving as Kenefer's link to Xipil, hung suspended from the top edge of the box, blocking Julpe's view of what the cat was doing.

"If I wasn't, do you think I'd be doing this?" Kenefer snapped.

"It's just that Mama said —"

"I know what your mother said. Your mother obviously had enormous sense . . . it is dangerous outside, but we don't have any choice." Kenefer dubiously poked a wire with a claw before reaching farther into the box. "We need to get inside the command area and have a look. Unfortunately, there are only two tunnels that are still open, and there are airlocks on both. Xipil hasn't been able to slip a single roach in. The only way in is via the surface. Now let me concentrate."

Julpe tried to ignore Kenefer's weight, and the pain he'd been feeling in his back for the past ten minutes. Kenefer was heavy. When he'd learned he was a member of the *Ejejatl,* the priestly caste, Julpe had imagined he wouldn't have to do this sort of thing anymore. It all seemed completely unfair.

"Done!" Kenefer said and leaped down to the ground. She stretched and arched her back. "Besides," she said when she'd finished. "I got Mirror to double check all the atmosphere tests myself. And it's not as though we're in America."

"We're not?"

Kenefer looked up at him, askance. "No, we're not."

"Then where are we?"

"England."

"And the difference is?"

"The difference is they are different countries." She sensed his confusion. "A country is a group of cities."

"And where's America?" He had become so intent on asking his questions that when the door of the airlock opened, he followed Kenefer into the small room beyond without thinking. As the door closed behind them, he flinched and looked around uneasily. It was cold in the room, and his breath frosted in the air in front of him as he breathed. There was a small window set into the door on the far side of the room. The glass was thick and heavily scarred and knowing that it opened onto the outside had him staying as far back from it as possible.

"It's on the other side of the ocean and no, I'm not going to play a thousand questions." She lashed her tail.

Julpe was about to ask what a thousand questions was when he realized he probably had a pretty good idea.

"Press the panel and open the door," Kenefer said.

Oh, so now he was useful, was he? "No, not until you tell me how you know it's safe."

Kenefer started to raise a paw, showing her claws. Then she seemed to think better of it and sat down to consider him for a moment. Julpe watched her warily.

"All right," she said, flicking her tail across her front paws.

"Just like that?"

"Yes." She scratched an ear with a back paw then sat up straighter. "The mother must teach her kits, and as your mother is dead, I guess I will have to. But first, tell me what you know of the history of your people."

"Why?" he asked suspiciously.

"Because if I'm going to have to explain why it's safe, I need to understand what you already know."

Julpe thought about it for a moment. That seemed to make sense.

"And sit down," Kenefer told him. "You're hurting my neck."

Julpe sat down and crossed his legs, placing his hands face up on his knees as he'd seen the storytellers do, took a deep breath, then paused. "What should I tell you?" he asked.

The tip of her tail twitched. "Why don't you tell me what you know of the creation myth."

"In the beginning," Julpe began, his voice unconsciously adopting the sing-song cadence of the old storyteller who had first told him the story, "the gods warred endlessly with the demons who had dragged themselves from the abyss. The gods were powerful, but the demons were beyond numbers. In time, only one god remained — the Sun-blessed-one. But the Sun-blessed-one did not possess enough strength to drive the demons back into the abyss by himself. Yet if he did not the demons would win, and the end of days would descend on the Earth. In time a solution came to him and the Sun-blessed-one lay with the Hutanga, the People of the Grass. From his progeny he selected those who by the power of prayer could dispel the darkness and drive the demons back into the abyss. Pleased with his creations he named them *Ejejatl* and marked them so they would forever be recognized. Then he created the *Tletl*, the *Atl*, and the *Tlalli*, the three castes, to support the Ejejatl in their endless struggle. Then, with the power of his own death, the Sun-blessed-one sealed the demons in the abyss."

Kenefer gave a slow nod. "And then what happened?"

"But then in time the demons found allies among the dissatisfied and while the evil Han rained fire down from the heavens the lowest, and those without caste, the *Tlalli* and *Macehualli*, led by the thrice-dammed Secularists rose up against those who struggled to maintain the seals and in the battle the Earth was destroyed."

Kenefer curled her top lip. "I suppose that is not *too* far from what really happened, although the Secularists were not the complete devils they're made out to be. Admittedly they did want to abolish the caste system and establish a demarchy, which didn't exactly make them popular with those on the top of the pile, but Xipil has certainly spoken quite positively of some she met."

"But Xipil is a priestess, and the Secularists wanted to kill all the priests!"

"Like all groups they had their extremists. But Xipil follows the teachings of Theresa, so she's a little more flexible about these sorts of things."

"Was Theresa a Secularist?" he asked, confused.

"Goodness no. She was a priestess. Some of her ideas were later suppressed as heresy but generally she's considered one of the great reformers. She died just under three thousand years ago, but even back then she believed the caste system needed to be reformed. And if Theresa thought it was bad then, consider what's happened to it over the last three thousand years."

Julpe sulked. He'd only found out that he was one of the *Ejejatl*, the caste at the top of the pile, and now he was told the pile was rotten.

"But you were certainly right about the Han," Kenefer said, starting to wash her face. "About two hundred years ago the Han launched a pre-emptive nuclear strike on the Nayarit Confederacy and its European allies. Unfortunately for the Han it wasn't 'pre-emptive' enough and the ensuring nuclear exchange resulted in a worldwide nuclear winter. Eventually rationing and abuse of the caste system in America led to a Secularist uprising that plunged the entire Commonwealth into civil war. England managed to avoid a lot of the damage America faced because their uprising was put down within a year. In America though, as far as Xipil can gather, it lasted for over seventy years, meaning the consequences were considerably worse than here."

"Why?"

"Why what?" She paused in her cleaning to look up at him. "Why did the war last so long in America?"

"I was going to ask how anything could be worse than here," Julpe said. "Although I'd like to hear the answers to both." For the first time in his life, he realized how much he didn't know.

Kenefer looked at the door then back to Julpe. "We need to leave soon," she warned him. "The temperature falls quickly at night, and you're hardly dressed for it. And the roaches would be totally useless."

He nodded.

Kenefer straightened herself. "There had been a coup by Techna nobles just before the Han attacked, which meant that the Naisre Commonwealth was 'converted' into an Empire, and that may have — Now what?" she demanded as Julpe raised his hand, her tail flicking in frustration.

"What, or who were Techna?"

"Techna is a country on the far side of America. No," she said, as Julpe started to raise his hand. "I'll show you a map, a drawing of where everything is when we're back. All you need to know for now is that the Techna nobles were a bunch of inbred cultists. Always had been. Seriously hung up on the divine right to rule. It was the Techna that invaded and conquered the

Han about thirty three thousand years ago, and it was probably the thought of that bunch of deviants back in charge of the Commonwealth that triggered the Han's attack. In their place I'm not sure I wouldn't have done the same thing. But even without the war, the Commonwealth —"

"I thought you said it was an empire?"

"— or Empire as it then became," Kenefer said with a warning stare, "were already on the path to self-destruction. Especially given that the new Emperor immediately demonstrated all the worst excesses of the 9th Dynasty, and none of its graces."

"What sort of excesses?"

"When you're older!" She narrowed her eyes at him, exactly as his sister did when she didn't want to answer a question. "But those excesses," she continued, "coupled with rumors that the new Emperor and his family had been provided with prohibited longevity technology, fed air to the fire of revolution. And that, coupled with those who'd had been edged out of the political center, meant that the secularist uprising had significant support from a number of groups who would normally have been expected to uphold the status quo."

"But why does that mean America is more dangerous than here?" Julpe asked, getting back to his original question.

The cat sighed. "Because the initial uprising was more successful there. The Secularist had access to many of the resources of the State, and certainly many of the population centers. So the weapons that had been intended for the Han were turned on the Empire. After seventy plus years of civil war there simply wasn't much left that could be described as life existing outside the domes, and if it hadn't been for the development of the K-Virus there wouldn't have been much in the way of life in the domes either. Then when the domes collapsed ..."

"Collapsed?"

"Someone developed a bacterium that broke down the rubber seals on the airlocks. It would have been a perfect weapon to have ended the war if it could have identified friend from foe. Unfortunately, it couldn't, although it did end the war, just not quite as planned."

"So, what happened here? I mean ..." He trailed off uncertainly.

"Just because the Secularist uprising was suppressed relatively quickly doesn't mean that England avoided the consequences of the nuclear winter, or whatever else leaked across the Atlantic. What it did mean was that once the initial uprising was suppressed the government was able to put all of its resources into building the shelters. This was actually one of the biggest. And now," she said, standing up and looking significantly at the panel, "we have work to do."

Reluctantly Julpe got up, unable to put it off any longer. Taking a deep breath, he closed his eyes and pressed his hand down on the panel. He heard the door grind open, and a chill wind gusted in around him, sharp and bitter. As he opened his eyes, he was stunned to find Kenefer sniffing at a body lying across the doorstep.

"I told you it was dangerous," Julpe said. "How long has she been dead?" he asked, hoping he wasn't going to have to touch her.

"She's not," Kenefer said, her ears pressed back to her skull, her tail bristling.

42

THE HUNT IS ON

(Monday Sultan Line)

"Zeki Miralay, the Kaymakan will see you now."

"Thank you," Zeki said, and as Emre's aide closed the door behind him Zeki came to attention tiredly.

Emre waved him toward a seat at the small table that had been shoehorned into the office he was presently occupying. "Can I offer you coffee?"

"Thank you." Like everyone else the Miralay had been operating on too little sleep, and too much caffeine since the attack.

"Coffee, Tulsa," Emre called loudly, then leaned forward. "I'll get straight to the point, Zeki. We think we know where the terrorists are. Or at least what line they're operating on."

"Where?"

"Nayarit."

Zeki frowned. "I've heard the name before, but . . ."

"It's the line where the Hraffor came from to conquer the Mainline."

"I thought it was dead."

"Apparently not."

"So, what are we doing?"

251

"*You* are off to Vienna. Your task is to establish a base on Nayarit via portal." Zeki nodded, as he accepted the cup Emre's aide handed him and took a cautious sip. "What have I got?"

"I'm still working on that. Your primary mission is to give us that forward base, but if you can identify where those jackals are hiding so much the better. I'm not holding my breath on that though; they have a whole world to hide on. And something else, the Vizier, and the C-T E's First Leader have decided this will be a joint operation."

"Oh wonderful, that worked so well during the last war."

Emre opened his hands placatingly. "The C-T E have not stinged on their aid this time."

"True," Zeki said.

Emre grinned evilly. "You should also know, though, that her most exalted majesty, Queen Victoire of the Angevin Empire is also making noises of providing support. She has taken the suborning of her intelligence service as a personal slight."

Zeki inhaled the coffee and exploded into racking coughs.

Emre gave him a moment to recover and catch his breath, then dropped the final bombshell. "I have a phone call scheduled with Colonel Randolph Scott of the Angevin Royal Marines this afternoon to discuss joint operations."

(Wednesday Etu Line)

Sonja stood at parade-ease, back ramrod straight, and stared at a spot just above the left shoulder of the Group Leader on the other side of the desk. Just why in all the shades had a Stores Officer in 'Stores and Victualing' been ordered to present with all her kit to the depot of the Clemhorn Rangers?

The Group Leader finished his perusal of her file. "Trooper Sonja Hawk."

She found herself straightening even more. "Sir."

"Your record says you enlisted with the Usurper's Mujahedeen during the war."

"Yes, sir?" she asked cautiously.

"And yet you refused demobilization when the regiment was disbanded. Why?"

"Because I wanted a career, sir."

"In Stores?" His tone was dry.

"It wasn't quite what I was expecting," she admitted.

"And five years without advancement — not much of a career."

"No, sir. There is a certain amount of understandable . . . prejudice against someone with my background."

He gave a non-committal grunt and returned his gaze to the file in front of him. "I understand you're fluent in Arabic?"

"It's a bit rusty, but —"

"And you drove a PAC during the war?"

"Yes, sir." Just where was this going?

He sighed. "Trooper Hawk, today is your lucky day."

"It is?"

He smiled. "You're aware of the situation on Sultan? I'm sure the news of the terrorist attack on Pesh has penetrated even into the recesses of Stores and Victualing."

"Yes sir. A million dead or wounded."

"Indeed. What you may not be aware of is that a force is being assembled with the intention of destroying those responsible. A joint force, Trooper, consisting of detachments from Sultan, the Mainline, and Etu. And the Rangers will be representing Etu."

She looked dubious.

"I suspect that you are now wondering how this decision affects a certain Trooper Sonja Hawk. As it happens High Command has decided in all its collective wisdom, that the detachment requires the services of a Squad Leader who can speak Arabic and is comfortable with motorized transport. And as it turns out you are the only soldier on Etu with those very specific qualifications."

"Sir, I'm not —"

"A Squad Leader? Yes, a mere trifle." He reached into his desk and produced two new shoulder-boards, and what looked like a Ranger's shoulder insignia. "Welcome to the Rangers, Acting Squad Leader Hawk. We're leaving in two days. Report to Sergeant Doughlas and get yourself kitted out, then take twenty-four hours leave."

"Sir," she squeaked.

"And don't disappoint me, Hawk."

"Sir, no sir!" she said, quickly recovering.

"Dismissed."

Outside the office she stood there a moment, stunned, then with a grin so broad it made her cheeks ache she headed off to find Sergeant Doughlas.

Thank you for reading FOR THE HONOR OF THE EMPIRE.
We hope you enjoyed it.

If you would like to be kept informed of further releases from
Hague Publishing why not subscribe to our newsletter at:

www.HaguePublishing.com/subscribe.php

And if you loved the book and have a moment to spare we
would really appreciate a short review. Your help in spreading
the word is gratefully received.

Now read on for an extract from:

FOR HONOR ALONE

BOOK 3 in *The Honor Series*

1

EXTRACT FROM
FOR HONOR ALONE

My Apologies My Lord Chamberlain

(Three Years Before —— Nayarit Line)

Xipil could still taste the bitter stink of the fire at the back of her throat, but at least the drugs they'd given her had killed the pain now. She could hear the quiet murmur of people around her, their voices faint and indistinct.

"This might hurt," a nurse warned her.

She wanted to scream denial. This shouldn't be happening. She hadn't been one of those selected, but the attack had disrupted all their plans. She felt the cold liquid entering her veins, a frigid wave moving up her arm, and with the last of her strength she grasped Margot's hand.

She woke from a disturbed, dream-filled sleep. For a while she lay there, eyes closed, trying to remember. She could remember the attack, the pain of the flames, and Margot's hand clutching hers, then nothing. She tried to open her eyes, but it was as though . . . she had to think what it felt like . . . it was as though her muscles had forgotten how to obey her. And there was something else, she could hear . . . breathing. It was a moment before she realized it was her own.

"Hello?" she tried, to be rewarded by a bare whisper.

"You're awake?" someone said. She didn't recognize the voice, but it was young and female, and sounded relieved.

"Can't move," she whispered.

"Hold on," the voice told her.

She felt a wet cloth pressed to her lips and sucked.

"What's your name?" she asked, as the cloth was removed to wet again.

"Mirror."

"Highness?"

Xipil jerked awake. "My apologies, my Lord Chamberlain," she said, tiredly squeezing the bridge of her nose. "You were saying?"

"Perhaps we should defer the rest of my report?" the small man said with a sympathetic smile. "I heard the princess didn't sleep well last night."

"The princess didn't sleep at all," the Empress said dryly. Her husband, sitting next to her, nodded his agreement, then covered his mouth to hide a yawn.

"But she is all right now?" the chamberlain asked.

"Sleeping like a baby," the Empress' Consort said. "Apparently, the trip to the park overstimulated her and we couldn't get her to settle."

"I can remember my first," the chamberlain said understandingly.

"Yes, well, you'd think that after a thousand years of watching other people's babies I'd be able to manage my own," Xipil said.

"I imagine that regardless of how many babies you watch, you're not prepared for your own," her husband said fondly.

Xipil nodded her reluctant agreement. She had wanted a baby but, until she met Edrai, had found no one she had wanted to have a baby with and had despaired of ever finding someone. The thought of artificial insemination had no particular appeal, and her oath to the order meant that she was unprepared for casual sex. She had considered adoption, but she had wanted her own child, someone of her own flesh and blood (or at least genetic programming) and then Edrai had led an Embassy to Earth. An ambassador from the Qunintain Confederacy, he was young and brilliant, with glorious green eyes and long, long legs that harked back to the time before her uplift. And he had cared about *her*, Xipil, not the Undying Empress and so they had married. At the memory of the ceremony, she reached out and gently squeezed his hand.

"Regardless," she said. "I would rather get this out of the way."

"As would I," the chamberlain admitted. "The celebrations for your millennium year are now less than three years away. And I feel grievously unprepared."

"We could cancel," Xipil offered hopefully.

"Majesty, don't even joke about it!"

"I wasn't joking," Xipil muttered.

"Majesty!" the chamberlain protested.

"Sweetheart," her husband said, patting her gently on the hand. "Please don't bait the chamberlain."

"Fine," she said, settling back into her throne. "Continue."

"As I was saying, in relation to the opening ceremony, we have received a request from the Centauri ambassador for permission to increase the official party."

"By how many?"

The chamberlain checked his papers. "They want to include another five hundred."

"So, doubling it?" She shook her head. "No. Transfer fees and security costs are already bad enough; let's not move into crippling, otherwise we'll be paying this party off for the next thousand years. If they want to send more people, they can pay for them themselves."

"I thought you'd say that," the chamberlain said with a smile.

And so it went. Finally, the chamberlain leaned back and closed the screen on his tablet. "That's it, my lady."

"For now," Xipil said dryly. "As always, your advice is much appreciated, but for the moment I believe my husband and I have some sleep owing to us."

"Of course, Highnesses," he said, standing.

Xipil followed him to the doors of the chamber, her husband a couple of paces behind them. As the doors slid open at their approach, Xipil's attention was caught by the guard standing stationary on the far side of the doors, with the empty audience chamber beyond him. "Priscus," she said, pleased to see him.

"Highness?" the chamberlain said uncertainly.

She gestured at the Imperial Marine in his steel-gray dress uniform standing motionless before them, his eyes fixed on the space just above her head

The chamberlain looked puzzled.

"Priscus," she repeated.

"I'm sorry, Highness. Priscus?"

"Our Captain of the Guard."

"What is it?" her husband asked, joining them.

The chamberlain's gaze moved uncertainly between them.

"Our chamberlain appears to have forgotten our Captain of the Guard," Xipil said perhaps more sharply than she intended, but she was tired. She looked at Priscus apologetically, but his gaze remained fixed on the same spot above her head. She turned to see what he was looking at, to find nothing there.

"Sweet?" her husband said, concerned.

She turned back to find that Priscus had not moved at all. She felt a frisson of fear. He could just as well have been a statue cast in carbonite.

"Priscus, he's just there," she said, pointing at him, but as her husband's eyes slid past the marine, he too shook his head.

"There's no one there," he said. "And who is this Priscus?"

"The Captain of the Guard," she said, eyes fixed on the frozen marine.

"Xipil, Xila, is the Captain of the Guard." He indicated the marine approaching them from across the empty chamber. "She's been the Captain for" – he blinked three times – "the last ten years."

The chamberlain nodded his agreement, but Xipil shook her head in denial. Her memory might not be infallible. After a thousand years there could often be a strong sense of déjà vu at times, but she distinctly remembered showing Priscus to her daughter just last week. She reached out to touch the marine's arm, but her hand closed on empty space. She stared, horrified, at her hand and at the marine who continued to stand frozen in front of them. "You can't see him?"

"Highness?" Xila said uncertainly as she reached them.

Xipil backed slowly away from them – something wasn't right. "I need to do something."

"Xipil?" her husband said, worriedly.

"I'll see you back in our quarters," she told him. Before anyone could say anything she started for the elevator at the back of the meeting room.

The door slid open at her approach. "Study," she said, ignoring the control panel.

The elevator dropped smoothly, quickly descending below the palace's public levels, and beyond it to the original level that predated the palace above. As the doors slid open again and she saw the small wood paneled room she let out a small sigh of relief – it was still there. Leaving the elevator, she stepped into a room that was on no plan of the palace, because it wasn't precisely part of the palace.

Wooden doors swung closed behind her. The study was lined with bookshelves on three sides, the roof at a height that to reach the top shelf she needed a small step. A mirror in an ornate wooden frame was set centered on the remaining wall. An old-style wooden desk was positioned in the center of the room facing the mirror. There was an intercom box on one corner of the desk, three pencils and a pad of lined paper placed slightly off-center. A computer screen and an old-style physical keyboard were the only other items on the desk. An adjustable chair had been pushed up against the desk.

Crossing to the mirror, she studied her reflection, which showed that of a young woman, pretty, but not beautiful, with short black hair. Finally, she had to acknowledge she was procrastinating. "Mirror, I need to speak with you."

The mirror shimmered, and its surface now showed another room.

A young oriental girl, with long curly orange hair and impossibly large eyes, was seated behind a desk. She looked up; her gaze sharpening as she recognized Xipil.

"Xipil," Mirror said in obviously pretended surprise. "It's been a while."

"Not that long."

"One hundred and twenty point five years, to be precise."

"Really?" Xipil frowned, trying to remember when she had actually visited last.

"Really," Mirror assured her seriously. "My congratulations on the birth of your daughter."

The memory of her daughter brought a smile to Xipil's face before she remembered the purpose of the visit. "So, what's going on?"

"Going on?" Mirror repeated guiltily.

Xipil simply looked at her.

"I was going to contact you," Mirror said.

"I'm glad to hear that," Xipil said dryly. "Perhaps you could tell me what you were going to tell me about."

"I've prepared a report," Mirror said hopefully.

"I'm also glad to hear that. And what does that report say?"

Mirror chewed on her bottom lip in the first sign of indecision that Xipil had ever seen in the AI.

"Mirror," Xipil warned her.

"That we have a problem," Mirror admitted. "I think you need to come over."

Xipil felt the hairs on the back of her neck rise in alarm. "Are you sure?"

Mirror nodded.

To leave, after all this time . . . But Mirror would not suggest that unless there was no alternative. That was what she had promised. Xipil swallowed. "You'll need to remind me how," she managed.

"Just close your eyes," Mirror said softly.

Xipil closed her eyes, then shivered. It might have been some subtle change in the air pressure, or temperature, but she knew she was no longer in the palace; was no longer even on the same planet. Some subtle memory of the first time she had been here brought back memories of her first awakening, the stink of the smoke still clinging to the back of her throat.

"You can open your eyes now," Mirror prompted.

Xipil opened her eyes to find that she was now standing in the room she had seen through the mirror, but now another chair awaited her before the desk. Mutely Mirror waved her into it.

"So, what's so serious you needed to pull me out?" Xipil asked, taking the chair and leaning forward.

"We're losing people."

"Priscus?"

Mirror nodded.

"You said – people. How many have you lost?"

"In the last two years, close to thirty-five million."

"Thirty-five *million*!"

"Given the population of the Empire, that's still less than half a percent," Mirror said defensively. . . .

Xipil winced. "Let's stick with the thirty-five million. You know I have a problem understanding percentages. More importantly, how could you *lose* thirty-five million people?"

"Well, I'm not exactly losing them."

Xipil looked at her.

"Something is affecting the computer's quantum memory store."

"Quantum memory?" Xipil repeated, not having the foggiest what Mirror was talking about.

Mirror rolled her eyes. "Look, you know what this is?" She held out her hand and a computer chip materialized on it.

"A computer chip?" Xipil guessed.

"Very good. And this . . ." A much smaller chip materialized next to the first, glowing with a faint blue light. "This is a quantum chip. It can hold one thousand times as much information as ordinary silicon memory. But it turns out that it's more susceptible to certain kinds of damage." The glow surrounding the small chip flickered, and died.

"So, what's causing the damage?"

"According to the simulations, something like this." Mirror closed her hand and when she opened it again the chips had been replaced by a disk of white fire with a black center that rotated slowly around itself, just above her hand. A second disk, linked to the first by a thin column of pure, white light, rotated above it in the opposite direction. Mirror observed them with a smile.

"And what's that?" Xipil asked, frustration tingeing her voice.

"Guess."

"Mirror!"

"You're no fun," Mirror complained. "It's a wormhole. According to my simulations, the most probable source for the damage I'm experiencing are random quantum effects within the event horizon of a black hole."

"A black hole! Are you serious?"

"Afraid so. At least the sort of quantum effects we're looking at dissipate quickly with distance, so it's got to be close. What!" Mirror demanded, noticing Xipil's face. "You've been using black holes to power your wormholes between systems."

"Mirror, I live in a virtual world!"

"A world based on projections of real-world physics."

"What are you talking about?"

"Xipil, I couldn't just make things up," Mirror said sincerely. "That would be magic. Besides, starting from the real world allowed me to reduce the computational resources that would have been required to create a whole new universe."

"So, what you're saying is that Nayarit could actually build wormholes to other systems."

"Well, it's a little more complicated than that. I mean Nayarit as a nation no longer exists, but the theory is sound, and given that someone appears to be operating some sort of gate nearby it certainly appears plausible."

"So, these 'black holes' are what's affecting your quantum memory?" Xipil asked, trying to get her head around what Mirror was telling her.

Mirror gave her an encouraging nod. She waved her hand and the wormhole disappeared to be replaced by a small hologram of a middle-aged woman wearing coveralls and a hard hat. The woman came to attention and gave Xipil a low bow.

"Meet Jane Dawson. She was the first to go."

Jane's face melted, sloughing off the underlying bone.

"The quantum effects result in damage to the individual character matrices. In most cases, the injury is self-limiting, but in other cases it can cause a complete disintegration of the character, with resulting damage to all those who knew them."

Jane's figure abruptly shattered into a million glittering pieces.

"Initially, I tried to repair the damage as it was occurring, but it was taking too long. The easiest solution was to lock out the damaged characters and to suppress or replace the memories of those who knew them."

"You couldn't try a restore?"

Mirror shook her head. "There's nothing to restore from. The world has been running so long and has grown so big that I've had to use the matrices originally intended for backup for main-time functioning."

Xipil frowned. "But what I saw with Priscus doesn't sound as though it fits the bill."

"That's because you were uploaded rather than artificially created. The Whole Brain Emulation has a separate matrix and backup. There's a level of complexity with you that means I'm simply not prepared to take the risk of fiddling with your memory. What you saw was an echo of Priscus."

"So, what are you going to do?" Xipil demanded, affronted that Mirror had even considered suppressing her memories. Once you started with that, where did you stop? She didn't like the idea of anyone having their memories doctored, but in this case the consequences of *not* doing that could be worse.

Mirror looked embarrassed. "I can't do anything. My programming has significant limitations built in that limit my ability to operate in or to affect the real world. If not for that I would already have been able to expand the memory matrix and we probably wouldn't be facing this problem. You, on the other hand . . ."

Xipil nodded, not really surprised. She had not left the world Mirror had created for her for over a thousand years, so for Mirror to have pulled her back into the 'real' world meant that any solution had to involve her.

"What do I have to do?"

"You need to find out where the disruption is coming from and stop it."

"And just *how* am I supposed to do that? If you've forgotten, I don't actually have a physical presence outside." She indicated her surroundings.

Mirror held up a hand. "No, you're right, you need helpers and I've already downloaded all the information your military and terra-forming departments have developed in DNA manipulation over the past thousand years."

"And just what am I supposed to do with *that*?"

Mirror actually grinned. "Before your Order took over the facilities to progress the 'upload project' they'd been used as a military research facility into genetically modifying animals to serve as military assets. I did, in fact, actually use their research as a basis for your own military laboratories. Therefore, the tools you need are already here."

"And they still work?" Xipil said disbelievingly. "They haven't been turned on for over a thousand years?"

"It's only been two hundred years in the outside world – you've been running on a fast clock of five to one. And when the military mothballed the facility, they wanted to ensure it could be turned on again."

Xipil frowned. She'd forgotten the fast clock thing; or perhaps she'd never been told?

"I've already ensured the links to the labs are functioning," Mirror continued, "and I've updated the communication protocols to provide you with access to the lab's tele-manipulators. As far as I can gauge, most of the facilities appear functional with minimum work."

"So, what, I need to grow some 'agents?'"

Mirror nodded. "Any ideas?"

"Perhaps start small?" Xipil considered the matter for a couple of minutes. "What are those things called my Empire used for exploration on new worlds? Roaches?"

"Sagitarian Roaches?"

Xipil considered the idea further, then nodded. The roaches, about the size of dinner plates, had been developed for First-In-Teams to serve as mobile environment testers. Hardy, they could operate in a far wider range of environments than their human masters. And with an inbuilt organic transmitter/receiver, that while having only an individual range of less than twenty yards, could be extended indefinately as they could pass messages between themselves in a rudimentary 'net,' making their final range restricted only by their numbers.

"How's this going to work, then?" she asked.

"I've built a virtual model of the labs," Mirror said. "Items that duplicate actual items in the real world have a soft halo effect. Here —" she turned the screen on her desk around so Xipil could see that there was in fact a soft blur of color around the edge of the screen. "I've placed the memory matrix into stasis and —"

"Stasis, already? I need to say goodbye?"

Mirror looked apologetic but defiant. "No, it was too dangerous. There's a higher static charge applied to the matrix when in stasis which should protect it. But I needed to do it as soon as I brought you through."

Xipil froze. Not to say goodbye to Edrai, and to their daughter. She wanted to protest, to tell Mirror she couldn't do this. But she knew that if she went back, she might risk their very existence and she couldn't, wouldn't do that. But to do what Mirror wanted her to do, without saying goodbye . . . But she was the Undying Empress, and if her one thousand years had taught her nothing else, it was that she *could* keep going, no matter what the consequences, no matter what the losses. And in this case, if she was successful, she wasn't actually going to lose them. And if unsuccessful perhaps it would be better that they never knew. But oh, how it hurt.

"You'll stay?" she asked Mirror finally.

"Of course," Mirror said, looking at her understandingly, with eyes that were much older than the young face she wore. They were all liars, Xipil thought, remembering her own wrinkled face and the soreness in her limbs when she had to wake each morning. At least she had not had to keep that for her reign.

"Then we need to start. The sooner we do, the sooner I can return."

2

EXTRACT FROM
FOR HONOR ALONE

Have You Set A Date Yet?

(Present —— Mainline New York)

"Ms. Louise to see you, ma'am."

"Thank you, Lauren. Show her in please," Margaret told the maid, not looking up from the report she was reading.

"No need, Mags," Louise told her, barreling in.

Margaret looked up, exasperated. "How many times do I have to tell you it's good manners to wait until you're shown into a room?"

Louise blew a raspberry. "If everyone had to wait until shown into a room, Mags, the world would grind to a halt."

Margaret winced. "How many times have I asked you not to call me Mags?"

"But if I don't call you Mags, what would we bicker about?" Louise replied as she dropped into a seat. Catching Margaret's glare, she sat up straight and arranged her dress demurely. "Better?" she asked.

"A little," Margaret allowed with a small smile. "So, sister of mine, to what do I owe the honor of your company?"

"I heard you were back in town and thought I'd drop by and see how you were. It's been over a month since I saw you last."

"And how did you hear I was back?" She, and the rest of the traveling circus she seemed to have gained, had only arrived back in New York yesterday, and she was due to take an airship to Naisre this evening, so Louise was lucky to have caught up with her.

"I asked your butler to phone me as soon as you returned."

"James?" She wouldn't have thought he would have been the type to divulge confidences. She might need to remind him of this.

"I worry about you," Louise said plaintively, seeing her face.

"I actually think it's the job of the older sister to worry about the younger one," Margaret pointed out.

"Not in this case. So," Louise asked when Margaret seemed willing to simply let the silence drag on. "How are you?"

Margaret considered the question seriously for a moment. "Surprisingly well, all things considered."

"You mean beyond getting kidnapped, killing your kidnapper, getting blown up by an atomic bomb, and then having to dig your way out of the basement they were holding you in. Did I forget anything?" She smacked her head in mock exasperation. "Yes, of course – there's also the fact you were diagnosed with severe depression and Post Traumatic Stress Syndrome from the war, and recently tried to kill yourself."

Margaret raised an eyebrow. "Put like that..."

"I'm not sure there is any other way, Mags. I've been worried sick. So has the rest of the family. Rajko's been keeping us up to date."

"I was wondering who'd drawn the short straw." Their brother was probably the best one for the job, Margaret thought. And if he'd already been in Naisre attending the Council of Leaders, Donald could have kept him up to date fairly easily.

"Unfortunately, his communications have verged on the terse at times. I saw the telegram he sent our parents. It wasn't quite as bad as: 'Margaret kidnapped on Sultan STOP More to follow STOP Rajko', but it came close."

"Couldn't he have arranged for a longer message to be couriered through the portal to Dontfrey? I know the fact you can't send any form of electronic message through a portal can be restrictive, but that's ridiculous."

"I think our mother read him the riot act." Louise looked at her sister. "Seriously though, how are you?"

Margaret gave a sigh, admitting defeat. "As I said, surprisingly well. I haven't seriously thought about killing myself since before the kidnapping. More importantly, my psych says I don't have to go back on the anti-depressants, which I'm thankful for, given how bad it was being forced to come off them cold turkey."

"You've recovered then?"

"Recovering. I have to see the good doctor every week when I'm in New York, and she's got me on an intensive exercise and yoga program that Jessie is taking with me."

"Jessie?"

"For an eight-year-old, she's a hard taskmaster."

"And Jade, have you heard anything?"

"No, not since we got separated. I'm hoping she's on Nayarit."

"You've got to be kidding!"

Margaret shook her head.

"But that line's dead!"

"Apparently not. Donald's got everyone digging through the records from the establishment of the Empire, trying to identify the line's coordinates."

"And when our esteemed cousin and First Leader finds it?"

"We go and get her back," Margaret growled.

"It might not be easy. She could be anywhere on the line."

"If she's there, we'll find her. And we've also had the promise from Sultan of two battalions of Janissaries. Between them and what the Empire will put into the field – "

"Just for Jade? I do like her, Margaret, quite a lot actually, but isn't that just a little over the top?"

"It was Nayarit who set off the atomic bomb on Sultan. Imagine if it had been New York rather than Pesh."

Louise grimaced. "Okay, so we do have to do something. And I can understand why you've been offered the Janissaries."

"Don't get me wrong," Margaret said, showing her teeth. "For all that we have to do something, this is very personal, both for Emre, who commands the Janissaries, and for myself. The bomb killed his sister and contaminated his city. Understandably, Emre wants those responsible hung, drawn, and quartered."

"And what do you want?"

Margaret grinned ferally. "They kidnapped me and placed Markus and Jessie in danger. Having them hung, drawn, and quartered would just be the beginning of what I want."

That was a side of her sister Louise hadn't seen before, although it explained what she'd heard about her during the insurrection on Dontfrey. Louise nodded, then decided to change the subject to the one that had actually brought her to the house. Well, that and the question of Margaret's health. "How is it progressing with Markus? Have you set a date yet?"

"Louise! We're not even engaged yet!"

"Why not?"

Margaret thought about it. "It's complicated."

"Oh, pish-posh." Leaning over, Louise rang the small silver bell on the table. "Lauren," she said when the maid appeared. "Is Mr. Ackov in?"

"Yes, ma'am," she said, with a doubtful look at Margaret.

"Please tell him we'd like to see him."

"Louise, what do you think you're doing – " Margaret started to say but was interrupted by Markus' arrival.

"You wanted to see me?" he asked.

"That was quick," Louise said.

"I was just coming down to say hello."

"Take a seat," Louise said, getting up and pulling the door closed behind him. Returning, she settled herself demurely in her seat. For a moment she looked at her hands before looking up at them both sitting there on the sofa. Margaret looked decidedly worried. "I will serve as the svakha." Seeing their looks of puzzlement, she added, "it's a Russian matchmaker."

"Louise," Margaret said warningly.

"Oh hush, Mags. You two obviously need help. You've been circling this matter for months. Besides, it was Mama's idea." Not exactly technically correct, Louise thought, but when their mother had phoned her to let her know Margaret was safe, she mentioned in passing that it was well past time that Margaret formalized her relationship with Markus, and that if they didn't, she was going to have to take steps. Having seen what happened when Margaret and their mother had locked horns in the past, it seemed obvious to Louise that if there was to be any progress on this matter, it would be a lot smoother if it occurred before their mother decided to directly intervene. She brought her thoughts back to the two individuals now sitting before her.

"Markus, I would like to introduce you to Ms. Margaret Peric," she said.

Margaret raised an eyebrow, while Markus just looked at her as though she were mad.

"She's loyal, intelligent, and has a present income of what?" She looked at Margaret, who simply raised the other eyebrow. She so had to practice that herself, Louise thought, then dragged her attention back to what she was supposed to be doing. "Considerably more than me," she finished.

"You obviously know what she looks like, tall, beautiful, et cetera, et cetera." She paused and regarded Margaret thoughtfully. "Hair color . . . variable."

Markus frowned.

"I dyed my hair red during the war," Margaret explained, as she touched the edge of her long, raven black hair. "This is natural."

"What you may not be aware of," Louise continued, "is that she actually has an extremely poor self-image."

"Louise!" Margaret snapped.

"It's all right, Margaret," Markus said with a smile, leaning back into the couch and crossing his legs. "I'd already worked that out."

"Really?" Louise said. "Already? It took me years."

Markus waved her on. "Please continue, I'm enjoying this." He shook his head warningly at Margaret.

"You're not going to when she gets onto you," Margaret said sourly.

Louise took a breath. "She is strong willed, and cares for those she considers herself responsible for, even when she isn't. That can make her very difficult to get along with, when what you want conflicts with what she thinks you need."

Margaret glared at her.

"Margaret, may I introduce you to Mr. Markus Ackov. Intelligent, with a penchant for chasing rabbits down rabbit holes, or in his case conspiracies across government departments. A powerful sense of duty and an annual income of . . . considerably less than yours."

Markus raised his hand.

"Yes?"

"I would just like to point out that my income has actually doubled over the past year as a consequence of what you have so quaintly described as my penchant for chasing rabbits down rabbit holes." He looked at Margaret. "I hadn't told you yet, but Intelligence has offered me a permanent job. Apparently, I'm good at spotting patterns." He sounded surprised.

"Well, of course you are," Margaret told him fondly.

Louise watched the exchange with a smile, then gave a small, let's move on gesture. She considered Markus for a moment. "Possibly too diffident, but with a core of steel. Which means that he will stand up to you when it really matters."

Margaret's glare lifted another notch.

"Oh tush, Mags, you can't always get your own way. That would be extremely bad for you."

"I do not always get my own way," Margaret muttered. "Just look at now."

"Only because I played the Mama card."

Markus snorted.

Louise smiled at him. "And given how his daughter has turned out, he seems ideal father material if you're looking for children. And if not, well, he comes with a daughter already in tow. In summary, in the view of this svakha, you are ideally suited. Do you agree? Margaret?"

TO BE CONTINUED

About the Author

Andrew spent much of his high-school years lost in the school library, exploring the worlds of Andre Norton, Robert Heinlein, and Isaac Asimov. His first commercially published series, *The Portal Adventures* (Peasantry Press), began as bedtime stories for his two sons. Now, with his children grown, Andrew lives in Perth with his wife and a fluctuating number of goldfish, writing science fiction, fantasy, and alternate history.

He has worked widely across the literary field, including as Principal of the Davies Literary Agency, editor and publisher of *The Western Australian Year Book*, and editor/writer for *Afterlife*—the online magazine for Atmosphere users.

Andrew's first published short story, *A Messenger to the Dragon*, appeared in *Aurealis* in 1992. His debut novel, *Trouble on Teral*—the first of *The Portal Adventures*, blending the spirit of Caroline Lawrence's *Roman Mysteries* with Andre Norton's juvenile speculative fiction—was released in 2018 by Peasantry Press. His adult alternate history series, *The Clemhorn Trilogy*, launched with *Nightfall* in 2019 (Zmok Books).

His alternate history short story *1827: Napoleon in Australia* was shortlisted for the 2021 international Sidewise Awards for Alternate History and won the Tin Duck Award for Best WA Professional SF Short Work the same year.

For more information, and/or you'd like a copy of the recipe for Carlos' Lemon Sponge why not subscribe to his newsletter at: www.andrewjharvey.com.

Hague

Publishing

www.HaguePublishing.com

PO Box 451 Bassendean
Western Australia 6934

www.ingramcontent.com/pod-product-compliance
Lightning Source LLC
Chambersburg PA
CBHW071238190726
48292CB00007B/2346